BIG TIME

BIG TIME

BEN H. WINTERS

MULHOLLAND BOOKS

Little, Brown and Company

New York Boston London

Mulholland Books / Little, Brown and Company
Hachette Book Group
1290 Avenue of the Americas, New York, NY 10104
mulhollandbooks.com

First Edition: March 2024

Mulholland Books is an imprint of Little, Brown and Company, a division of Hachette Book Group, Inc. The Mulholland Books name and logo are trademarks of Hachette Book Group, Inc.

The publisher is not responsible for websites (or their content) that are not owned by the publisher.

The Hachette Speakers Bureau provides a wide range of authors for speaking events. To find out more, go to hachettespeakersbureau.com or email hachettespeakers@hbgusa.com.

Little, Brown and Company books may be purchased in bulk for business, educational, or promotional use. For information, please contact your local bookseller or the Hachette Book Group Special Markets Department at special.markets@hbgusa.com.

ISBN 9780316305778
Library of Congress Control Number: 2023948291

Printing 1, 2023

LSC-C

Printed in the United States of America

*It's probably considered eccentric to
dedicate a book to its editor,
but I'm willing to risk it for Josh Kendall —
a generous giver of time.*

Time is what we want most, but what, alas! we use worst.

— William Penn, *Fruits of Solitude*

BIG TIME

PROLOGUE

i.

Wait a second, wait a second, wait a second," Allie called from the back seat.

The driver didn't answer. The woman had said not one word this entire time, which was part of what was so terrifying about the whole thing. She just drove, not turning around, not answering Allie's questions, acting like Allie wasn't even back here. Allie tried to get her to engage, Allie had been trying the whole time, since the moment this lady had grabbed her from the bench at the edge of the playground and forced her across the sidewalk and into the back seat of her silver SUV.

"Hi, could you—I'm sorry, would you just talk to me? Can you look at me? Please."

Allie tried to stay calm. She was trying to stay calm. It had been— what?—an hour? Two hours? The sun was going down. They were driv- ing south, or at least that's what Allie thought, she thought they were driving south, she had tried to look for landmarks but the windows were tinted and it was hard to see.

"Can you tell me where we're going? Can you just — I'm sorry, can you just *talk* to me?"

The driver — the kidnapper — this strange and terribly quiet and oddly witchy woman — still refused to answer. She just drove, keeping to an even highway speed, no talking, no radio, no sound but the muted rush of the wheels. Allie stared at the back of the woman's head, at her long black hair pulled back in a tight ponytail, at her pale thin neck.

Calm. Allie was working so hard to stay calm. You have to be rational. You can't panic. You have to stay calm.

"Okay, look. Here's the thing. Whoever it is that you think I am, I promise you it's not me. You've got the wrong person. Can you — I'm sorry, can you hear me?"

Allie knew it was useless. A waste of words. A waste of time. If this lady, whoever she was, if she was going to respond, if she was going to take pity on her, if she was going to pull over and untie her wrists and apologize for the misunderstanding and let her go, then she would have done it already. Right?

But Allie kept talking. Kept trying. Because, yes, she knew it was useless, but she also knew that if she *stopped* talking, *stopped* trying, she would collapse into despair, she would start crying and not stop crying until this lady either killed her or dropped her in a dungeon or threw her in a hole or whatever the hell she was planning.

"Can I just tell you something? Seriously. I'm not rich — okay? — I'm not some, like, heiress or anything like that, if that's what this is. I'm just a person. I'm just some woman. I'm a teacher." And as if to prove that she was a teacher, just a regular boring middle-school teacher, Allie was talking in her most pleasant voice, earnest and teacherly, carefully explaining what everyone needed to know for tomorrow's quiz.

"My name is Allie Zerkofsky. Allison Bridget Zerkofsky. My maiden name is Brownlee — Allison Brownlee. I'm originally from Ohio, and

I'm twenty-six years old, and I teach at Dalton Kruger Middle School in Bordentown, New Jersey. I live near there with my husband, Lucas, and — and —"

Allie stopped. She couldn't think of the baby right now. She couldn't say the baby's name. If she said the name out loud, then despair would over-rush her, she knew that it would, and that would be it.

"I teach science and math to sixth- and seventh-graders," she said instead. "The kids call me Ms. Z. I'm not rich. I'm in debt, actually! I have over forty thousand dollars in outstanding student loans."

Allie paused. She breathed hopefully. She didn't know what else to say. Her kidnapper did not seem interested in her student-loan debt.

"I'm wondering if maybe you've got me confused with — I don't know — some kind of drug dealer or — or — or Mafia person?"

Nothing. No answer. Allie's wrists chafed where they were cinched tightly, one against the other. She felt panic building in the back of her throat.

The driver guided the SUV through a series of turns. It was getting darker outside, but Allie felt like they were still going south, south and west, skirting Philadelphia. She thought she could make out the tops of the bridges that connected New Jersey and Pennsylvania.

What if they were going into the woods? Weren't there all those hardwood forests in the rural northern part of Maryland, just over the state line? That's what they do, isn't it, when they're going to kill you? Drive you over the state line and into the woods.

Was Allie going to cry again? Was she starting to cry? She moaned softly, tilted her head up, working overtime to keep from crying. Working as hard as she could.

"Please," she said. "Please don't kill me. Are you going to kill me?"

"I am not," the driver said, and Allie gasped at the shock of the woman's voice after the long miles of silence. The voice was cool and flat and

7

uninflected, a voice to match the high black ponytail and the pale thin neck.

"I am not a killer," the driver continued. "I am a delivery person. I pick up a package and deliver it. Killing and death do not come into it, barring some problem or issue." The driver looked into the rearview mirror and made quick, grave eye contact with Allie. Her eyes were large and perfectly green, and Allie—insanely, under the circumstances—looked back at her and thought: *God, she is gorgeous.*

"Is there going to be some problem or issue?"

"No," said Allie. "No, no, no."

A delivery person, though, what did that mean? Who could have ordered that Allie be . . . delivered? She thought again that this had to be one of those horrifying situations you see in the news, some tragic gangland mix-up where regular people are murdered for no reason at all, and you shake your head and go, *Those poor people,* except now it was Allie, Allie was those poor people.

Lucas was probably getting home from work at this point, going from room to room in their little house on Myrtle Avenue, starting to freak out, calling, "Honey? Hon?" and thinking, *Where is she? Where's the baby?*

Oh, no. Oh God. The *baby.*

Rachel.

At the thought of Rachel, Allie could see her, could *smell* her, the sweet-soap smell of her scalp. She could feel her tiny wriggling weight.

Allie started to cry.

"Please, ma'am," she said, her voice a ragged quaver. "Miss. Please. Can you just tell me if the baby's okay?"

The driver flicked her eyes up to the rearview mirror again and gave Allie a brief questioning glance, but then she looked back at the road without answering. Allie kept talking.

"Her name is Rachel. She's fourteen months old, and she has this—

she drinks a special formula, because she's got a milk allergy, and — it's serious, so —" Allie broke off. The thought of Rachel and her formula set her crying again, big hitching sobs she couldn't hold in.

They had been at the playground on Maslow. Rachel was in the sandbox. The stroller sat parked nearby, with the diaper bag hung on its handles. Allie had taken her shoes off despite the cold because Rachel liked to pack Mommy's toes in little dunes of muddy sand.

Allie was fully sobbing now, her face hot with tears.

"Oh my God, wait, though, you have to *tell* him," she said to the driver. She leaned forward against the seat belt. Her upper arms ached from being tied. Why hadn't she thought of this already? Why hadn't it been the first thing she'd said when the lady put her in the car?

"You have to call that man. Please can you just call him?"

"What man?" said the driver sharply.

"The — the man," stammered Allie. There had been two of them. The woman who had taken Allie and an accomplice, a broad-shouldered man in a gray overcoat and heavy black boots. "The man who took my baby."

"What baby?" the driver said, and Allie felt a terrible pain erupt from her chest and she cried out. It was like something was gnashing against itself, deep inside of her, close to her heart. Like bone grinding against bone. Startled, Allie jolted in her seat and her head banged hard against the tempered glass of the rear window.

"Hey," said the driver, and turned in her seat just as Allie fell over sideways, her body locked, her teeth gritted. She was trying to scream but she couldn't scream, it hurt too much, something was scraping inside of her like a rusted gate. A sound escaped from her in a strangled gurgle.

The driver craned further around, murmuring, "The hell?" just as a deer drifted into the road. She turned back only at the last instant, jerking the wheel hard to the left in time to avoid the animal, sending the SUV skidding off the pavement and colliding at high speed with one of the dark trees that lined the shoulder. The driver was thrown back hard in her seat as the airbag exploded open and slammed into her chest. The hood crumpled and the right headlight shattered and steam came out of the engine in a plume.

Allie was tossed forward and then flung back as the seat belt snapped tight against her chest. "Oh my God," she said. "Oh my God."

The grinding internal pain that had erupted inside of Allie receded just as quickly, and now in the stunned silence after the accident she acted without thinking: she slid out from under the seat belt onto the flat carpet of the seat well and inched forward, hands bound, until she could clamp her mouth around the silver door handle and, with an awkward clutch of her teeth, yank it inward, clicking the door open.

Then she pushed forward on the door with the top of her head and tumbled gasping into the roadside mud.

Frantic, Allie stumbled up from her knees onto her feet and lurched into a run, remembering that she had no shoes on only as her foot came down on a thick jagged piece of headlight.

The pain was shocking and intense, and Allie staggered as, from the corner of her eye, she saw her kidnapper pushing open the driver's side door. *Oh God,* she thought. *Oh no.* It was a nightmare. It was a horror movie.

Allie crouched to pull out the shard of headlight just as the driver got to her and grabbed a tight fistful of her hair.

"Come on," said the woman coldly, but in that instant Allie, with a sickening tug, yanked the piece of headlight from her foot, and then — thinking only of Rachel, only of her daughter's flashing eyes and fat little body — she straightened up out of her crouch and jammed the bloody glass into the woman's face, her screams mingling with the startled screams of the driver as Allie drove the shard into her eye.

Allie let go, leaving the broken piece of headlight where she had planted it in the driver's face.

And then she ran.

ii.

Desiree breathed through the pain, calculating how much time this was going to cost her.

That was her name, the striking green-eyed woman in the black pant-suit who had taken Allie from the New Jersey playground: Desiree.

The shard of broken headlight had penetrated deeply into her eye, and the pain was extraordinary, the pain of a sharp, cold, inorganic object embedded in her eyeball.

Desiree wasn't really her name. In Desiree's line of work, real names were a liability, and she hadn't worked under her own in many years. The name Desiree was one she had selected, and it would be discarded at the conclusion of the assignment.

The conclusion of the assignment that would now be delayed. Desiree hated delay. She loathed it. She started the timer on her watch when each new job commenced, and Desiree knew without consulting the watch that she was already over four hours on this one. In a perfect world, a simple delivery such as this would not require more than eight hours in total. This was not a perfect world.

Desiree's preference would have been to chase the woman through the woods, but this was impossible. Before doing anything else she would have to remove the foreign object from her eye. She would have to seek medical attention. Desiree breathed slowly, in and out. Blood spurted and then dripped and finally merely trickled from her face. Twilight was almost concluded. The roadside was darkening. Time was escaping through the trees.

She had taken her eyes off the road. Turned halfway around in the driver's seat to look at the girl. Why had she done that?

Desiree knew why: It was the way the girl had screamed. She had said something about a baby and Desiree had said, "What baby?" and then the woman had made this spine-shivering scream, like no scream that Desiree had ever heard. Which, in her line of work, was saying something.

Desiree brought herself up onto her knees, fighting off a wave of nausea and dizziness. She braced herself with one hand flat on the muddy ground. With the other hand, she reached up and took hold of the protruding end of the shard of polycarbonate plastic still stuck in her eyeball and began to pull it out.

The pain, which had begun to subside, intensified. Desiree's body buckled and shook.

She did not scream. She breathed evenly.

The jagged triangle at last came free, accompanied by a final cascade of blood and vitreous fluid. Her hand still pressed against the ground, Desiree allowed herself one long, muted groan of angry pain.

Then she stood, holding one hand over the wound while her other eye blinked rapidly to adjust to the bleary country darkness. She made her way to the rear door of the SUV and opened it. She squeezed a water bottle to irrigate the wound, then opened her first aid kit. She packed the wound with gauze and then made an X of surgical tape to secure it.

Desiree performed these tasks very quickly, with maximum efficiency. Her every movement was charged with impatience. Every moment she was not chasing the girl was a moment lost. Every moment, Desiree's search radius got wider.

"Are you all right?"

Desiree turned and saw a young man who had come out of the woods and was behind her, a few feet from the rear of the rented Buick Enclave. Desiree smiled tightly, thinking she had no time for this. The boy was sixteen or seventeen, in athletic shorts and a T-shirt that said PROPERTY OF LINCOLN HIGH SCHOOL. A ridiculous jogger's headlamp was strapped to his forehead.

"I'm fine," she said, but the teenager stood there gawping.

"Are you sure? Looks like you got in an accident."

"I'm fine," said Desiree again, but the boy was shaking his head, his silly headlight bobbing back and forth.

"You stay here," he said. "I'll go and get help."

He turned to jog away and Desiree pulled the 9-millimeter pistol from the pocket of her coat and shot him one time in the back of the head. He fell directly to the ground, his gangly late-adolescent body collapsing like an accordion beneath the weight of his head.

She stood over him for a moment. A second bullet wasn't necessary.

Desiree, who was much stronger than her small frame suggested, lifted the jogger into the rear of the Enclave. His eyes stared up at her while she arranged his body in the cargo hold. The headlamp had gone off.

This would take yet more time. Now not only did Desiree need to deal with her eye, she had to swap out this vehicle as soon as possible, before some state trooper pulled her over to ask about the collision damage.

There was a car lot she knew that dealt with these kinds of situations. But it was in Perth Amboy, in the exact opposite direction of where she was supposed to deliver the girl.

Desiree checked the timer on her watch. She had been working this job for four hours, nineteen minutes, and thirty-two seconds. Thirty-three seconds. Thirty-four. Time flying forward, burning itself away.

She had to find that girl, and she would find her. As soon as possible.

iii.

Allie crashed haphazardly through the woods until she emerged on a narrow hiking path. She followed this path, taking rapid, terrified breaths, looking back over her shoulder every few yards, running in the darkness even though her body burned from the strain, running and running even as the wound in the sole of her foot cried out each time her foot struck the ground. She paused only long enough to get her hands free, tearing the cloth against the sharp broken end of a jagged branch, and then she continued to run.

The ground was cold. Allie's whole body was cold. She was lost in the woods in mid-November, and it was so cold.

Allie sternly lectured herself not to panic. "Don't panic," she said, and she could hear herself saying it to a roomful of seventh-graders losing their shit about state testing or whatever it was: *Don't panic. Remain calm.*

She had to find her way out of here, that was all. She had to find a phone. She had to call Lucas.

He'd be absolutely losing his mind by now. He'd be calling all of their friends, calling her parents.

And what about Rachel?

No, thought Allie fiercely, *don't. Do not.* She couldn't think of Rachel, of her fragile little peanut, wailing and confused, surrounded by strangers, probably soaking wet. No — it was unbearable to think of Rachel, so Allie commanded herself not to do it, to ignore that particular terror and keep going, stay calm and focused and find her way through the forest and to a phone that she could use.

And as all of these thoughts cascaded through Allie's mind, as she fled through the darkness with her foot pulsing in fiery pain, every once in a while she remembered the terrible grinding sensation that had rolled through her body before, when she was in the back seat and her captor had pretended not to know she had a child.

Thinking back, it had been *like* pain but not pain exactly. It was more like a kind of pressure exerting itself, a feeling like something dissolving, like something being destroyed. It was strange even to be thinking of it as Allie fled deeper and deeper into the moonlit forest, in the midst of this miserable ordeal — but what on earth could that feeling have been?

WEDNESDAY

1.

Grace Berney had a moment, just a moment but kind of a long one, where she thought she might actually go insane.

Not really, of course. Not literally. She was going to be fine. It wasn't a big deal.

It was just her mom, just Kathy being her same old Kathy self, just her dear old mother driving her out of her mind, and her dear old mother had been driving her out of her mind for going on forty-six years already. So what was one more night?

Grace took a nice long breath and let it out slow and said, "Hey, Mom? I think maybe you're making this harder than it needs to be."

"Everything is harder than it needs to be," Kathy said tartly. "That's just called life."

Or maybe Grace *would* go insane. Maybe tonight was the night!

Kathy made an agitated little grunt and shifted her soft bulky weight backward into Grace's arms. Grace dug her heels into the carpet and jammed her hands into her mother's armpits and succeeded, although just barely, in keeping both of them from toppling over.

"Ach," said her mom. "That *hurts*."

"Sorry," said Grace. "You okay?"

"I guess."

"Can we keep going?"

"Well, gimme a damn *second*. Let me catch my *breath*."

Grace's mother looked a lot like Grace, or at least what Grace was resigned to looking like thirty years and fifty pounds into the future. Grace had heaved Kathy out of her armchair to maneuver her, step by labored step, across the tidy living room of the town house to the bathroom. Now they were paused at the halfway point, directly below the Smithsonian Institution print of wildflowers that hung between the front windows. Grace noticed that the windows were smudged and needed cleaning, even though she had cleaned them maybe three days ago. After she got her mom to the toilet, she should grab a wet paper towel and swipe those clean. Maybe do the fireplace mantel too; it had been a while since anybody cleaned the mantel.

Or I could just die, thought Grace as she stood contemplating chores while her hands were getting grossly warm in her elderly mother's armpits. *Dying is another option.*

Theoretically Kathy MacAlister was perfectly mobile so long as she had her cane, but lately Kathy had begun leaving the cane in random places around the house and forgetting where she had left it, requiring that she be assisted in getting from one spot to another. Grace didn't know if this new habit represented the first stirrings of senility or was simply the latest manifestation of a lifelong streak of selfish stubbornness. Neither prospect was particularly heartening.

"Come on," said Grace. "We're almost there."

"I can see that. I'm old. I'm not *blind*."

22

Grace made the decision to ignore her mother's tone, a decision she made many times over the course of any given day. All Grace wanted was to skip ahead to the part of the night when she was alone in front of the TV, slowly drinking the single glass of wine she allowed herself when all the day's responsibilities had been discharged. Grace was not a boring person, but she had boring habits. She was aware of that. It was fine with her. Life was short. She liked wine and she liked TV.

"Okay, Mom. Here we go."

Grace and Kathy took a big clumsy step together, and then Grace's phone rang from the kitchen, playing the jaunty preset ringtone Grace kept meaning to change. Kathy stopped abruptly and the two of them nearly toppled over.

"Oh, for God's sake!" said Kathy. "What is that noise?"

Grace rolled her eyes as she regained her footing. Kathy was old, but she wasn't *that* old. She had heard *phones* before.

"Someone's calling me. Ignore it."

The ringtone played again.

"I can't *ignore* it. It's driving me out of my gourd."

"You're fine. Walk."

They kept going, and the phone stopped mid-ring, but then a second later it started again, insistent and bright, and Grace craned her neck to try to see the phone where it lay on the kitchen counter, to see who on earth would be calling her at 7:30 on a Wednesday night. *Nobody* called her. It was probably someone wanting to extend her car's warranty or a robot with an exciting loan opportunity. River was the only actual human who regularly called her, but River was getting a ride home with friends and was very unlikely to do something as lame as call to check in.

"You know what?" said Kathy. "You're so intrigued, go answer it. You can set me down here."

"You mean just . . . lay you down on the floor?"

"Yes. I'm fine."

"Mom. I thought you had to go to the bathroom."

"I'll make it. I'll crawl."

"Mom."

Kathy waved an irritated hand and let out a long groaning *uch*. It was one of her most impressive old-lady tricks, to remain so haughty and commanding even in the most undignified positions, such as being dragged like a sack of flour across the floor by her adult daughter.

Soon, Grace knew, it would be time to figure out a new situation for her mother. She and River couldn't attend to Kathy's needs much longer, and the space of the townhome increasingly felt too small for three. The first floor was really just one big room: a front hall that nosed into the living room, a kitchen separated from the front by a narrow breakfast counter. Behind the kitchen was a stairwell leading to the second floor and its three bedrooms. Grace liked to call her place "compact." Kathy — snidely but probably more accurately — called it "cave-like."

Kathy had been living with Grace and River on a "temporary basis" for close to five years, since her series of small strokes had coincided conveniently with the ending of Grace's marriage.

"The timing really just worked out" is what Grace's brother, Danny, had said then, transparently relieved at being spared the burden himself.

Figuring out where Kathy could move (and how to pay for it) was just one item on the big list that was constantly revising itself in Grace's mind: the list of things that had to happen that she had no time to make happen. Make a plan for Mom. Start the college-search process with River, because somehow it had become fall of junior year. Research a new car; actually make a decision about a car.

Grace hated the list. The list never stopped growing. The list was her closest companion and her greatest enemy.

At last they made it to the bathroom door and Kathy disappeared inside and Grace did not go with her. Kathy did not yet require any help *inside* the bathroom, and thank the Lord for small miracles. Grace's phone rang again, and she speed-walked to the kitchen to answer it, but it stopped ringing as she got there. She scooped it up and peered at the screen, frowning.

"Well?" hollered her mother from inside the bathroom. "Who was it?"

"No one."

Grace scrolled back through the recent calls. Four missed calls over the past fifteen minutes, all from a 301 number she didn't recognize.

"Well, it wasn't *no one*," Kathy called, the annoyed brassiness of her voice muted by the bathroom door.

"No," said Grace. "It wasn't. Oh, weird," she murmured. Because actually, she *did* recognize the number. "It's my office."

And then, a little louder, so Kathy could hear: "It's my work." Grace checked the time on the phone. Half past seven. So weird.

"Work?" called Kathy, and then coughed thickly. "Why is your work calling?"

"I have no idea, Mom."

"So? Call them back."

"I will in a minute."

"What if it's important?"

"Nothing at my office is important." Grace stared irritably at her phone. For God's sake. She had gotten home only an hour ago. "I'll call in a sec." She sighed. "Let's just make sure you're okay."

"I'm urinating, Grace. I'm not having heart surgery." The door opened a little, and Grace saw her mom's pinched features scowling through the crack. "Call them."

Grace stood with her phone in one hand, absently rubbing her lower back with the other. Why was work calling? The one good thing about having a job where nobody cared was that nobody was supposed to care. When the day ended, you were done. You were free to go home to your leisure-time pursuits, such as dragging your cranky mother to and from the bathroom.

"Oh, good," said Grace, suppressing an eye-roll as Kathy emerged from the bathroom. "You found your cane."

"Yeah, I found it," said Kathy airily, as if this had been her plan all along. "It was in the bathroom."

Grace let her eyes flutter shut for a moment, accepting the things she could not change. Then she pressed the green button to dial the most recent caller, and the front door slammed open, and River stormed in, sloughing off the outrageously expensive backpack Grace had just bought and hurling it against the wall.

"Hey, sweetie," said Grace as she ended the call.

"Marni is being *extremely* annoying," River announced, throwing open the door of the refrigerator and glaring into it.

"I'm fine, thanks," Grace said. "How was your day?"

"Come on, Mom," said River. "Don't do that. That's annoying."

River, Grace's only child, was at a high boil. They snapped shut the door of the fridge and turned with arms crossed tightly, displaying an exasperated scowl. River was sixteen, and their default reaction to every question or comment was to act as if falsely accused of murder.

"When you come in the house, you say hello," Grace said firmly. "We've talked about this."

Many a time, in fact. Many a time had they talked about it.

"*Hellooooo*," sang River with aggressive cheer, throwing in a big fake wave for good measure. And then they added immediately, "What's for dinner?"

"*River,*" said Grace sharply. "Say hello to Nana."

26

"Oh my God!" River erupted, but then turned and offered a long elaborate bow in the direction of Kathy, who was hobbling determinedly back to her armchair, leaning heavily on the oaken cane. *"Helloooooo, Nana."*

"Hello, dear."

River glared at Grace — *Satisfied?* — as Kathy picked up her book of sudoku and settled back into her big armchair. For all the complaining she did both to and about Grace, Kathy was remarkably tolerant of River's belligerence and insubordination. Grace suspected that Kathy took her only grandchild's salty attitude as a tribute to her own.

"I wish you wouldn't be such an asshole, honey," said Grace sweetly, and River stuck their tongue out and said, "Don't swear at me. Or I'll go live with Dad."

"Oh, you will not."

"Yeah, no," conceded River, "probably not." Then they pretended to laugh but actually sort of did laugh, and Grace gave River the finger and River gave it back at her, a conspiratorial interchange between the best friends they still were, secretly, beneath all of this parent/child bullshit. Grace hugged River, and River suffered themselves to be hugged.

"So, wait, though," they said, pulling away. *"Is* there dinner? Or no?"

"Yes. Obviously," said Grace. There would be dinner, of course — it wasn't like they could just *skip* dinner — but she hadn't gotten that far yet. "I thought you were eating with Marni."

"Marni stayed late at chorus to flirt with Seth."

"I thought Marni was gay."

"Marni is *pan*, first of all, and second, she isn't really into Seth, she's just trying to get help with chemistry. Can we order pizza?"

"I don't know. Hold on. I don't know if I have any cash."

"Oh, well, maybe we can use Apple Pay because this isn't the early nineties?"

The phone rang again, and all three of them looked at it, Grace and River in the kitchen and Kathy from her armchair, pencil and sudoku in hand. River glanced at their own phone and then looked up, confused. "Wait," they said to Grace. "Is someone calling *you?*"

"Looks that way."

Grace gave River a wicked smile, holding up her phone and waggling it smugly. But it was just her office again, of course, and Grace felt a fresh wave of annoyance. It was nighttime, for God's sake. Her family needed her. Someone had to formulate some kind of plan for dinner. Someone had to clean the kitchen. And then it would be time for wine and TV.

"Hello?"

"Hey, there, Grace. It's Lou. All good on the home front?"

"Oh. Uh . . ." Grace instinctively pulled away from her mother and her child, hunching over slightly and putting her non-phone hand over her ear. "I'm doing okay. How are you?"

"Can't complain. You know how it is."

"Sure."

Lou Fleming, Grace's boss, betrayed no urgency in his tone. He spoke in his usual tone, casual and overly friendly, which Grace always found irritating but now found extra irritating.

"Can I help you, Lou?"

"You sure can," said Lou. "Little something brewing here, and I could use your expert input."

"Uh — okay."

Grace slipped out of the kitchen and into the narrow stairwell that led up to the second floor. She sat down on the third step, too fast, jolting her tailbone.

What is this? she thought. The intrusion was a small thing, but it wasn't a small thing. It was galling. There were only so many hours in the day, and only so many of them did Grace get to spend away from the third floor of Building 66 on the White Oak Campus of the Food and Drug Administration in Silver Spring, Maryland.

"So, listen, Grace," said Lou amiably. "You cover portacaths, isn't that right?"

"I do, yeah." Grace rubbed a thumb between her eyes.

"I thought so. Score a point for me, right?"

Lou made a throaty, self-deprecating chuckle, but the whole thing was a strange and self-conscious performance. Lou had been working at CDRH for twelve years, only slightly shorter than Grace's own fourteen-year tenure, and for all his faults, he was no dummy. He knew very well which reviewers were responsible for covering which of the various medical devices that fell within the department's purview. *What is this?* Grace thought again with sharp annoyance, leaning her head against the stippled white wall of the stairwell. Was it some kind of test?

And had she really been working at their little branch of the FDA for fourteen years? That was a long time. It was, objectively, too long. When she thought about how long it was, Grace felt a brick of sadness, heavy and dense, settle in the pit of her gut. "So you had a question about ports, Lou?"

Lou didn't answer right away. There was instead a burst of typing in the background, and then a brief muffled noise like Lou had covered the phone with his palm to talk to someone else. Grace waited, feeling the minutes seeping away. From where she sat, three steps up, she could see River in the kitchen, texting, laughing; God forbid the kid at nearly college age could take some initiative and organize dinner. Kathy was settled among the nest of books and supermarket puzzle magazines in her chair, clutching her pencil and watching Grace with undisguised curiosity.

Grace retreated a couple more steps up the stairwell, like a turtle disappearing into her shell. They'd be waiting for her, both of them, the moment she got off the phone. Waiting to hear what the call had been about; waiting for dinner, for attention, for her time.

"Hey, you know what?" said Lou, clearing his throat. "Don't hate me. But it might be easier if you came back into the office. Would that be all right?"

2.

Grace came off the elevator and there was Lou, sitting in his glass-walled office, waiting. The main part of the floor, a maze of cubicles and low pony walls, was empty and dark. She was the only other person here, just her and Lou, who was beckoning to her, heavy and pink-faced and blandly earnest.

As Grace approached, her low heels echoing flatly in the darkness, she made a minor adjustment to her black Ann Taylor skirt, tugging the front of it more toward the front. Quickly and grudgingly she had gotten dressed again for work, putting back on her skirt and shirt and black pumps.

"Hey, hey," said Lou. He was smiling awkwardly and unwrapping a Snickers bar. "There she is. You're my hero, Grace."

He was awaiting her behind his desk, scratching at his mustache and pulling the Snickers free from its clingy brown wrapper.

"Oh. Shoot." He looked at the candy bar as if it had just appeared in his hand. "I just went to the vending machine. I coulda got you something."

"I'm good," said Grace through her impatience. She was, in fact, pretty hungry, but the last thing she wanted was a stupid Snickers. She wanted actual *food*. Before she left, she'd given River her Postmates password and instructions to stay under forty bucks and please keep in mind Kathy's various dietary restrictions and opinions. God only knew what the two of them would end up eating.

Lou was in some terrible Frankenstein's-monster combination of home and business attire: a lumpy sweatshirt that said ALASKA over a cartoon of a moose, paired with pleated khakis and scuffed white tennis shoes. Lou's mustache was thick and black and unironic; he looked like a state trooper in a seventies movie. He was one of a breed of middle-aged family men who were ubiquitous in the federal civil service: competent, polite, and dull. In Grace's experience, each of these men had some very specific outside interest, be it pickleball or stamps or World War II. Lou's particular avocation, Grace was aware, was fantasy football.

"Okay," said Lou. "So. You're my expert on all things portacath."

"I guess I am."

"Something kinda...came in over the transom, as they say. Hoping you can take a peek."

Lou set down his candy bar and rested his hand on a manila envelope, the kind with the fiddly metal clasps at the top. Now, before Grace could answer, he opened the envelope, pulled out a set of photographs, and laid the stack down on the desk.

"Voilà."

On top was a fuzzy color printout of a photograph showing a woman's naked upper chest. Grace flushed, glanced up at Lou, then quickly down again. The picture was not pornographic, but it was uncomfortable to be looking at it alone with her boss. It was a medium close-up, showing just the woman's upper torso, from the breasts, which were covered by the subject's crossed arms, to the bottom of the chin.

There was something grim and dehumanizing about the photo, poorly framed and washed in yellow hospital light. The subject was a very thin woman, small-chested and bony, pale-skinned and dotted with small freckles. There was a tattoo high on her left arm, disappearing over the rise of her shoulder.

"You see what I'm seeing?" said Lou, and Grace murmured, "I do, sure." There was a telltale bump high on the right side of the woman's chest, a flat raised patch maybe three centimeters in diameter. Grace looked at Lou, then back at the picture.

"She's got a port."

"Yes, ma'am," said Lou, taking the picture by the edge and flipping it over like a card magician, revealing the next one in the stack.

It was another printout, this time of a chest X-ray, which Grace presumed to be of the same woman, and now the medical device implanted on the right side of her chest was visible in blurry radiological outline. It was a small oval of plastic or metal, bulging out slightly on one end. This bulging section was unusual, but otherwise Grace could tell exactly what she was looking at. A portacath was a medical device that was surgically inserted beneath the skin, usually in the chest or upper arm; connected to a catheter, it provided direct access to a central vein. Based on the placement of this patient's port, the line would go to the right internal jugular.

Grace studied the two pictures, the snapshot and the X-ray, side by side. Some tender emotion had been triggered in her, something close to pity. A girl; the inside of a girl. *Poor thing.*

She looked up from the pictures. Lou was waiting, scratching his mustache.

"Yeah, so, basically," he said, tapping the X-ray with one fingertip, his voice now betraying a slight trace of impatience, "we're being asked if we might be able to *ascertain*"—he said the word slowly, smiling

33

self-consciously, acknowledging the fancy diction—"the origin of this particular device."

"Being asked by whom?"

"Direct request from the hospital. It appears this, uh, this young lady was brought to an ER in, uh, let's see—Hanover? You know where that is?"

Grace shook her head.

"Up near BWI. Baltimore County. The, uh—" He glanced at his computer screen. "The Hanover Regional Medical Center. Midsize county hospital. Couple hundred beds, but it's the primary emergency center for its region. Apparently this gal was brought in really early this morning. They found her unconscious on a train car. Exhausted, dehydrated. Totally out of it mentally, it seems like, plus with a nasty gash in her foot."

"Oh, dear," Grace murmured, but Lou only scowled at the interruption and plowed on. "Plus she's got this port in her, and the site's infected."

Grace lifted the first picture again and looked closer, thought maybe she could see the telltale ring of swollen redness at the edges of the bump. She wasn't sure.

"Docs admit the Jane Doe, treat the infection with antibiotics, but they're tryin' to get some medical history on her."

"And they can't just ask the patient?"

Lou shrugged. "Apparently not. Apparently she is"—again he slowed down, put heavy self-conscious emphasis on the medical jargon—"*obtunded.* Meaning, like I said, basically out of it or what have you. Doesn't know which way is up."

"Jeez," said Grace, and Lou shrugged. Grace could tell he was getting bored. He was ready to go.

"So, bottom line, big finish on this, some brilliant doctor over there says, 'Maybe we call the medical-device folks, trace this funky device, find out where and when this gal got ported, then we can figure out who the heck she is.'"

"What does that mean, *funky device?*"

"Well," he said. "You tell me."

Lou moved the X-ray picture from the top of the stack to reveal the next one: a zoomed-in section of the X-ray, centering and enlarging the port. Grace murmured, "Huh."

"Yeah," said Lou. "Huh."

If there was one thing Grace had learned in her years at the Center for Devices and Radiological Health, it was that one of the hallmarks of medical-device design was regularity. The clients were physicians, and what physicians wanted was a device — whether it was a stent, an insulin pump, or a dialysis machine — that worked like they and their patients expected it to, exactly how it had worked in the past.

But this port, with its odd little bulge on the side, was not like other ports.

Without thinking about it, Grace pulled a legal pad from her bag and drew a diagram of the port. She surveyed the little sketch and furrowed her brow. "Do we know who the manufacturer is?"

"Nope," said Lou. "Not yet." He smiled, and Grace said, "Oh," and then "Oh" again, realizing with a kind of frozen horror what Lou was about to ask.

"And you know how the folks up on the sixth floor have been pushing us to be more responsive to direct requests from the patient-care community."

"Uh, no," said Grace. "I did not."

"Well, they have," Lou said, and patted the desk a couple times. "So. Can you stick around a bit, do some digging on this? Be great if we could get them a quick answer, earn some brownie points with the folks upstairs."

"Right," said Grace, thinking, *No*, thinking, *Come on*. But what she actually said was "I mean, Lou . . . It's, uh . . ." But she couldn't even say *It's pretty late*. She couldn't even find it in herself to say *Can't we do this tomorrow?* She just let "It's, uh . . ." trail off and hang there, and Lou waited, until finally, crushed under the weight of the silence between them, Grace sighed and said softly, "Sure. Yeah. No problem."

Lou beamed. "Fantastico," he said, and gave his desk a last happy tap before standing up to go.

Grace looked back at the stack of pictures. There were more pictures under the three that she had seen. She wondered, in passing, what they were. She wondered what kind of consent this anonymous young woman had given to have her picture taken, shirtless and vulnerable in her hospital bed. Did she know the pictures would end up on the desk of some bureaucrat in Maryland?

"Bet you'll figure it out too," said Lou, slipping into his puffy North Face jacket and wrapping himself in a scarf.

"Well, I'll do my best," she said.

She was already tired, and she felt a sudden gnawing need for home, to see River, her only child, whom she saw too rarely as it was. But the words had just tumbled out — *Yeah. No problem* — and now it was too late.

Although of course, some pathetic, people-pleasing elf had already started scurrying around in Grace's mind, rubbing its little hands together as it brainstormed how to handle this assignment: pull all the regulatory applications for ports, work backward from the present, try to match the technical specs from the applications to what was in the photo . . .

"I'll poke around a bit, Lou. But, uh, if I can't find anything in an hour or so —"

"Of course. Absolutely," Lou said, raising a hand to cut her off. "Listen, give 'er an hour, two or three tops, see what you can do. I just wish I could stay and keep you company. But I got something I need to do at home."

"Oh," said Grace. "Is Patty okay?"

"Patty?" Lou furrowed his brow as if he couldn't quite place his wife's name. "Oh, yeah, Patty's fine. I gotta hit the waiver wire."

Lou patted his pockets for his keys, moving with clumsy haste. "So, listen, like I said, take the time you need, there's no one here to bother you, and hey — if you come in a little late tomorrow, my lips are sealed, okay?"

The phony smile slipped from Grace's face as she made her way across the big main floor to her own tiny office, glancing once over her shoulder at the elevator doors as they closed behind the escaping Lou.

Grace was not high enough on the third-floor org chart to merit an office of her own. She shared with Kendall Johns, their desks and computers mirror images of each other. Even though Kendall wasn't here, she was careful to respect his side of the space. She took off her coat and folded it neatly over the back of her chair. Then she sat down, sighing, and took off her striped winter hat with the little woolen ball on top that she now realized she had been wearing for that whole conversation.

Then Grace sat vacantly staring into space as her ancient government desktop chugged grudgingly to life.

She couldn't believe she was about to put in more labor — unpaid, uncounted labor. It made her feel small and mocked. To be trapped at her desk doing Lou's grunt work when she should be spending time with her family, or watching TV, or whatever she damn well pleased.

As she sat waiting for the Dell's screen to resolve out of blackness, Grace felt the galling irony: she had once longed for a job that pulled you in at all hours, urgent in its call to duty.

When she went to law school, it had been with the idea of one day wielding the sword of justice against corporate malfeasance. She'd met David in first-year torts at GW Law—David, who would become her husband and River's father and, eventually, her ex-husband. Together they passed endless hours in the bowels of the law library, occasionally emerging to walk the streets of DC, flush with young love and naive exuberance, imagining without embarrassment a life spent fighting various good fights. Grace's dream was to be a capital defender; David would run a firm specializing in class actions against corporate polluters.

But life did its thing. They both graduated from GW with loans to repay. They had a kid. By the time of the divorce, David was firmly ensconced at Palmer, Phelps, in a gray building in Northwest DC, specializing in complex securities transactions and churning his way toward partner. And here was Grace, in her good and steady and unremarkable job with federal benefits and a shared office on the third floor. She wore the same sensible ensembles every day of the week, ground through an endless stack of 510(k) intent-to-market applications for medical devices, and watched Netflix at night.

That's what we're all signed up for, as Grace's mother liked to say in her caustic way. *Life takes you where it takes you, and it leaves you there.*

Grace sighed. Kathy had always been a real fount of encouragement.

The truth was that somewhere along the way, Grace had gotten very good at this job. The fact that she was a prized employee, efficient and accurate and reliable, gave her a sour kind of pride—how marvelous it was to have become so accomplished in the intricacies of medical-device regulation: what differentiated a class 2 from a class 3 device, what the requirements were for each class of certification. Grace could only reflect, with a sad retrospective horror, on all the time and effort she'd put in to become an expert at this stuff. All those hours; months' worth of hours; *years* of hours.

At last the screen of the Dell glowed to life, requesting her password. Grace cracked her neck, one way and then the other, and got started.

And as the minutes passed and yawned into hours, as Grace trawled the relevant applicant-history files, maneuvering expertly through decades of 510(k) applications for portacaths and related devices, she imagined herself in the disapproving company of the person she'd set out to be but never managed to become.

The Grace of her youth, righteous and wrathful and ambitious, standing at her shoulder, astonished with disappointment.

3.

Hello? Hi? Can someone come in here, please?"

Allie was awake. She had been asleep and then sort of awake and then asleep again, or not, she wasn't sure, but now she was suddenly very awake, awake and terrified in a hospital bed with no sense of how long she'd been in it or how she'd gotten here or where *here* even was. She was utterly, confoundingly disoriented, with panic fluttering through her bones.

Allie jammed her thumb down on the little button beside the bed. She had been pressing it and pressing it, but no one would come and help her. Come on, come *on*, why wouldn't they *come*?

"Hello?" She raised her voice so maybe someone would hear her out in the hallway, and the strain of shouting made her cough. *"Hello?"*

The hospital room had beige walls and a beige floor, and the blanket on the bed was beige, too, and there was a light lemony smell of cleaning fluid. On the wall there was a small dull watercolor: a grove of pines all listing slightly left. There was a TV bolted to a metal arm above the door.

There was, too, a clock ticking relentlessly as the second hand made its endless sweep, and it reminded Allie with a pang of her classroom, of how certain restless kids were constantly eyeing the clock above the door, counting down the minutes to the end of the day.

Her mouth was dry. She coughed again. Why was her mouth so dry? How long had she even been asleep? There was some kind of line coming out of her arm — was it taking out blood? Was it putting something in?

Oh my God, Allie didn't like this. She didn't like this at all.

She tapped on the button again like she was playing pinball and raised her voice louder and louder, calling out into the hall.

"Hello? Can somebody come in here maybe and help me? Please?"

This was insane. She had to get out of here. She still hadn't called her husband. Her husband —

Allie's racing mind stuttered and stopped. A spasm of pain clutched her chest and then let go, and then —

Lucas.

Her husband's name was Lucas.

Yeah. God. She had to call Lucas and tell him she was alive, she was okay.

Was she okay? She didn't know how long she'd been here, how long she'd been unconscious. *Had* she been unconscious? Or had she merely been sedated? Was one of these machines she was hooked up to pumping some kind of narcotic or anesthetic or whatever it was called directly into her veins?

Allie could see the clothes she'd been wearing folded neatly inside a plastic bag on a chair on the other side of the room.

She remembered now. Early this morning — late last night — whenever it was they'd brought her in here, they'd been asking her for her name, asking her what had happened, and she'd said she had to call her husband. She'd *tried* to call her husband.

Her husband? She didn't have —

Again, the pain in her chest, and then again, release.

Lucas.

It hurt — not as bad as it had hurt in the SUV last night when she'd cried out and jerked and banged her head into the window. But it *hurt.*

Lucas! Yes, Allie, God, yes! Your husband. Her husband's name was Lucas.

That's right, her husband had a name, and she had tried to call him from the phone beside the bed. She'd dialed 1 for an outside line but then she couldn't remember the number — well, of course not, why would she? All her numbers were saved in her phone. But he must be looking for her. Right? He'd be making all kinds of calls, checking the area hospitals. He'd be frantic by now.

Oh my God, thought Allie. *Unless they got him too. Unless they —*

Who?

The people. The people who got you.

Right, right, right.

There was some sort of very unusual conversation going on inside Allie's head. She didn't like it. She mashed the call button some more, pressing it and pressing it. She needed water or, like, ice chips or something. Weren't hospitals supposed to give you ice chips? Allie's students were going to be so worried. Next week was a week of standardized testing before the Thanksgiving break. Allie kind of felt like maybe it was best for her to close her eyes and go back to sleep, but on the other hand she felt like she had been asleep forever and all she wanted was to be awake and get the hell out of here.

Maybe she should just climb out of the bed and wander into the hallway and find someone who could help her. The problem was that she was hooked up in at least two different ways — there was a thin tube under her nose and there was an IV line running into her arm, pushing fluid into her veins from one of those balloon-like plastic bags that hung from a metal frame beside the bed.

She thought she remembered being brought in in an ambulance, barely awake, barely alive, phasing in and out of understanding as they asked her a million questions.

Trying to call someone. Who had she tried to call?

Before that, she remembered fleeing through the woods, every step sending agonizing pain up into her wounded foot — she remembered attacking that scary woman driver, remembered the SUV crashing — and she remembered being in the playground with the stroller parked at the edge of the sandbox when the two of them came out of those cars, the woman and the man who had taken Rachel —

Rachel.

Allie sat up straight and screamed, "Help! Somebody please *help* me!"

Finally — *finally* — a doctor came, practically bounded into the room. He was a round white man with a gleaming pink scalp and a breast pocket jammed with pens. A nurse trailed behind him, wearing pale pink scrubs covered in cartoon mice.

"Good, good," said the doctor cheerfully. "Look who's back in the land of the living."

"Okay," said Allie. "Thank God. Hi. Listen —"

"One sec," said the big doctor, stretching out the word *one* in a patronizing super-syllable. "Just gimme ooooooone sec."

The doctor had some sort of tablet tilted in front of him like a restaurant menu, and he was scrolling through it, apparently in search of Allie's chart. The nurse, two heads shorter than the doctor even in her sturdy black shoes, bustled over to the monitors beside the bed and jotted down readings.

"Hi, wait. Whoa, whoa." Allie jerked away from the nurse, who had unscritched a blood pressure cuff and was trying to wrap it around her skinny upper arm. "I need to get out of here. I need to *go*."

"Goodness. Sick of my bedside manner already. I think that's a record." The doctor chuckled and glanced up from the iPad. "I haven't even *said* anything yet."

Allie blinked up at him. She felt like she was going to cry.

"My life is in danger. I said when I got here. When they brought me in. There's this lady, I don't know why, but she's *after* me. Can we call the police? We have to call the police."

"Actually," said the doctor, "the police already know you're here. So that wish, at least, has been granted. Now, in case no one did so already, allow me to welcome you to Hanover Regional Medical Center in lovely Hanover, Maryland. I'm Dr. Steven Adomian, but folks call me Dr. Steve. At least, that's what they call me when I'm in earshot."

He gave her a cheery wink, and Allie felt a wash of utter dismay. She had known men like this before, men like her current vice principal, Mr. Wellman, confident and self-satisfied and blithe, and could see with immediate clarity how this whole encounter was going to go: Dr. Steve would half listen and make dumb doctor jokes and check off boxes on his iPad, and meanwhile that lady was out there, the small evil woman with the green eyes who had snatched Allie from a public park and from whom she had only barely escaped with her life.

I stabbed her, recalled Allie with a jolt, and the horrified recollection brought sickness up into her throat. *I stabbed her in the eye.* She could feel it in her hand, the silvery surface of the shard she'd plunged into the woman's face. Allie turned her head to one side, looked at the painting of listing pines, then looked back at the big doctor.

"What I am trying to tell you, uh, sir? Sir? I'm trying to tell you that I am in imminent danger," said Allie. "And so is my child. Can you help me?"

"Of course," he said. "That's what we're here for. But first I want to just get everyone caught up, okay? So, very early this morning, you were brought in by an amazing team of EMTs and a couple of lovely cops, and given your condition when you were found on . . ." He checked his notes. "On a regional train car, the first thing the emergency docs did was put in a line and give you a liter of normal saline. Then they decided the prudent move was to numb up your foot and have Dr. Shah sew it up. Speaking of which . . ."

Dr. Steve lifted Allie's foot with one paw and held it gingerly while he inspected the bottom, frowning with concentration. His scalp reflected the lights up toward the ceiling tiles. The clock ticked while he examined the sutures.

"Stitches are looking pretty tidy. How's it feeling?"

Allie rolled her foot around, flexed her toes. "It's fine," she said impatiently. "It feels fine."

"Okay, then," said the doctor. "Ten points for Dr. Shah. We're still giving you fluids for the dehydration and an IV antibiotic. This says you told my colleagues this morning that you aren't allergic to any medications—is that right?"

Allie nodded.

"And that you called family members and friends but were unable to reach anyone?"

Allie blinked. She couldn't remember. Had she tried to call Lucas? Why hadn't she been able to reach him? He—

"Wait," she said, but Dr. Steve was already moving on.

"Can you confirm your name for me?"

"It's Allie."

"Okay! Great." Dr. Steve jotted it down with his stylus and then waited, eyebrows still raised. "And is there a *last* name that goes with that?"

Allie opened her mouth and then closed it again. She considered for a moment while Dr. Steve waited, stylus clenched between two thick fingers. "I can't . . ." Allie trailed off.

"Sorry, Allie . . . your last name?"

The pain subsided. Allie took a breath. "I'm afraid I can't remember."

"Well, hey, that's okay." Dr. Steve seemed unfazed. "I'll put *TBD*." He grinned. "Wouldn't be the worst last name, right? Allie TBD? Sounds like a rapper or something, huh?"

It was exactly as Allie had feared, this guy's casual, condescending air, but that was sometimes a thing you had to deal with with doctors, wasn't it? The most stressful day of your life was just another day at the office for them. She remembered laboring with Rachel, grunting and straining, feeling like her body was turning itself inside out, and it was hour, like, *fourteen* of what ended up being eighteen, and there she was, soon to be a single mom, no one there to help, and some doctor kept making the same sort of isn't-life-funny jokes, and she had just felt like, *Dude, come on! This is the hardest thing I've ever done, so maybe stop acting like everything is fine. Everything is not fine.*

"Allie?" Dr. Steve was smiling blandly at her. "Do you know what year it is?"

She told him.

"Great. Do you take any street drugs, Allie?"

She shook her head. She moaned. She needed to get out of here.

"And are you employed at present?" Dr. Steve asked her.

"Yeah. I work at a — a —"

She had almost said *ice cream parlor,* which made no sense. Allie did science. Allie was a — a scientist?

She felt it then, suddenly, as she lay there trying to remember something she had inexplicably forgotten, what she did for a living—a tightening around her chest, an incipient version of the brutal pain that had seized her last night in the kidnapper's back seat. She brought a hand up to her chest, wincing. It hurt. *Goddamn,* did it hurt—

"I'm a teacher," Allie blurted out, relieved. The word had just come to her. For a moment she had had no idea.

What is happening, Allie? What is going on?

"I teach at a middle school."

"Where?"

"I . . . I told you." Allie blinked. "At a middle school."

"Great," Dr. Steve said, dutifully writing on his iPad. "Good for you."

Allie didn't answer. She felt afraid. Confused and afraid. A few moments ago, thinking back to the day that Rachel was born, she'd been picturing herself alone in that hospital room. But she hadn't been alone. Her husband had been there when their daughter was born, hadn't he?

Wait. Husband?

Allie's head throbbed. She did have a husband, didn't she?

Yes.

Or—

Yes.

But now she couldn't remember his name.

Allie squeezed her eyes shut tight, tears forming behind the lids. *Name, name, name—what the hell is his name?*

But there *was* no name, actually, only a—a *feeling,* a *sensation* of a bowling shirt and a bowling bag, a way of laughing in the back of the throat, and even as those impressions swirled and receded in Allie's mind, the grinding pain returned to her chest, straining across her ribs, and this time it lasted, stretching out for one second, two seconds, three, while Allie gasped and clutched the bedrail and moaned.

"Whoa," said the doctor. "Whoa! Allie? Hey!"

"I'm okay," she said at last. "I'm okay."

Allie took a series of long ragged breaths, reeling from the pain that was only now passing, as Dr. Steve or whatever his damn name was scrawled away on his stupid iPad.

"Hey, Dorothy?" His brow furrowed as he addressed the nurse. "I'm ordering some labs for our friend here. Can you head up to the sixth floor, see who's at the wheel up there?"

Dorothy nodded unsmilingly and bustled out of the room, heavy shoes squeaking on the tile. Allie hated the tubes and wires that were connecting her to the machines and the IV bag. She wanted to leave. It was all a tangle. The lady in the silver SUV, with the green eyes and dark hair. These inexplicable waves of pain. What the *hell* was happening?

"Now, Allie," Dr. Steve continued. "It's not quite clear from the notes here how you got the laceration on your foot."

"I told them already. This morning."

Had she told them?

"Right, right." Dr. Steve frowned. "According to what you told the docs this morning..." Dr. Steve consulted the iPad. "There was a woman, quote, 'dressed all in black, in a silver car.'"

"Bigger. Not a car," Allie corrected. "It was a—like an SUV."

"The woman had green eyes," Dr. Steve went on, still reading. "And a ponytail. That's the person who took your baby?"

"No, no."

"No?"

"She took *me*. Just me. The other one took my baby. Her—I don't know. Accomplice, or whatever. There were *two* of them."

"Two of them. Okay."

"He had boots on. Black boots, or—"

Allie squeezed her eyes shut, trying to form a picture. When she opened them again, the doctor was writing something down, and Allie was sure that whatever he was writing had nothing to do with the words she was saying. He was writing *Confused and disoriented,* or maybe he was writing *Out of her goddamn mind,* or simply *Nutjob.* It was no use; the doctor had slotted her into a category. He had put her in a box. Anything else she said about the terrible danger she faced would only prove that she was a crazy person, a hysterical woman ranting about imaginary dangers.

"Sorry, wait," she said. "Can you just look at me? Instead of writing?"

"Of course." With patronizing exactitude, Dr. Steve clipped the stylus to the underside of the iPad. "So, your child—sorry, what's the child's name?"

For a frantic moment Allie could not remember, and every cell in her body vibrated with horror, and then she shouted it: "Rachel!" She was practically panting. "*Rachel.* We call her—sometimes we call her Ray-Ray. I know it's silly."

"We?"

"What?"

"You have a husband or a partner?"

Allie didn't really see how it was any of this guy's business, but she answered anyway, just a curt "No. No, it's just me."

She pursed her lips momentarily while the details of her life swam around in her mind, unable to settle, and then she shook her head, because who cared, why did any of this matter?

Allie was thinking only of little Rachel now, her bright red cheeks, her funny little sweep of strawberry hair. She had a birthmark high on her right temple. She had all these allergies, but she was also in the seventy-fifth percentile for weight and height, which, to Allie, who had always been so skinny and small, seemed like an astonishing sign of vitality. She kept growing and growing, her little feet always straining against the toes of her onesies.

Allie thought of Rachel with a kind of wild desperateness, like she had to see her, she had to see her *now* or she would lose her forever. Like the thought of Rachel was all that was keeping Allie connected to the earth.

"Okay, Allie, well . . . thank you so much," said the doctor, snapping closed the iPad and tucking it under his arm. The nurse, Dorothy, had slipped back into the room and now stood waiting directly beneath the clock, with her hands clasped in front of her.

"So here's the plan. We are going to keep you nice and comfortable for the time being while we try to figure out who you are and what exactly happened to you."

"I know who I am," Allie said. "I know what happened to me."

But Dr. Steve just nodded, smiled pleasantly — *Sure, sure* — and moved on as if she hadn't spoken. "Last thing," he said. "What about the port?"

"The — the *what?*"

"The port. Portacath?" he said. "May I?"

Without waiting for an answer, Dr. Steve moved aside the neck of Allie's gown, revealing a hard flat bump on her chest below her clavicle and just above her right breast. Allie looked down at it. She reached up and touched it. It felt like a callus. Like a stone beneath her skin. Her fingertips began to tremble.

"What *is* that?" she said.

"A portacath. A medical device."

Allie looked down at her chest again, holding her chin at an awkward angle against her body to try to see the strange patch of skin. "Why did you put that in me?"

"Whoa," said Dr. Steve. "It was there. It's a little infected, and we're gonna go ahead and pop it out tomorrow. But we'd like to know when and why it got put in in the first place. Might help us figure out who you are."

50

"I told you who I am."

"Well — you didn't, really, though, did you?"

"What?" said Allie, and then she remembered about the port.

She remembered when they'd done it —

— a hand on hers, a reassuring voice: *Don't worry, honey. You're in good hands.*

Allie shivered, baffled and homesick. Whose voice was that — what hospital — when *was* that? The moment was faded at its edges, sweet and honey-lined and aching in her memory, a whisper of the past.

The present interrupted. Dr. Steve, squinting down at her, the pink dome of his scalp. "Allie? You okay? What are we thinking about in there?"

Allie didn't answer. She couldn't. She tugged up the neck of her gown.

"You know what?" Allie said. She lay back. She let her eyes drift shut. "I need to rest. Can I rest now?"

Allie said that suddenly she was very tired, and she would like to go back to sleep — which was, of course, exactly what Dr. Steve wanted to hear.

But Allie was not tired, and she did not go back to sleep.

When Dr. Steve had left the room, when the sound of his labored big-man breathing and the nurse's squeaking shoes had faded down the hall-way, Allie opened her eyes wide. In the hospital light, in the beige room, she was entirely awake.

She reached gingerly inside the neck of her gown and laid her fingers again on the hard flat patch of skin that marked the site where the device was implanted.

What had he called it? A port. Portacath. She touched the spot cautiously, as if it were a mouth that might bite her.

She and Missy were riding their ten-speeds around and around the cul-de-sac at the end of Kenwood, getting this close to the parked cars, daring each other to crack the side mirrors or scrape the paint. Couple of budding little hoodlums hurling insults at each other, laughing like idiots, each demanding that the other go faster, go further. Ten years old? Twelve?

Her stepdad on the front porch, framed by the quiet interior light, his big friendly face bearing the sad trying-hard smile he'd worn since Mom got sick. "Gals? You wanna come in and eat something? Remember eating, ladies? It's one of these things we humans like to do"—

Allie gasped. The pressure in her chest was like hands, dozens of hands, pushing up on her ribs from inside.

The memories were like radio signals. Missy shrieking, tossing handfuls of gravel into the spokes as she sped past; the big red-brick house on Kenwood Drive at the end of the cul-de-sac loop, stately in the twilight. Her stepdad's thick hair, his voice cheerful but streaked with melancholy.

Allie lurched to the side and vomited over the bedrail, clutching her chest and panting—

—because she had grown up in Logan County, Ohio, in a dot of a town called Bellefontaine, where her parents operated a filling station. They had a wood-sided house on a country lane with cornfields visible from the yard, and there wasn't a big red-brick house in the whole county, and she'd never had a friend named Missy, and she'd definitely never had a stepfather. Allie's parents were Douglas and Kelly Brownlee and they'd been happily married her whole childhood and were to this day.

Calm down, Allie insisted to herself, *you have to stay calm,* but then she told herself to shut up because calm wasn't really happening anymore, no one was buying calm.

Her hands were trembling as she picked up the phone to call her parents, asking herself why she hadn't done it already, as she dialed one and then dialed the number she still knew by heart. But anyway she knew what would happen and it did happen — the phone just rang and rang, which made no sense because Douglas and Kelly Brownlee were always at home in the evenings and even if they weren't, their voice mail should have answered.

Allie slammed the phone down and picked it up and tried again, and this time the operator's dead robot voice came on to tell her that the number she was trying to reach did not exist.

4.

It was almost midnight, and Grace was still at her desk on the third floor of CDRH, still researching the funky portacath.

She had set the timer on her iPhone, fully intending to stick to her guns and give this objectionable nighttime project the single hour of effort she'd committed to and not a moment more. But when the timer went off, she set it for another half hour and kept working, and then did so again, and then once more.

She was close — she knew it. There were only seventeen major manufacturers of portacaths and a scattered handful of smaller companies that had entered the space over the past several decades. Her detective work in discovering the maker of the specific model implanted in the Hanover mystery woman was largely a process of elimination. She just had to keep chugging away.

And as much as Grace resented sitting here in the middle of the night solving someone else's problem for no extra compensation or reward, she found that she couldn't leave the task unfinished. Meaning she was either admirably dedicated to the notion of a job well done or pathetically desperate for the praise of people who didn't care about her one way or the other.

"Potato, potahto," Grace murmured, and yawned, and set the alarm one last time.

At last Grace sat back, stretched her arms out to their full length, and announced to Kendall Johns's collection of desk plants that she was done. She uploaded the document summarizing her findings to the shared Dropbox where Lou Fleming liked to see finished assignments.

What she had discovered was that the port had been produced between 2008 and 2011 by a medical-device company called Goldenstar Therapeutic Technologies, known as GTT, headquartered in Delaware but with its primary manufacturing plant in Singapore. The portacath in question, with the model number GTT798, was notable for two innovations: an unusual oblong shape, designed to optimize fluid flow to and from the catheter, and an embedded electronic transmitter, allowing ported individuals to be tracked as they moved through different sections of the hospital.

Late in 2011, Goldenstar Therapeutic Technologies had been absorbed by a larger entity called KRG Holdings, which itself had filed for bankruptcy in 2013 and disappeared. But during GTT's brief existence, the GTT798 had been sold to a handful of vendors, mostly in the north and northeast United States. Six of the buyers had been small hospitals, including two apiece in Cincinnati, Ohio, and Lexington, Kentucky; three were outpatient centers with names like Sunset Ridge Pain Management Associates; two were big public universities with large scientific-research faculties and teaching hospitals; and one was some sort of private academic facility called the Substance Material Group.

"And that is that," said Grace as her summary document uploaded to the server. "Nailed it." Then she smiled, thinking what a dork she was for taking such pleasure in the satisfactory completion of Lou's irritating assignment, imagining how savagely River would roast her if they were here. But Grace couldn't help it; yes, this had been unwelcome work, but at least she had done it well.

Grace stood and stretched, putting her hands on her hips and twisting her upper body back and forth. Lately she had developed a small but increasingly worrisome pain in the small of her back. Her primary care doctor had, six months ago, cheerfully informed her that back pain was just "one of those things that come with age" and could be "awfully tough to address." In the end, she had handed Grace a pamphlet with exercises in it, which she dutifully if skeptically performed whenever her back acted up.

When she was done half-assing her way through the stretches, Grace slipped her bag over her shoulder and went to Lou's door to stick a Post-it note on it telling him her report was in the Dropbox. That way he'd have it if she took him up on his offer and came in late tomorrow — though Grace knew perfectly well she would never do that.

As she stuck on the Post-it, Lou's door crept open slightly, and Grace saw into his office, the familiar furniture and art dimly visible by the half-lights on the floor. The manila envelope with the pictures in it was still sitting on his desk. There were more pictures. She remembered that — there had been more pictures in the envelope, more printouts, that Lou hadn't shown her.

As Grace stood there staring into the office, a thought struck her with sudden force and clarity: *I have to see.*

She wanted to know more about the girl in the hospital, who she was and how she had ended up there, the whole bizarre situation. Grace didn't know why she wanted to know, but she did. She *needed* to know.

The thought so clear, it was like a picture in her mind, like the words hung suspended in the air before her.

I need to go in there.

I need to see the rest.

As soon as Grace had the thought, she knew she was going to do it. As exhausted as she was, as ready as she was to go home, she was going to go and look. It was as good as done.

She edged Lou's door open the rest of the way and slowly walked in. She felt the absence of the world. All day, every day, the third floor was noisy with chatter, with people's phones ringing and beeping, with the occasional *ker-chunk* of a soda dropping down from the vending machine, with the braying laughter of Terry Baumgarten, who sat right outside Grace and Kendall's shared office.

It was different now, at night. All was settled and still. The deep hum of electrical systems murmuring to each other.

Grace had no business going into Lou's office, of course. It wasn't her office, and they weren't her pictures to look at. Plus it was time to go home. Well past time, in fact. Grace looked at her watch; it was 11:55. The day itself was almost done.

But this also meant that her mother and her child were asleep at home. This particular opportunity for quality family time or for peaceful alone time or for whatever kind of time it was going to be had already been lost and could never be recovered.

And the photographs from the hospital were calling out to her somehow. This was silly, and Grace knew that it was silly, but it was also true. She had this urge that was not an urge, exactly, but more like a kind of insistent foreknowledge: There was something interesting going on here, and interesting things were rare, and she deserved to know more. Even more than that, what Grace deserved was some kind of compensation for being summoned tonight just to save poor Lou the trouble of doing the

57

work. She deserved to feel, for one half of one second, like she was a person with her own will in the world.

She was in. She had done it. She had her bag over her shoulder; she had her legal pad clutched under her arm.

She sat down in Lou's chair, at Lou's desk.

On the top of the stack of photographs was the one she had already inspected: the framed torso of the young woman, arms crossed protectively over her breasts. Her freckles and her tattoos and the small oblong circle of raised skin indicating where the port had been inserted subcutaneously. Grace moved that picture aside and saw the X-ray and then beneath that the picture that was zoomed in tightly on the port site, the odd shape like a question, like a mistake.

She lifted that picture by its corner and flipped to the next.

It was the girl's face.

Not a girl — Grace immediately corrected herself with a self-accusing eye-roll. A woman.

A young woman, to be sure, twenty-five or twenty-six at most. Grace lifted the picture and looked at it closely. It was framed tightly from the chin to the top of the scalp. The face was small and angular with a turned-up nose and thin, sharply defined cheeks. This photograph made Grace unaccountably sad, and it took a long moment of staring at it to say why. It was the eyes. The girl — the *woman* — was staring directly at the camera, her eyes soft and out of focus, and there was something unnameable deep in her expression that seized at Grace's heart.

"God," she said softly, not knowing exactly what she meant, "what *happened* to you?"

Grace slipped her phone from her pocket and began taking pictures of the pictures, one by one, wanting for reasons she couldn't quite explain to create her own record of what she was seeing. When she was done, she set her phone down and again held the picture of the face, just the face, caught in the tight framing of the photo. She traced the piece of printer paper with two fingers, as if she could reach through it, pierce the membrane of time, touch the woman's skin directly.

Then Grace asked her question again, in a slightly different way.

"What have they done to you? What have they *done?*"

5.

Desiree, whose name was not really Desiree, stood alone in an empty patient room in a rural Maryland hospital. She was preparing to inject a dose of antibiotic into the muscle of her thigh.

The overhead lights in the room were very bright. There was a full-length mirror on the back of the door of the room.

The antibiotic was called Rocephin. She loaded a vial of it into a hypodermic syringe, then removed her pants in order to access her thigh. She located the best site to insert the needle the way she'd been instructed to over the phone by Dr. Ashberry, whose name was not really Dr. Ashberry and who might not actually be a doctor. He had warned her that if she did not do the intermuscular injection correctly, it would A) hurt like a motherfucker, and B) not work. It would make a lot more sense for her to come see him so he could do it himself. But Dr. Ashberry's practice was out of his studio apartment in Queens, New York, and Desiree did not have the time to make that trip at present.

She just had to do it. She had to do it and get back to work.

So Dr. Ashberry had provided instructions over the phone, along with a list of antibiotics that would do the trick. He had suggested it would be easiest to steal the necessary dose from a hospital pharmacy.

This was convenient, because Desiree had been traveling from hospital to hospital looking for the targeted individual who had run from her after the car accident in the Maryland woods.

So far this job had taken Desiree over twenty-eight hours. Twenty-eight hours and thirty-seven minutes, as of the moment she had checked the timer on her watch, just before closing the door of this patient room. When she was done with the business of the injection, it would be closer to twenty-nine hours, an absolutely miserable total.

Desiree worked for a flat fee, no expenses, and thus what she earned on any given assignment had to be amortized out over the total time required to complete it. It was the merciless math of time and money, and there was no gray area. A typical job took six to seventy-two hours, depending on the difficulty level, and earned her $45,000 to $250,000, with the rate varying based on a number of factors, including the nature of the assignment, nature of the target, locale, and potential for danger.

On the high end, then, Desiree could earn as much as $41,667 an hour, but such cases were extremely rare. More typical was something close to five thousand an hour, although a particularly time-consuming project might net her as little as five or six hundred. One way to compensate for this variability in pay was to complete each assignment as quickly as possible, which not only maximized the money earned on that particular assignment but also allowed her to move swiftly to the next one and its resultant payday.

This current job was taking too long. For what it was, it was taking way, way too long.

When Desiree had contracted for this seemingly routine assignment she had told the client that she would bring the targeted individual from the pickup point to the destination point within twelve hours. And Desiree had considered this to be a conservative estimate, given that the distance between pickup and drop-off points was only 166 miles. A twelve-hour total would have made her $65,000 fee amortize out to $5,417 an hour.

But now she was looking at thirty hours, at the very least, which meant an hourly amortized take of $2,167, minus the unconscionable $1,200 consult fee she now owed Dr. Ashberry plus whatever the repair cost ended up being on the first Buick Enclave.

It had taken Desiree several hours to locate a suitable place to rid herself of the gangly corpse of the young jogger. Then there had been the round-trip time to Perth Amboy, where her car guy had whistled and shook his head before taking possession of the cracked Buick and providing her with a replacement, Desiree the whole time staring balefully at him, staring balefully at her watch, staring balefully at the sun rising over industrial New Jersey.

Only late this afternoon had Desiree been able to begin looking in earnest for the targeted individual, the surprisingly spirited girl who had managed to escape from her. She had returned to the site of the collision and easily found the path of the girl's frantic run from the scene; she traced her to a fence that separated the woods from a regional train station. It seemed likely, then, that the escapee had found her way onto a train; this galling fact, coupled with the many hours that had passed, vastly expanded the radius of potential places Desiree now had to look.

But the girl had been badly injured. She was scared and disoriented. Desiree would find her.

Meanwhile, the client had been calling.

He had called, indeed, three times since her initial ETA had come and gone. Desiree reported frankly that the targeted individual had slipped the leash, for the moment, but that she remained confident in her ability to quickly find her. The client sounded nervous, maybe even close to alarmed, but Desiree did not think he was the type to outright cancel.

But one never knew. And if the client indeed chose to bag the whole operation and void their contract or if the target popped up before Desiree could find her, then Desiree would be left with only her up-front fee, a financial hit she was in no mood to incur.

Desiree's best hope was that she would find the young woman in a hospital, given how badly she had been injured in her escape. Surely she will have alerted her doctors to her ordeal, and surely the hospital will have contacted the authorities. But in the meantime she would remain a patient: isolated, injured, and vulnerable. Nor was it impossible, for someone of Desiree's determination and ability, to seize a target back from the control of law enforcement. It didn't matter where the target was. If Desiree could track her, she could take her.

It would be risky, but such risks were in the nature of her work. And if she quit, or if she failed, it would all be for nothing.

She had to hurry. Keep moving. *Go.*

Desiree crouched, carefully inserted the needle into the pale meat of her thigh, and depressed the plunger.

When all the fluid was gone from the hypo, she withdrew the needle. It came out with a single pulse of pain at the site.

When she rose from her crouch, Desiree was confronted with the jarring vision of her face reflected in shadow in a mirror hanging above the sink of the small hospital bathroom. Her eye was still covered with gauze. She had not looked yet to see the extent of the damage.

She was — or had been — a conventionally attractive woman. This was not arrogance on her part but a fact. She knew it because people were constantly telling her so; she knew it because she had been able, over the course of her professional life, to use her beauty as a lure or a distraction.

It was impossible yet to say what her face would look like when it healed. She could not yet know to what extent this change in her physical appearance would affect her earning power. She knew there was something about a small and physically attractive woman who did this work that potential clients found intriguing. She earned a premium for it, which she now assumed would be reduced.

Another reason to work harder. Work faster. She had to keep going.

Desiree retrieved her pants and was preparing to slide them on when the door opened. It was a custodian, a short beefy man in deep blue coveralls. He stood, startled, with one hand on the doorknob and the other on the handle of a large, wheeled plastic garbage can.

"Hey, now," he said dully. He looked at her legs, then up at her eyes. "What're you — what're you doing in there?"

The custodian had a walkie-talkie on his belt and he was reaching for it when Desiree grabbed him firmly by the front of the coveralls and yanked him off his feet and dragged him back into the room.

"Hey," he managed before Desiree got her forearm across his neck and started to squeeze. She maneuvered herself around his body, tightening her arm as she kicked shut the door behind them.

Desiree was small and the custodian was large but she was an expert. She dropped down onto one knee, bearing the man's thrashing weight before her, until she let him go and his own weight sent him down hard, and his head banged against the floor with a grim thud. Then Desiree straddled him and wrapped her small arms around his large neck, finding the compression points on the sides of his neck, not the center. She needed not to kill him but to put him to sleep. He gurgled and thrashed and finally stopped moving.

Desiree stood up, panting, gingerly patting the bandage over her eye, making sure it was still in place. The wound site throbbed. It hurt, but not badly.

The custodian made a groaning sigh and shifted slightly on the floor, his arms sprawled out, a felled giant. Desiree stared at him until she was satisfied he was indeed unconscious.

She had maybe half an hour before he regained consciousness and alerted the authorities to her presence, and that was a tight window. She considered putting a bullet in his head, but she knew that the downside risk of a murder was not worth the extra time it would buy her.

She would just have to be quick. She needed to be quick. Time was charging forward. Every passing moment was chipping away at what she stood to gain.

Go.

Desiree finished dressing and slipped out into the hallway. She would clear this hospital and then move on to the next one. She would begin at the emergency department, making polite inquiries about a young woman who might have been brought in for a nasty gash on her left foot. Desiree had already searched and eliminated seven local urgent-care facilities and hospitals out of a total of nineteen she judged to be likely candidates based on the location of the accident and the hours that had passed since.

She pressed the button for the elevator and waited impatiently for it to arrive.

THURSDAY

6.

"What about Sylvia Canning? You remember her?"

"Um — I'm not sure," said Grace. "I think so?"

"Oh, of course you do." Kathy scowled. "The Cannings were in that ugly green house on Barber Street? Sylvia had kind of a weasel face? Her oldest boy had the wobbly eye?"

"Mom, can you lift your elbows, please?"

Kathy obliged with a grunt, and Grace rushed a wet rag across the counter. Last night had been exhausting, her sleep fitful and uneasy. Today had started only half an hour ago and she already felt behind the eight ball, trying to get enough of the kitchen cleanup done so that she wasn't leaving a sticky counter and a sink full of dishes for the later version of herself, the poor exhausted lady who'd be straggling home from work ten hours in the future.

"Well, anyway," said Kathy. "Her cancer's back. Sylvia's." She tapped the side of her head with her forefinger. "It's in her *brain*."

"That's awful," murmured Grace, absently crossing herself.

69

"Eh," said Kathy. "I never liked her."

Grace cast a hopeless glance toward the coffee maker, which had been gurgling petulantly for half an hour at this point without producing any actual coffee. *Come on,* thought Grace, and then went to the foot of the stairs and shouted for River. It was a school day and the first bell was in a half hour, meaning that River was having trouble settling on an outfit, which meant that when at last they emerged, they'd already be in a mood.

"What about Janice? You remember Janice Rutherford?"

Oh, for God's sake, Grace thought, but just said, "I think so."

"She worked at the diner. She had that stupid hair?"

"Yes. I think so. I don't know, Mom. Hang on." She turned to shout up the stairs. "*River!* Where are you? What are you *doing?*"

No response, only stomps and slams from the upstairs bedroom. Drawers being flung open; outfits considered and then angrily discarded.

"Apparently she slipped on her front steps. Went down—shattered her hip."

"I think you told me that one already."

"No, I didn't. This just happened. It was on Facebook."

It was all on Facebook, of course. For Kathy, social media was just a slow-rolling horror show of death and disfigurement, and she loved it. The coffee machine beeped sharply three times, and Grace threw up her hands as if celebrating a field goal, but the liquid that had emerged was in no way coffee. It was just hot, tan water.

"Oh, come on," said Grace to the coffee machine, and Kathy said, "I told you not to buy that damn thing," and Grace said, "No, you did not," and River at last came tumbling down the stairs, arms full and overflowing: backpack, gym bag, phone, ice-skating gear.

"Is there coffee?" they said.

"Back up," said Grace. "Try again."

"Good *morning*," River sang flutily, and dropped all the bags in a heap on the floor. "Is there coffee?"

"No. It's being weird."

"Are you kidding me?" said River.

Grace smiled as big as she could and kept cleaning.

Sometimes sharing a home with her mother and her only child was like living in a house of mirrors: Grace was always catching glimpses of herself around the corner, in a different light or a different mood. Here you are as a child; here you are grown old. Obviously she was lucky, and she knew she was lucky, to share quarters with the two people she cared for most in the world — but also it would be very nice, sometimes, to be alone.

"River, just as a heads-up, we are leaving in nine minutes."

"I *know*," said River, stomping around the kitchen. "Stop *telling* me."

"I just told you. You just came down."

"You tell me every day. Literally, same conversation. Every day. So, are we stopping at Starbucks or no?"

Grace glanced at her watch and said no and River moaned.

Kathy, meanwhile, had tilted on her stool to examine River from above the rims of her round glasses. "What the hell is she *wearing?*"

"*They,*" said Grace before River could say it, but River still said it: "*They,* Nana. It's seriously not hard."

"Fine," Kathy said, waving her hand. "Sorry, hon." And then, to Grace again: "What the hell are they *wearing?*"

"Come on, Nana," said River, planting their hands on their hips. "Don't be judgmental."

Once upon a time, River had been the kind of kid you saw in greeting cards, a pudgy magical creature in a sailor dress, adorable ringlet curls, and wide, awestruck eyes. Then for a while, late in elementary school and into middle, they'd been a tomboy, favoring a short ponytail and overalls, and then for a year or so, it was a baroque form of emo, with jet-black hair and embroidered jeans and painted fingernails.

In retrospect River had always been drifting closer to what they were now, or rather what they had always been and now felt comfortable announcing: nonbinary, floating free between or above both genders. Today they were in a shapeless button-down shirt. Their hair was spiked up, dyed black but with the natural blond peeking in at the roots; lately they had begun wearing black horn-rimmed glasses with nonprescription lenses.

"I think that shirt is actually pretty cool," Grace said to Kathy and then smiled at River. "Seriously. I dig it."

"Great news," River said sarcastically. "I'm so relieved."

Grace dumped the old coffee grounds in the countertop compost bin and started the brewing process over, and—amid all the gentle chaos of the morning—moving through her, just under the level of conscious deliberation, was the last picture from the pile on Lou's desk: the close-up of the young woman in the hospital, too skinny and too pale, her eyes dazed and unfocused.

Grace was trying not to think about it, because what good would that do, and after all it was none of her business. And there was some part of her still wondering if she had dreamed it, if maybe it hadn't been there at all.

But she hadn't dreamed it, she knew it had been real, and now, although she was *here*, rushing and cleaning and arguing and living, still she was *there*—bent forward over Lou's desk in the darkness, choked up with empathy and wonder.

"Now, what on earth is *this?*" Kathy said sharply.

"What is what, Mom?"

Kathy, her elbows again propped on the counter, was reading from the yellow legal pad that Grace had tossed there when she finally got in last night. Grace felt a bolt of confused panic at the sight of the pad, and she leaned across the counter to make a grab for it. "It's nothing," she said.

River snatched up the pad before she could reach it. "Whoa," they said, scanning the page. *"Mom."*

"What?" said Grace, and then: "Can I have that, please?"

She reached again for her pad, feeling oddly exposed, as if some mean kids had found her high-school diary and were passing it around. But even as she tried to snatch back the legal pad, Grace didn't really understand what was on there that was making her feel so violated. She thought back frantically, flushed with confusion and embarrassment: What had she written?

As if reading her mind, River said, "What did you write on here?"

"It's nothing," she said.

"Well, it ain't *nothing*," said Kathy. She was unfolding her half-moon reading glasses from her breast pocket to perch them on the bridge of her nose.

"It's work. It's boring. You should not be looking at that."

"Well, which is it?" River asked. "Is it nothing? Or is it a boring work thing we shouldn't be looking at?"

"You are such the child of lawyers," said Grace, and River grinned wickedly and shrugged. "So?" they said. "Sue me."

Kathy snorted with laughter, and Grace exhaled heavily, pushing her hand up into her hair. These two, the two of them together, instinctively teaming up to push her buttons. It would have been sweet if it weren't so annoying.

"It's just some notes for a project we're working on," Grace lied. "That's all."

Grace couldn't remember having written anything down while she was looking at those pictures. Now, though, she could see the scrawled notes on the notepad from last night's conversation with Lou Fleming. She could see where it said *direct request from hospital.* Beneath that, the words *totally out of it mentally.* There, too, was Grace's meticulous small marginal drawing of the port made by Goldenstar Therapeutic Technologies.

River looked up from the page and stared at her. "Mom? What is this about?"

She stared at the page.

"It's sort of . . ." she said. "It's hard to explain."

"Why are you acting weird?" demanded River, and Grace said, "I'm not," and River just stared at her from behind their costume glasses. Since they were little, River had hated being lied to, and since they were little, they had always known when Grace was lying.

"I'm going to the store today," announced Kathy, out of nowhere, and began to stand up very slowly, gripping the countertop for support.

"What?" said Grace. "How?"

"What do you mean, how? In my damn car."

Kathy looked at Grace challengingly, and Grace took a deep breath. They had had this conversation so many times.

"Mom, you're not driving right now. Remember? The doctor said."

"That doctor can kiss my fat ass."

"Yes. That's what you told the doctor."

"Hey, Mom?" said River.

"Hang on," said Grace, and kept her eyes on her mother. "Dr. Aaronson said you need to see a gerontologist—"

"Dr. Aaronson, first of all—"

"To assess your capacity, and in the meantime—"

"My capacity is fantastic. My capacity needs to go to the damn Costco."

"*Mom.*"

"What?"

"This is freaking me out."

Reluctantly, Grace turned away from her mother and toward River. "What? What is freaking you out?"

"*This.*"

River pointed at the pad, and Grace stared at the words. It said <u>WHAT HAVE THEY DONE TO YOU</u>, thickly underlined. She realized with a kind of dark red horror that she had written them.

Grace stared at the words. "Jesus," she muttered.

She remembered thinking that exact thing. When she crept back into Lou's office to look again at those pictures, when she had found the close-up of the patient, staring ahead, her eyes strangely unfocused. And Grace had thought, *What have they done to you?* It's just that she didn't remember writing it down. Not until now.

It was as if she had wanted to make sure that she remembered.

Kathy meanwhile had pulled open the junk drawer and was sifting through all the shit that had accumulated in there: postage stamps and loose thumbtacks and screwdrivers of random sizes. The sight of the mess filled Grace with anxiety. She had to clean that, she really did. And the basement. She had to clean the basement.

"Mom, can you stop?"

"I need the keys."

"I hid them."

"Mom, is someone in trouble?" River wanted to know.

"You did not hide my keys," Kathy said.

"I did."

Everyone was talking at once now, Kathy bitterly demanding to be allowed to drive to the damn Costco, given that she was seventy-four damn years old, and River asking again if someone was in trouble, and who it was, and what did that mean, *What have they done to you?*

"Stop," said Grace. "Stop." She waved her hands in the air and told them both to be quiet. "River, we have to go. We're both going to be late. Mom, I love you. I'll take you to Costco tonight."

"Just tell me where my damn car keys are!"

Grace grabbed her stuff, and River grabbed theirs, and Kathy was still complaining loudly about being a prisoner in her own damn home as the two of them rushed out the door. They were already late and there was no time to stop at Starbucks, and as River groaned and begged, Grace tuned them out and thought instead of what she'd meant when she'd written *What have they done to you*—and the obvious question that went with it: Who were "they"?

7.

Kendall Johns glanced up from his computer. "Oh. Good morning."

Grace was more than a little late today, but it didn't matter; Kendall was always there when she got in, and whether she was thirty seconds late or half an hour, he did the same thing: glanced up and furrowed his brow very slightly, as if he had forgotten he had an officemate and was slightly perplexed by the interruption.

"Hi, Kendall," she said as she arranged her purse and coat on the wall hook beside his. He always took the leftmost two hooks, and she always took the right. "How are you doing today?"

"Fine, fine," he said, fixing his eyes back on his computer. Kendall was a soft-spoken African American man from Northern Virginia; he and Grace had always been perfectly collegial, but they weren't friends. "Would you like me to turn my music down?"

"No, Kendall," said Grace. He always asked, and she always said no. Kendall listened to classical music on a small portable Bluetooth speaker, the violins as quiet as insects humming in a field. "I don't mind at all."

Their daily ration of conversation thus concluded, Kendall returned to his work, the very tip of tongue poking out from the corner of his mouth like a cartoon character's. Grace had no real sense of Kendall's life outside of the office, but she gathered he was childless and unmarried. Once, in the relatively informal setting of the break room, she had mentioned her gay cousin Thomas as a prelude to a potential setup. Kendall's response had been polite but uninterested, and she had never brought it up again.

Grace sat down, booted up her own computer, and logged in.

"Oh, come *on*," she said, and Kendall flicked his eyes over.

"Is everything all right?" he asked quietly, and Grace said, "No. I mean, yeah. It's fine." She stood up. "I'm fine."

"Good," said Kendall, and kept typing. Grace walked out of their little room and crossed the open-plan office and tapped on Lou's door. Immediately she was annoyed at herself—she should have just barged in. Instead, she stood gently rapping like a dummy, presenting herself like some kind of simpering peasant, until Lou swiveled his chair toward the door and beckoned her in.

"Lou?" she began.

"That's me." Lou beamed at her, leaned back in his chair, and laced his fingers behind his head. "How's everything in Graceland this morning?"

"You know," she said pointedly, "I'm a little tired."

"Yeah?" he said with a small frown of annoyance—clearly he hadn't intended his casual "How's everything?" to elicit a reply. "Sorry to hear that."

Grace fought to keep the smile on her face. "Hey, so, Lou? I noticed you didn't open the Dropbox file."

"The—the what, now?"

He had forgotten all about it. She had been here till midnight finishing the stupid research project, and he'd forgotten the whole thing.

"The—"

Lou snapped his fingers.

"God! Right," he said. "The portacath business. Yeah, I saw you had gotten that in there. Thanks for working so quickly."

Grace's smile hardened. It wasn't as if she had really been given a choice in the matter. Lou was wearing a cable-knit sweater with a loosely knotted tie underneath. He took a sip from his coffee mug, which said BOSS JUICE.

"Don't you need to look at it?" she asked. "Pass along the results to the hospital?"

"Uh—no." At last, Lou had the decency to look a little embarrassed. "Funny thing. It's actually no longer an operational request."

"What?"

"Yeah, I should have told you." His smile was at least half wince. "That's on me. By the time I got home last night, I had a follow-up e-mail from that hospital in, uh . . ."

"Hanover," said Grace. "Near Baltimore."

"Yes. That's right. Hanover. Turns out they don't need the info after all. So we can go ahead and cancel that."

"Well, I, I—" Grace stammered. The thoughtlessness was sort of astonishing. She flushed with embarrassment and annoyance. "I can't cancel it. It's done. I already did it. You told me to work late and get it done."

"And I cannot tell you how much I appreciate it. Absolute rock-star behavior." He paused for a sip of boss juice. "I appreciate it. And by the way, when they sent that request, they did say it was urgent, but I guess they changed their minds. Shame on us for taking them at their word, right?"

"Right," said Grace absently. Under the surface of her irritation, a new feeling was moving. She could see the face again, the girl's face, bewildered and stricken. "Hey, so, Lou," she said. "Did they say why?"

"What?" Lou was dabbing at his mustache with a wad of napkins.

"Was there a reason why the request was rescinded?"

"Nope. No, I don't think so. I just got a second e-mail from the fella at the hospital, just 'Thanks anyway,' something like that. No explanation. You know how these doctors are." Lou grinned awkwardly as if they shared some long-running joke about the way doctors were. "But listen. Again. Thank you so much. You can return to your regularly scheduled programming. I owe you one."

Lou dismissed her with a little salute, which she half-heartedly returned, thinking that his "I owe you one" was worth exactly nothing; thinking of Kathy, of one of Kathy's favorite dark adages: *The world is like a minefield, except instead of mines, it's assholes.*

Grace made her way back to her little office, offering perfunctory smiles and quiet *Good morning*s to various coworkers on her way. Terry Baumgarten, as usual, was perched on the edge of Shiva's desk, the two of them laughing at something obviously non-work-related on her screen. Randy was in a sharp blue suit, dressed to impress, as usual, still young enough to think there was anyone here worth impressing.

She stopped in the break room to coax a pale, tasteless cup of coffee from the machine. Then she slipped back into her office and sat down; Kendall didn't look up.

Today she was supposed to be reviewing the 510(k) filing for something called the Sleeper's Friend, a respiratory device for sleep-apnea sufferers that was, for all intents and purposes, identical to any number of other respiratory devices for sleep-apnea sufferers currently on the market.

When it came to innovation in device manufacturing, the companies tended to talk from both sides of their mouths. In physician-facing communications (i.e., marketing), they would convey that such-and-such device was wildly new and different, so much so that every serious-minded doctor should switch to the new product immediately. To the FDA, they claimed that the device was basically the same as other products that had already been approved, meaning that the expensive and time-consuming de novo certification process wasn't necessary.

It was Grace's job as a reviewer to evaluate such claims, a task exactly as enthralling as it sounded.

Grace had a sip of the grim coffee and tried to clear her head. She thumbed through the thick packet of relevant supporting documents for the Sleeper's Friend, which included about three dozen schematic diagrams, at least five of them richly detailed in their illustration of the nasal cavity.

"Oh boy, oh boy," she told herself wanly. "Away we go."

Grace picked up the first page of the document packet, read the title — "A Review of Inflammatory Patterns in the Nasopharyngeal Passages" — and immediately put it down again. "Or maybe I'll just kill myself."

This earned a curious look from Kendall. "Hmm?"

"Nothing. Sorry."

"Okay."

"I'm good."

"Great."

Kendall had not stopped typing through this brief exchange, and now his eyes returned to his screen.

Grace navigated to the Dropbox, opened the research document, and began to read through the info she'd found for Lou late last night. It was done, the project was concluded, Lou had told her to forget it and move on, but Grace was unwilling, even unable, to do so.

"That's weird," she said a minute later.

"I'm sorry?" said Kendall, his voice tinged with annoyance. "Did you say something?"

Grace said, "Ignore me."

"Yes, ma'am."

Grace was reading through the list she'd assembled last night of all the companies that had purchased the unusually designed portacath briefly manufactured by Goldenstar Therapeutic Technologies. The fourth purchaser listed was the one called Substance Material Group, based in North Carolina's Research Triangle. In the midnight bleariness of the assignment, Grace hadn't really clocked what an odd name it was.

Substance Material Group?

"What on earth is *that*?"

Abruptly, Kendall stopped typing, slid open his top desk drawer, and took out a pair of over-the-ear headphones. He adjusted the headphones, and the music disappeared from the speaker. Smiling tightly, Kendall resumed typing. Grace ignored this performance; she Googled the words *Substance Material Group,* then tried it again after remembering to put the name in quote marks. The first hit was a link for the company's home page, and she clicked it.

"Well," said Grace, not bothering to keep her voice down now that Kendall was ensconced in his headphones. "Well, shit."

There was no website for the Substance Material Group; at least, not anymore. The URL redirected to a hosting company called YourSiteUnlimited, which inquired of Grace, in a bright red font and with multiple exclamation points, whether she might be interested in buying the domain. *Uh, no,* thought Grace. *No, thank you.* She leaned back in her chair and stretched her arms all the way up in the air, feeling like maybe she still hadn't woken up all the way. Grace had a sip of awful coffee, sighed, and set down the mug on top of the thick stack of sleep-apnea documents. She glanced at the top page on the stack, but then — blinking away a quick flicker of guilt — looked back at the missing website and the bright red text asking her if she wanted to buy it.

Then she dug around in her pocketbook until she found her phone.

Hey, Grace typed. Her thumbs moved clumsily across the screen — somehow she was the one person who still hadn't gotten used to the ungainly thumb-typing required to send a text. What's the name of the website where you can look up web pages from a long time ago?

Grace waited, holding the phone loosely in her palm. After a moment, River texted back. I'm in class Mom what R U doing.

Grace rolled her eyes. No phones were allowed in class, but River had told her that everybody had Messages on their computer, and everybody texted all day long.

Jan Ko, another reviewer, slipped into the office with a thick stack of manila folders and a question for Kendall or, more likely, to pursue the unreciprocated crush she'd had on the man for the better part of a decade. Grace hunched forward, blocking Jan's view, and kept texting.

Don't be an a-hole, Riv. What's the website called?

The three hovering horizontal dots appeared to let Grace know that River was composing their reply. Grace watched the dots, then peeked up at Jan and Kendall, who had taken his headphones down to answer whatever her question had been.

Grace looked back at her phone, where the three insolent dots at last resolved into words. JFC Mom tell u later.

"Oh, for fuck's sake," Grace said loudly, and tossed the phone down on her desk. Kendall and Jan swiveled their heads toward her and stared. "It's okay." Grace tried to make an offhand smile. "Just my idiot kid." She pointed at the phone on the desk as if her child were trapped inside it, too much of an idiot to escape.

After Jan wandered out and Kendall retreated back inside his head-phones, Grace tried River one more time and got them to cough up the simple piece of information: the name of the website that River and their friend Mallory had been discussing after dinner one night as part of researching the history of a new English teacher they found to be, quote, "balls hot."

When Grace at last found her way to the website as it had been archived in 2012, it wasn't much more informative. The home page was a bland pale blue with the three words *Substance Material Group* across the top in plain Helvetica, with no links or tabs or drop-downs. The familiar empty phrase *More info coming soon* sat in the center of the page, where obviously no more info had ever arrived. There was nowhere to click for Contact Us or FAQs. No mailing address. Nothing.

Grace took a last sad sip of her coffee, which by now was not only bad but cold.

It was weird. Any kind of research facility or clinic, any operation with the wherewithal to be sourcing portacaths from a med-tech com-pany, you might expect to have a more professional website or one that at the very least indicated what sort of business it was in.

The other question for Grace was what the hell was she even *doing?* Her workday was sighing away, and if she was going to have a provisional recommendation on the 510(k) for the Sleeper's Friend ready by 5:00, she'd better get started.

Yeah, but the problem was, she didn't want to. All she wanted was to figure out what the Substance Material Group was and what connection it had to the girl in the picture. She didn't know why she wanted it so much, but she knew she couldn't stop. Not now.

Grace picked a bit of coffee-grind grit out of her teeth and stared again at her computer screen, thinking. Then she clicked the Back button to return to the original search-engine results, where she'd entered *Substance Material Group*. This time Grace scrolled down to the second hit, a link to a PDF from a publication called the *Journal of Applied Metaphysics*. "Good Lord," murmured Grace; the *Journal of Applied Metaphysics*? The article was from the Spring 2004 issue, and it had been written by someone named Dr. C. P. Stargell, described in a brief biographical sketch as the "founder and chief scientific officer of the Substance Material Group."

Grace puzzled over the unusual name—Dr. C. P. Stargell—and the article's even more unusual title: "Incarnating the Arrow: Toward a Substantive Vision of Time."

"What does *that* mean?"

She clicked on the article, but as the page began loading, she heard someone saying her name. Kendall was standing over her desk holding his black faux-leather coat and jaunty driver's cap.

"Oh," she said. "Hi."

"Yes. Hello."

"Hey, real quick: Can the word *incarnate* be a verb?"

"Yes," Kendall answered immediately. " 'To endow with concrete reality.' A small group of us are going to lunch. Would you be interested in joining?"

"Oh." Grace rubbed her eyes with her fingertips. "Is it lunchtime?"

"Yes, Grace," Kendall said cautiously. "It's lunchtime." He examined her with his head tilted, eyebrows slightly raised. "Are you quite all right?"

"Yeah." She smiled. Her fingers were twitching. She wanted him to go so she could read the article.

"Can I bring you something from Panera?"

"Panera? No." She smiled again, very politely, not really paying attention.

"Incarnating the Arrow: Toward a Substantive Vision of Time." The *Journal of Applied Metaphysics*. "I mean, what the *hell*."

"I'm sorry," said Kendall, slipping into his coat. "Are you talking to me?"

"No," she said. "No, I'm not."

Then she started to read.

8.

Desiree scowled at her phone. The phone was vibrating. She waited for it to stop, and it did, but as soon as it stopped, it started again.

The client kept calling. This was understandable but irritating. For this client, clearly desperate to have the girl brought to him, the delay must be excruciating.

As it was for Desiree herself.

It was midday on Thursday, and the last time she'd looked at her watch—which was just moments ago, when she parked the Enclave in this hospital lot—it had informed her she'd been on this job for forty-one hours and seventeen minutes, which worked out to an hourly rate of roughly $1,574—a relatively paltry fee, growing paltrier by the moment.

It was cold outside. Frost sparkled on the black asphalt of the parking lot. Desiree answered the phone.

"What?"

"Oh, yeah, hi," said the client in the anxious wheedle that Desiree was already tired of. "How are ya? I'm just hoping for a status update."

"I will call you when I have something to report."

"So — so, no report yet?"

"Correct."

Desiree hung up before the man could say anything else.

The client, Desiree had gathered, was not a professional in this business. He was some kind of scientist or doctor. Desiree hadn't gotten the name. Whenever possible, she didn't. The client had been referred to her, which was how she got most of her jobs, and she was not interested in any details unrelated to the job itself. She didn't know the man's name or what the target was to him: lover, daughter, employee, friend. None of it mattered.

She was in the lobby now, itching to get back to work. She looked at her watch — forty-one hours, nineteen minutes; $1,573 an hour. Desiree looked around the soaring atrium. There were bright murals on several walls and a low underlying burble of conversation. A woman in pink scrubs was pushing a slumped-over man in a wheelchair. A smell of cheap hot lunch drifted in from an adjoining cafeteria.

"Well, hello," said an old woman in a kiosk with a bright blue ASK ME ANYTHING badge on her lapel.

"Hello," said Desiree.

If the old lady had any particular reaction to the surgical tape and gauze over Desiree's right eye, she did not show it. Vivid external wounds were par for the course in a hospital lobby. The old lady smiled brightly, showing a smudge of red lipstick on her teeth.

"Welcome to Hanover Regional Medical Center."

9.

There Allie stood on the even black pavement of Kenwood Drive, right in the center of the circle of the cul-de-sac, right where she and Missy used to ride their bikes.

But who was Missy? Allie had no friend named Missy and never had. She kept telling and telling herself that, standing by the mailbox at the end of the walk, gazing up at the pair of sturdy curved aspen trees that flanked the front door. She remembered climbing those guys. She remembered the rough feel of the bark on her palms. She remembered sitting in the crooks of the boughs. Her mom calling her Little Ms. Monkey Pants when she was still well enough to chase her around the trees.

Allie felt the pain in her chest again, felt it groaning and shifting inside her, threatening to erupt. Not only had she never been on this street before, she had never so much as set foot in Maryland before, except maybe when she was growing up in Ohio — *You grew up in Ohio!* — and had gone on a grade-school trip to Washington, DC. Four yellow buses full of giggling farm kids. So, yes, maybe she'd passed through Maryland, but that was it. Allie tried now to remember the names of her friends growing up, the kids she'd sat with on the bus trip, the boy she'd had a crush on until he'd asked someone else to the sixth-grade dance.

What were their names? Where were their faces?

She and Missy riding their ten-speeds, around and around the cul-de-sac at the end of Kenwood—

Her stepdad on the front porch, framed by the soft interior light—

Allie was cold. She was wearing the same clothes she'd been in when she got to the hospital. She had slipped back into them before she left in the middle of the night, adding a pair of well-worn sneakers, a windbreaker, and a baseball cap she borrowed from the nurses' station. Allie hated having taken things that didn't belong to her, and she swore to herself she was going to bring it all back when this was over, but when would that be?

What was happening?

Allie felt the gentle heat of tears in her eyes. She blinked them away. She struggled to make sense of the world.

Because she had never been here, never been to Kenwood Drive, but she could feel the hard plastic of the bike seat digging into her butt, could see Missy streaking past, Missy laughing, Missy's thick brown hair catching the wind like a sail. Allie had grown up in Ohio, had gone to college and grad school there before moving to New Jersey for her first teaching job, but standing here on Kenwood Drive in suburban Virginia, shivering on this green lawn in front of this red-brick house, sent a warm rush through her body that felt exactly like coming home.

She looked up and down the pleasant suburban street of handsome colonial homes, lawns mowed up to the curb, basketball hoops bolted above garage doors.

"You gotta take a breath, kiddo," Allie instructed herself softly. "You gotta puzzle this out."

Allie was still talking to herself like she talked to her kids. Not her *kid*-kid, not Rachel, who was just a baby, but to her sixth- and seventh-graders, who were constantly in need of reassurance as they cycled through the various dramas at—

Allie blinked. A cold breeze brushed across her cheeks. Where? Where did she teach?

The name of the school had dropped out of her head, but obviously that didn't matter. Not right this second.

"Calm, calm, calm. Calm it on down."

Her heart was racing. It was too much. Whatever was happening, it was happening too quickly to process, too quickly to try to understand. It just *was*.

More memories were coming, blinking to life like light bulbs. The red-brick house looked different than when she was little, that was for sure. There had been no silly mailbox then like there was now, painted to look like a miniature replica of the house. And the house had just plain white window shades, but once upon a time her mom had insisted, over her stepdad's gentle objections, on installing venetian blinds on every window. She could *hear* her mother saying the word, playful and musical, the way she loved to practically sing certain words, *venetian* . . .

Allie hugged herself tightly like she was holding herself in place, keeping her body from disassembling and drifting off into the atmosphere.

She'd been up all night, which was maybe part of the problem, why she felt so spacey and insane, but she knew there was another part too. She had tried calling her parents three more times before sneaking out of the hospital, and for good measure she had tried her friend Joan, who lived a couple doors down and was also a single mom and who sometimes watched Rachel for her.

But no one picked up when she called Joan, and as the phone rang and rang, Allie wondered whether she had put the number in wrong, then whether Joan still lived nearby, and finally whether she had a friend named Joan at all, until, confused and uncertain, she hung up.

In the lobby of Hanover Regional Medical Center she had borne the chatty advice from a cheerful lobby lady with an ASK ME ANYTHING button on who frowned slightly at the name Kenwood Drive but said, in that sweet way of old ladies still charmed by the internet, "Why don't we have a look on Google?"

There was a Kenwood Drive in a place called Spring Valley, California, and one in Alexandria, Virginia, and Allie had known right away that yes, that was it. Alexandria was right. It was familiar.

The ASK ME ANYTHING lady calmly instructed her on how to get by bus from the rural Baltimore County hospital all the way to suburban Washington, and from the bus depot Allie had taken a Metro train. From the Metro stop she had walked four miles in the shoes that were too big for her, some poor nurse's purloined Nikes. She winced and then gasped as the pain in the sole of her foot burned back to life, but she walked unerringly. Her body knew which way to go.

Now she stood crying before the Kenwood house, bent forward, her palms planted on her knees, remembering more and more as she stood here. She'd moved to this house when she was five, after her mom met her stepfather, and later her mom had gotten sick, and then she herself—

She — she herself —

Pain slammed into her like a crashing wave, and for a brief half an instant she had no name at all.

Her name had gone.

And then it was back, had clicked right back into place. *Allie.*

Her hand flew up to the raised hard circle on her chest. The *port.* She touched it. It did not seem to be doing anything, it was just *there*, a strange hard dead piece of plastic inside her body — but it was doing something to her — something was *happening.*

No. Something had *happened.*

New truths were drifting in and affixing themselves to her conscious-ness like bits of ash after a bombing, and other things — Allie things, the bare facts of her life — were burning away in the chaos. She gripped tightly the fact that she had a daughter, and her daughter's name was Rachel.

"Rachel. Rachel."

Whatever was happening, things were leaving and things were chang-ing, and she did not want Rachel to leave or change. *"Rachel,"* she said loudly, tossing the word up to the sky. "Rachel!" She thought of her baby and her baby was named Rachel, and she had brown curly hair.

Brown?

Brown?

Was Rachel's hair brown?

"Oh, no," said Allie softly, and then she jumped at the sound of a garage door rattling open across the street. A car was backing out of the driveway. A man was sitting in the driver's seat of a blue Audi, a ruddy white guy in his seventies with a golf hat on.

He saw Allie and rolled down his window. His words made puffs of condensation in the early-morning air.

"Excuse me?" the man called.

Allie stared at him.

"Young lady?"

Allie recognized him right away. It was Al McDermid, Missy's father.

Before she could figure out what to say to him, Mr. McDermid's face softened with old affection, and his eyes opened wide.

"My God," he whispered. "You look just like her."

10.

Grace read "Incarnating the Arrow: Toward a Substantive Vision of Time" very slowly, trailing one finger along the words like a child puzzling her way through a test. She had tried to read it online and found that to be impossible: The text was too dense and the subject matter too unfamiliar to scroll through. So Grace had printed out all thirty-two pages, standing nervously by the printer and praying there'd be no paper jam or other malfunction so she wouldn't have to summon help from IT Ronald and explain what this was.

Reading it on paper didn't help much. Yes, the article was in English, but it used so many unfamiliar words and phrases, so many complicated concepts, that Grace was unable, at first, to make much sense of the whole.

It started with the origins of the universe, the development of the Big Bang theory and the idea of space-time, and the complex interrelationships among the four fundamental forces that governed the physical world. Grace strained to recall her high-school physics, struggling through the complex vocabulary, and then, just when she was beginning to understand, or thought she was beginning to understand, the article's tone completely changed.

There was a section break marked by a row of asterisks, and then the author refocused his attention — there was no other way to describe it. What had been a dense scientific article on astrophysics became more of a literary treatise, an intellectual history of one abstract concept: the concept of *time*.

It has been proposed, wrote Dr. C. P. Stargell in a new and different mode, *that time is akin to a river, bearing its subjects forward, willingly or unwillingly, through the spatial and sensory experiences that are perceived as "existence." Another equally poetic notion frequently encountered is the concept of time as a tunnel — not something that bears us forward but rather a structure through which we pass.*

Grace found this literary-historic stuff only slightly easier to follow than the complex science that had preceded it, and she had no idea what the connection might be between the two. But she rubbed her eyes and persisted, hunched forward on her chair and squinting at the pages. At some point, when she could smell that someone had dumped out the dregs of the morning pot and put on an afternoon one, she went to the break room to get more coffee.

She pressed on toward the end of "Incarnating the Arrow," grasping at bits and pieces of understanding, and as she read, it was like a fog rolled slowly into the room, a thick distorting quality to the air, enveloping her and holding her close. There was another row of asterisks and the article reverted abruptly to scientific language; Dr. Stargell made a series of connections — as best as Grace could understand — between the principles of astrophysics and the molecular structures of the human body.

"This is — I mean, this is bonkers," Grace murmured as she puzzled through the dense paragraphs.

But it wasn't bonkers. It was all starting to make sense, and when she reached the end of the article she returned to the beginning and started over, reading with a pencil in her hand this time so she could underline and circle or just tap the tip of it against her teeth as she concentrated.

When she was done with her second read-through, she started in right away on her third.

Grace stumbled again and again through Dr. C. P. Stargell's description of the universe's origins, through Dr. Stargell's review of all the metaphors for man's relationship to time and their respective insufficiencies, and into Dr. Stargell's explanation of space-time and its constant, continuing expansion, which included a complex mathematical description of the relationship between the perception of light and the passage of time.

It was only on her fourth and last reading that Grace was pulled up short by a single paragraph close to the end of the final page. She had circled the paragraph on her third read, and now, on her fourth, it seemed to lift off the page and dance before her eyes:

Yes, there is such a thing as time, *THE CONCEPT, which we perceive in various ways (as noted above). But there is also such a thing as* time, *the PHYSICAL PHENOMENON OF THE UNIVERSE, which we do not perceive but possess.*

Grace double underlined the last section of the sentence — *we do not perceive but possess* — and held her breath as she read on.

For clarity I would suggest that this latter meaning of time *be denoted by a separate descriptor, for which I propose the term* durational element, *or DE.*

The next phase of this project must be directed toward confirming that the durational element can be identified, isolated, and manipulated.

Grace stopped reading. She had been tracing the words with her forefinger, but now her finger stopped moving and rested on that final word:

Manipulated.

Grace felt a wild murmuring in her heart. Her finger trembled on the page.

It was like a key had been turned, a door opened. Now that Grace grasped the central idea, Dr. Stargell's article wasn't confusing at all. It was simple. The amount of time a person had was theoretically quantifiable. Which meant that eventually — *in time* was what Stargell had written, whether the pun was intentional or not — scientists would be able not only to measure it, but to isolate it and remove it. And, eventually, to *transfer* it: to take time out of one person and give it to another, like a skin graft or an organ transplant.

Grace stood abruptly and almost immediately sat down again. Her legs were weak.

She was thinking again of the photograph from the Hanover hospital. The picture had shown the torso of a young woman, her arms crossed protectively across her breasts, the telltale sign of the port just below her clavicle. The port had been made by Goldenstar, and Substance Material Group (with Dr. C. P. Stargell its founder and chief scientific officer) had been the ones using those ports.

Grace pictured the girl's face. Her sad eyes, staring off into nothing.

"Grace? Are you okay?"

Kendall was standing over her desk again, in his faux-leather coat and driver's cap. She peered at him through the fog that still seemed to surround her.

"Kendall," she managed. "Hi. You're back from lunch."

"Yes," he said, with a curious smile. "Four hours ago. It's five o'clock, Grace. I'm leaving for the day."

"Oh."

Behind Kendall, through the window of their office, Grace saw people putting on their coats, shutting down their computers, arranging the items on their desks in preparation for tomorrow.

"Of course. Me too. I'm just gonna—" She widened her smile. "Gotta make a quick phone call."

But when she called the hospital in Hanover, they could tell her nothing. The woman on the switchboard put her through to the emergency department, and the person who answered had no patience for a non-emergent question and asked her to hold, and she held and was eventually transferred back to the switchboard.

On her second try, the switchboard again connected her to the emergency department, and the nurse again told her to hold, and then the line went dead.

Grace caught Lou Fleming as he was putting on his thick North Face jacket with all kinds of pockets and zippers. She said, "Hey, Lou?" as she knocked, a little more firmly than she had this morning, and saw he was on the phone. He looked up at her, his brow furrowed with concentration. He pointed at the phone. Grace made a *Sorry* face and started talking anyway.

"Lou, this is gonna sound crazy, but I think we oughta check on that woman. From the hospital in Hanover."

He squinted at her, half listening.

"I think there is something really strange going on. I'm —" She took a breath. Steadied her voice. "I'm worried about her."

"Hey, hang on one sec," said Lou into the phone, then put his hand over it and said to Grace, "That's all wrapped up, remember?"

"Yeah, no, I know."

"Great. See you tomorrow, Grace."

He turned away, zipping his coat, back on the phone. "You wanna waste the money on a kicker," he said, "knock yourself out. But don't come crying to me . . ."

Thirty seconds later Grace got off the elevator and emerged into the parking lot; the cold flushed her cheeks and a sharp wind agitated the flags on the flagpoles. She pulled out her phone.

"Hey, kiddo," she said to River. "Listen. I need you to do dinner again tonight."

"What?" River was aghast. "No! Wait! Are you kidding?"

"I am not kidding." She was speed-walking to her Altima. The late-afternoon air was crisp and cool. "I think there are frozen pizzas in the freezer if you don't feel like dealing with Postmates again."

"Ew. Mom. Those pizzas are so bad for you. Also, I ate them already. Me and Marni ate them after school on Monday."

Grace beeped her key fob to unlock the Altima. "I'm sure you can figure it out. I love you. Tell Nana I love her too, okay?"

"Wait. *Mom.* Hey!"

Grace hung up. She started the car.

River would figure it out. Her very bright sixteen-year-old and her seventy-four-year-old mother would figure out something to eat. She stared out the windshield and held tight to the wheel, pushing her family out of her mind, thinking instead of Dr. C. P. Stargell and that young woman in the ER.

Her mom would be fine. Her kid would be fine. They would eat. They would sleep.

It was dusk, so Grace clicked on her headlights. Tall street lamps lined the highway. They flashed by like beacons.

11.

At forty-six, Grace didn't feel old most days, but there were definitely times when she felt it coming, certain evenings when she could feel oldness seeping in around the edges, making sure she knew it was waiting for her.

Like tonight, like now, halfway through the hour-long drive from Silver Spring to Hanover, when she began to get sharp angry twinges from the pain that had lately taken up residence near the base of her spine. The lower back pain, some kind of pinched-nerve thing, had been precipitated by nothing, no specific exercise or accident. It had just kind of started one day, like a little gift from the gods. *Hey, lady? You're in your mid-forties? Here's something special for you!*

"Shit," Grace said over the drone of the NPR host somewhere near Annapolis. "Fuck. *Ow.*"

The pain started to creep up from the small of her back, up the lower rungs of her spine. Grace scooted her butt back and forth on the seat, trying to find a way to sit that didn't hurt. Then she just sighed and waited for it to pass, which it usually did after a few minutes.

This, then, was what it was like to feel middle age arriving in your body. The back; the trouble sleeping; the whole business of having to hold a restaurant menu at a steep angle and peer down at it until you could make out the names of the desserts. It all came with the territory. In recent years, Grace had more or less made her peace with the twenty excess pounds she had been carrying around since age thirty. She had accepted that at a certain point, these extra pounds were not "extra" but part of the new settled shape of her body.

Getting older wasn't the end of the world — except, of course, that it was. Eventually, it literally would be.

Along with all the physical changes had come a certain barely perceptible change in her understanding of life, the world, and her future. Without thinking about it, without really having time to think about it, Grace had let go of certain possibilities concerning what life might still hold for her. No longer did she think of her life as building up to something else. *Here's how things are,* she thought now, if the thought ever really occurred to her at all. *Here is how things will remain.*

When she stopped for gas, somewhere around Laurel, Grace dutifully performed the series of dopey stretches her primary care doctor had recommended for her back pain. She bent deeply at the knees, extended one hand, and arched slowly to one side and then to the other, doing a series of air chops like slow-motion karate.

All of it — the pain in her back, the news on NPR, doing the exercises by the side of the car, smiling politely at the bemused stares of her fellow motorists — were distractions from the insanity of what she was doing, taking this spontaneous journey after sundown on a weeknight to try to find a woman from a picture for some reason that Grace could not explain, even to herself.

"Steve Adomian," said the doctor, a large white man in late middle age with a moon face and a sizable paunch beneath his lab coat. "But everybody around here calls me Dr. Steve. Well—that's what they call me to my face, anyway."

The doctor glanced up from the iPad he was scanning to see how his joke had landed, and Grace smiled obligingly.

"Grace Berney," she said. She held up the laminated ID card around her neck. "I'm from the FDA."

"Oho," said Dr. Steve, dropping the iPad on his desk and tugging officiously at the sleeves of his white coat. "Guess I better watch my p's and q's, then. Here. Sit."

He swept his arm to the other chair in the office, and Grace sat down and tried to decide how to begin. She'd walked into the hideously overlit lobby of the Hanover Regional Medical Center ten minutes ago, and after an urgent visit to the ladies' room, she had been informed that visiting hours were over. When Grace explained that she was not family but a government official here in response to a request from an attending physician, the gray-haired woman with the ASK ME ANYTHING badge had tutted approvingly and directed her to the third-floor office of Dr. Adomian.

Grace settled in the chair across from him and placed her bag at her feet. "Well, so . . ." she began uncertainly. "I'm sorry to drop in on you like this."

"Not to worry, not to worry." Dr. Steve took a quick final swipe at his tablet, where he had been rapidly checking things off with a tiny stylus. "Although I certainly hope we don't have a drug-diversion issue. We had a problem three years ago with an obstetrics nurse and fentanyl, but I think since then—"

"Sorry," said Grace, rushing to interrupt. "I'm not from the *DEA*. I said the *FDA*. I'm sorry."

"Oh. Huh," said Dr. Steve, his expression changing in an instant from concerned to confused. "What *part* of the FDA, exactly?"

"CDRH?" Grace said with a little question mark at the end. Dr. Steve's face was a polite blank, so she hastened to clarify, "The Center for Devices and Radiological Health."

"Can't say I'm familiar."

Grace held up her laminated ID badge, and Dr. Steve gave it a cursory examination and then again murmured, "Huh." His desk was totally bare save for a handful of Post-it notes lining its edge. The walls of the office were similarly empty; there was a single narrow bookshelf with nothing on it but a few medical-supply catalogs. Clearly this was a space where no one spent enough time to set anything down or hang anything up.

"So, what can I do for the department of, uh—what was it? Lotions and Potions?" Dr. Steve chortled softly.

"Actually," she said, "you called us. Someone from your hospital sent an e-mail to my boss asking for our assistance in identifying a medical device."

"Oh, yeah? No kidding." Dr. Steve reached up and scratched his ear, clearly mystified. "Someone from *here* did?"

The doctor's frankly uncomprehending expression sent a wave of embarrassed confusion through Grace. Was she at the wrong hospital? Had she misread the report somehow? She began, haltingly, to explain the request Lou Fleming had received the night before for help in identifying an unusually shaped portacath, and suddenly Dr. Steve smacked a hand down on his desk so hard that Grace jumped.

"God!" he said, and laughed, a heavy laugh like a seal's. "The port! Of course. Of *course*. I know exactly who you're talking about."

Grace exhaled with relief and leaned forward avidly. "You remember her?"

"Oh, sure." He beamed. "She was pretty memorable, that gal. *Pretty memorable*—"

Dr. Steve was interrupted by a burst of static from the boxy speaker between the light fixtures in his office. "Dr. Weiss to the ED, please. Dr. Weiss." Dr. Steve made his hands into a bullhorn. "You hear that, Dr. Weiss? Tear yourself away from the nurses' station and go do your job."

He chortled and winked at Grace, who tried to stay on topic. "So you do remember her, then? The patient with the port?"

"I do indeed. I'm just wondering who reached out to you folks."

"Oh, gosh," said Grace. "I'm afraid I don't know."

Clearly Dr. Steve was turning over the HIPAA implications of discussing the mystery patient's info. Grace wondered if she should call Lou Fleming and ask him for the details of the hospital's request—it would only be fair, after all, to call him at home in the evening. But then Dr. Steve snapped his fingers loudly, beaming with the sudden realization. "Oh, you know who I bet it was?" he said. "Who it was that called you guys? Bet it was Dr. Shah. Young guy. One of the emergency medicine residents. Yup. Arjun Shah." He shook his head in delighted amazement. "Young man is a comer, I'll tell you. He must've figured we'd want to know what the deal was with that port, decided he'd show a little initiative, send a note down to the FDA."

"I think that's it," said Grace, the half-lie leaving her mouth without her even thinking about it. "That sounds familiar. Yeah."

Dr. Steve shook his head, very impressed with young Arjun's initiative. Grace reached into her bag and pulled out a legal pad. It was the same pad she'd used last night, the one where she had written *WHAT HAVE THEY DONE TO YOU* and underlined it. She flipped to a clean page and readied her pen. "So, what can you tell me about this patient?"

"I mean, what can I say? They brought her in late Tuesday night or sometime real early Wednesday morning, I think? It was before I got here."

"Who brought her in?" said Grace. "A friend, or—"

"No, no. It was the paramedics. I think one of the, uh—what do you call 'em? The train cops? Amtrak cops? They called 'em. I'd have to check. I do know the EMTs said she was found on a commuter train, and she was in real bad shape. Looked basically like she crawled away from some kind of car accident. Skinny thing, bony as a rail, all sharp elbows. Big gash in her foot, like from broken glass or something. When she was admitted, she already had the foot stitched up, and that was probably Dr. Shah also." He chortled, sighed. "Boy, when *I* was a resident? Forget it. I was lucky if I could keep from killing anybody for twenty-four hours."

Dr. Steve gave her an aw-shucks self-deprecating grin, and Grace realized that the man was flirting with her. She smiled again, tugged the collar of her blouse closer to her neck. *No,* she thought. *No, thank you.*

"And what—sorry—did you get a name?"

"Aubrey, maybe? No—Allie!"

"Allie." Grace wrote it down.

"No last name, in case you're going to ask. I'm guessing short for Allison, but who knows?"

His goofy chortle turned into a sigh, and then he dropped his voice confidentially and said, "Between you and me, Ms., uh—"

"Berney."

"Of course, of course. Sorry. Between you and me, Ms. Berney, our friend Allie was more than a little bit—what's the word?" He sighed again. "Recalcitrant. You know what I mean?"

"I guess. I think so."

Grace wrote the word down: *recalcitrant.*

"Didn't remember a lot, or didn't want to say a lot if she did. Possibly under the influence, although I don't think anything came up on the tox screen. I can check on that. She was very focused on the idea that someone was after her."

105

Grace stopped writing. She felt her heart beating, three precise beats, like the tolling of a clock.

"I'm sorry. You said—someone was after her?"

"Well. No." Dr. Steve raised one finger. "I said she *thought* that some-one *might* be quote-unquote 'after' her. Some kind of sinister character. By the way, we get this. This is a thing. 'I'm being chased, they're com-ing to get me.'" He paused. "Oh, Ms. Berney. Oh, dear."

Whatever the look was that had come over her, it made Dr. Steve chuckle, gently and patronizingly.

"You're gonna wanna take that with a grain of salt, okay? A big grain. I don't think this young woman was entirely well. Mentally, I mean."

"Sure." Grace forced another smile. She wrote down the words *after her*. She wrote *sinister character*.

"Did she say anything else? Anything at all?"

"Wait. Crap. Hang on."

Dr. Steve's computer had begun to emit a series of urgent chimes. Now his phone did too.

"Crap," he said again, more emphatically. He jumped up and scooped the tablet off the desk. "No rest for the wicked."

"I understand. Can I just—"

"Sorry, gotta leave it there, for now," said Dr. Steve, interrupting. And now he made his move, leaning in toward her, too close, as he tugged his lab coat more snugly around him. "But I would *love* to talk again sometime."

"I need to see her."

"What?"

Grace stood up too and put herself between Dr. Steve and the door. "I need to speak to her *now*."

"Yeah, well," he said flatly. Something about her sudden forthrightness and abrupt movements had taken the flirtatious interest out of his voice. "You can't."

"Why not?"

"Because she's gone."

Forty-five minutes later, Grace was driving back home.

The woman, Allie, had disappeared from the Hanover Regional Medical Center at some point last night, leaving behind no address, no phone number, not even a full name. Dr. Steve would check, but what he figured was that when the enterprising Dr. Shah discovered this disappearing act, he'd withdrawn his request from the FDA.

Whatever brought the woman to the hospital, whatever had happened to her in the past or was happening to her now, she had slipped away, and Grace felt this loss not just as a disappointment but like a vanishing. Like it was the disappearance of herself from herself; like it was her whole soul leaving her body.

Grace drove back home in silence, listening neither to NPR nor to any music. Alone in the car, with her back once again aching, she asked herself questions she hadn't asked herself on the way here. They were the questions raised by "Incarnating the Arrow" that its author hadn't addressed: If time really could be taken from a person and given to someone else, how would that manifest itself? Would it just . . . add an hour at the end of a day? Add a year at the end of a life?

Grace shook her head slightly, blowing out air from the cheeks. *It's not real,* she told herself. *It's not like it's* real. *So who cares?*

The nearly empty highway rushed past. Her eyes squinted in the halogen darkness.

What *was* real was this girl, this young woman, who had been at this hospital and now was gone. What *was* real was that Dr. C. P. Stargell's company had bought specialty portacaths from Goldenstar Therapeutic Technologies at some point prior to 2013. And now, in 2024, this young woman, with one of those ports in her chest, had turned up in a Hanover hospital, uncertain of who she was or what had happened to her, fearful that someone was trying to track her down.

This is a thing. Dr. Steve, skeptical and patronizing. *I'm being chased, they're coming to get me.*

Grace drove with her hand pushed up into her hair, with her eyes open wide and bulging, staring out at the southbound lanes of 295.

Another question about transferring time that the article hadn't addressed was simply what would become of the person it had been taken *from.*

12.

I have chills," said Missy McDermid. "Feel my arm. Here. Feel it. I have literal fucking goose bumps."

Allie smiled awkwardly at the woman with the thick brown hair — it was Missy, Allie knew who it was, it was *Missy* — standing there staring at Allie with unvarnished astonishment, her mouth wide open, her eyes gleaming with fascination.

"I mean, can you feel that?" Missy took hold of Allie's hand and pressed it onto her forearm, and Allie shivered at the coolness of Missy's skin, which was indeed pebbled with gooseflesh. "It's wild. You look *just* like her."

"Yeah, that's — that's what your dad said."

"My dad," said Missy, and snorted in a funny caustic way that made Allie's heart ache with old joy. "My dad's a fucking tool, by the way. I'm sorry you had to deal with him."

Classic Missy. Allie's heart was in her throat. She reached out and clutched the doorjamb to stop herself from swaying, from collapsing onto the stale carpeting of the apartment building hallway. She had never seen this woman before. She loved her. It was Missy. It was a stranger. She wanted to hug her, wrap her up with bear-hug tightness and let Missy lift her up and spin her around. But that would obviously be a little strange.

Missy put her hands on Allie's shoulders and peered into her eyes. "Your eyes aren't the same as hers. Although, I mean . . . no, they're not. Or — God. I don't know, dude. It's fucking weirdness, though. Sorry to totally flip out on you. But, like — I mean — you look *just* like her. Whoa — you all right?"

No. Uh-uh. Allie, if she even was Allie, was *not* all right. Her body ached with tiredness and confusion, and her feet hurt inside the stolen sneakers. She was still wearing the sneakers, the ball cap, and the windbreaker she'd stolen from the nurses' station. She hadn't slept, not really, in almost two days.

Still holding tight to the doorjamb, she reached with her other hand to clutch her chest, where the grinding sensation of gears turning slowly against each other essentially churned nonstop, not acute but persistent, a constant low discomfort that sometimes rumbled up into pain. It hadn't really subsided since she'd stood on Kenwood Drive and recognized the two-story red-brick home, which she'd never seen before, as the house where she'd grown up.

"Okay, so, wait," said Missy, shaking her head, but not unfriendly. "What are you doing here, exactly? What do you need from me? I guess I don't totally understand who you are."

You and me both, thought Allie, but she just mumbled, "It's kind of a long story."

The truth was, Allie wasn't sure what she was doing here, what mystery she thought she was trying to solve. But the old/new memories had been so vivid, of Missy and of Kenwood Drive, of her mom calling up to her through the branches of the Chinese elm — and especially of that voice in the hospital: *Don't worry, honey. You're in good hands. This is Dr. —*

But none of that was real. What was she doing here? What she had to do was go home, get home, back to — to —

To —

Who did she have to get back to?

Allie now hung on the doorframe with both hands, head down, fighting a wave of nausea. Missy stepped forward, alarmed.

"Whoa," she said. "Come on, come in." Missy dragged her inside. "Sit. Sit, sit, sit. Come on. Sit down."

Missy swept a bunch of laundry off a fat cheap armchair and pushed Allie down into it, then went to pour them each a glass of water from the kitchen, really just the other end of the one big room that constituted the entire apartment. As Mr. McDermid had tartly warned Allie this morning, Missy's College Park studio was above a Thai restaurant, and the place smelled redolently of peanuts and fish sauce.

"Thank you," murmured Allie. "Thanks so much."

"De nada," pronounced Missy, handing Allie her glass and settling herself in the sofa next to the armchair. Missy's hair was twisted up and secured atop her head with a single chopstick, just like Missy had worn it when they were younger. She had a sweet round face and almond eyes and she wore a long denim skirt and a fuzzy gray sweater.

Allie sipped the water and steeled herself against an upswell of pressure in her chest, intensifying and receding, leaving behind new memories, one by one: Missy at age thirteen winding her hair into a single long plait and piercing it expertly with the chopstick she kept in her backpack while the boys in English class pretended not to stare; she and Missy on a narrow stage, Missy shouting into a microphone and bouncing on the balls of her feet.

"Sorry about all the junk," Missy was saying now. "My boyfriend and I split like six months ago, and he was a total chaos agent. I'm still kind of in recovery mode. Okay, so. Let's start at the top. Your name is Allison, my dad said?"

"Uh . . ." It took her a brief half second, an instant of struggle, before it came, before she could find the word. "Allie. It's Allie. Allie, uh—"

Allie reached for a last name but couldn't find it. It slipped from her fingers as she grasped for it, like a marble disappearing down a drain.

"Okay, Allie," said Missy, leaning across her squat black coffee table. A thick strand of hair had fallen forward, and she took it in her hand and curled it around her finger. "So, seriously: Who are you, and how did you end up on Kenwood Drive?"

"Okay, so, I mean—it's weird."

"Weird is okay," said Missy. "I fuckin' love weird. As you—"

Missy stopped herself. She had been about to say *As you know* or *As you well know,* and Allie saw the words falter and fall away, and Missy bit her lower lip with stunned confusion.

"Go on," Missy said softly instead. "I'm all ears."

"Okay, so," she said. "Like I said, my name is Allie."

And then Allie just talked. Haltingly, she explained what had happened to her in the past couple of days. The parts of it that she understood or remembered. How she and her baby daughter had been kidnapped from a park near her home in New Jersey, how she had escaped from the car, how she had spent a terrifying night in the hospital before escaping from there too.

And then—blinking back tears by now, shaking her head—she said she wasn't sure if it was even safe to go home and that she'd had a strangely hard time reaching anyone who might be able to help her. And then—cautiously, looking down at her hands, knowing exactly how it sounded, she talked about how the memories had begun to appear in her mind: memories of Kenwood Drive, of her mom and her stepdad, of a whole childhood that wasn't her own. This part Allie was reluctant to talk about, how these impossible things were happening inside her head, how new memories seemed to be forming themselves and old ones burning or sliding away. But the thing was that she knew she could tell Missy everything. Missy was her best friend. She had known Missy her whole life. Yeah, except that no, no, she had never met this woman before, she—

"Whoa," Missy said, staring unblinkingly at Allie. "Fucking intense, dude."

"Yeah," said Allie. "I know."

It actually felt really good to talk, to just say all of these things out loud. She felt as calm and relaxed as she had in many hours. She felt like an actual human being. She smiled nervously. Missy smiled back but didn't say anything. She drew out the chopstick and began to slowly rewind her hair. Allie could tell that she was processing. Digesting.

"Welp," said Missy. "I can't explain it."

"But just to . . . just so I know," said Allie, leaning in. "You grew up on that street? On Kenwood? And you— you rode bikes and all that with this friend, this girl? I just mean, the things I'm remembering . . ."

She trailed off, but Missy was nodding. "Oh yeah," she said. "A hundred percent."

The memories were real. They weren't *Allie's,* but they were real. "So, your friend—" Allie started, but Missy interrupted her.

"Hang on," she said. "Back up one sec. I mean, because— just hold on."

Missy stood and took two steps away from the sofa as if she suddenly needed to put space between herself and this stranger. She set her hands on her hips and peered at Allie. "So you were kidnapped, you said?"

Allie nodded.

"You said your baby was kidnapped also?"

"Yeah."

"But not— with you?"

"What?"

"No, I just mean..." Missy peered at her cautiously. "I just mean, where is she?"

"There was...it was..."

Allie tried to remember. She squeezed her eyes shut tight and tried to remember. "There was another car."

"There were two cars?" said Missy. "You said one before."

"No, there were two. And, um, two people—a woman and a man."

"And the man took the baby?"

"Yes." *Rachel,* Allie thought adamantly. The baby's name is Rachel.

"Was the other car also an SUV?"

"I can't—I'm not sure."

She stopped. She couldn't picture the second car at all anymore.

She shook her head. She gritted her teeth. She strained to remember, but the memories were peeling away, dissolving out of her mind.

"Okay," said Missy abruptly. "Break time. Did you want a beer?"

"Oh, uh—no," said Allie. "No, thanks."

What Allie really wanted, she suddenly realized, was food. She'd had a few bites of miserable chicken from a hospital tray twelve hours ago and nothing since. But it didn't feel right, asking Missy to, like, cook her a meal or order in something. How long was she going to be staying here? What did she want from this person?

"So, look," Allie said when Missy sat back down with her beer. "I don't entirely understand what's going on here."

"No shit." Missy took a swig.

"But whatever it is, I think it's obviously, you know, somehow connected to your friend. The one I look a little like."

"Not a little," said Missy firmly. "Exactly. You look like Ana if she'd grown up."

Ana. The name crashed into her like a wave.

Just like it had crashed into her when Mr. McDermid had said it this morning. *Ana.*

"Right." She said it herself. "Ana. Your father said that Ana, um — that she was — "

She stopped. She couldn't say it. But Missy — good old Missy, frank and firm and fearless — was way ahead of her.

"Dead," said Missy. "She died in an accident. A little over ten years ago."

Then Allie just couldn't hold back anymore; she slipped out of the armchair and got down on her knees before Missy and fell into her chest, and Missy held her tightly and kissed her on the head. Allie was crying, and she felt from the rise and fall of Missy's body that she was crying too.

And while they hugged Ana was thinking, *I love this chick and I missed her so fucking much,* and at the same time, slashing and overlapping, Allie was thinking, *No, no, this is wrong — this is wrong — no.*

Allie pulled out of the hug. Softly, she said, *"Rachel."*

"Whoa — " said Missy. "What?"

Allie said it again. She had to say it. She had to know it. She had to remember it and keep remembering it. "Rachel."

"Why are you saying that?"

"It's my daughter," she said. "Rachel is my baby's name. I have to say it because . . ." She shrugged, pushing tears out of her eyes. "I'm just weirdly forgetting all this stuff and that's the one thing I do not want to forget. I really do not want to forget Rachel's name."

Missy was staring at her.

"What?" said Allie.

"Well," said Missy. "You ready for this?"

"What?"

"Rachel was Ana's mother's name."

115

*　　*　　*

A little later, Missy declared that Allie was going to spend the night. She got up from the couch, went back into the kitchen, opened the freezer, and surveyed its contents.

"So here's the story. *Something* is going on here. I don't know what it is, and neither do you, but we're not gonna crack it tonight." She took a frozen pizza out of the freezer and waved at the sofa with it. "That thing is a pullout, believe it or not. We're gonna eat pizza, and you're gonna stay here tonight. My shift tomorrow isn't till twelve, so we'll get some sleep, clear our heads, and in the morning we figure out where you need to go and how to get you there. Okay? And in the meantime, I'm gonna take a lot of pleasure in sharing space with someone who reminds me so much of the person I loved the best in the whole fucking world. Sound good?"

Allie nodded. "Sounds good."

Missy nodded too, then tore open the pizza's flimsy cellophane wrapper with her teeth. "I feel like I'm high, I swear to God. Do you feel high?"

"No, I, um . . ." Allie smiled. "I don't know. I never really did drugs."

"Seriously?" Missy laughed with astonishment. "Okay, well, then, you're definitely not Ana. My girl liked to in-*dulge*."

"Was that . . . the drugs?" Allie asked. "Is that how she died?"

"No," said Missy, and then, "Yes and no."

"So how did she . . ." Allie stopped. The pain in her chest was there, grinding on steadily, like a machine. Like a machine that was wearing something away. She heard the voice again in her head, calm and reassuring, a man's voice: *Don't worry, honey. You're in good hands. This is Dr. — Dr. —*

She tried to remember more. Tried to find it. A hospital smell. A bustle of activity. Bright lights behind her closed lids. Pain somewhere. And the voice, reassuring and distant, someone patting her . . . *good hands. This is Dr. . . .*

Allie breathed shallowly. She could almost remember. It was so close. "Tell me," she whispered. "Can you tell me what happened?"

"She was a fucking wild child is the basic answer," said Missy. "Ana's mom was sick, had been sick for a couple years, and her stepdad was, like, consumed by it. So Ana was kinda acting out. We were—I don't know. Fifteen, sixteen. We had a band. Punk rock. Just fucking around. And one night Ana gets plastered after a show at this place on Q Street and she decides she's going to walk to the Metro. Alone. And I—"

Missy had been telling this story in the casual tone that was so familiar to Allie, funny and coarse, but suddenly she stopped, and her face hardened, and when she continued, her voice was roughened by emotion. "I met a guy. At the show. So, like, where what I should have done was say, you know, *No. You're not going to do that, you're not going to fucking walk by yourself to the Metro in the middle of the fucking night, Ana, because you're drunk and you're a girl and you weigh maybe a hundred pounds on your heaviest day,* instead what I said was, you know . . . 'Bye. Good luck.'"

Missy's voice had tightened and slowed. Her nostrils flared.

"Anyway, she got hit by a car on Q Street. A hit-and-run. She made it to the hospital, but they couldn't save her."

Allie reached for Missy but she said nothing. She couldn't. Allie was there again, in the hospital, confused and scared. *Don't worry, honey. You're in good hands. This is Dr. —Dr.—*

Allie blinked. The scene swam. The past appeared and disappeared, and it wasn't her own past.

"Hang on," said Missy. She turned away and slid the pizza into the oven as the last piece of the sentence landed in Allie's mind.

Stargell.

You're in good hands. This is Dr. Stargell.

"Holy fuck," said Allie with a voice that was not her own voice. She

117

was almost back there. She could almost see. The bright hospital lights. The whir of machinery. *It's me,* she thought. She understood. *I'm her. I'm me. I'm Ana.*

And then—

"Who the fuck is Dr. fucking Stargell?"

13.

At last Desiree arrived at Kenwood Drive in suburban Alexandria, Virginia.

It had taken her longer to get here than she would have wished. It always took her longer to get anywhere than she wished. But Desiree always drove at the speed limit. Any time the imperatives of a given assignment urged her to go faster, she reminded herself that every mile above the speed limit incurred an incremental risk of drawing the attention of the law and that such attention could carry consequences that would derail not only the current job but potential future ones.

But the passing of time was eating away at her. She had to find this girl. She turned onto Kenwood Drive, parked at the end of the cul-de-sac, and killed the engine.

She had been working on this job for fifty-one hours and twelve minutes.

Two hours ago she had finally caught the scent of the missing woman. A confused Jane Doe with a laceration to her left foot had been brought into Hanover Regional Medical Center at one or two in the morning on Wednesday but had left unexpectedly, without being discharged, very late that same night.

Using the persona of a concerned family member, Desiree had gathered this information from a succession of people who had no business giving it to her. It was an occasion in which Desiree's physical appearance worked very much in her favor: petite and pretty, plus now with a sympathy-attracting injury to her eye.

She selected a house at random on Kenwood Drive and approached. Desiree had grown up in a house like these. A good deal smaller, and in another state in another part of the country, but spiritually the same. A quiet street, suburban and dull, each home identical to its neighbors. One never knew what was happening inside these houses. Desiree's father, for example, was an exemplary employee of a regional food-and-beverage marketing company as well as a Little League coach and a member of the Jaycees; on weekend nights, however, he drank himself into a dark fury and slammed Desiree's mother against the wall.

It was in extracting herself from this situation that Desiree had taken the first steps that led eventually to her current occupation. She had always located her father's misery — and the misery he inflicted on those around him — in the shame and agony of his working life. Every morning he had to go somewhere and sit, all day long, performing menial tasks and pretending they mattered, his life and his family's life perpetually dependent on the whims of some boss or just on the health of this large entity, "the company," over which he exercised no direct control.

Desiree had built a career where she could choose her own projects. Make her own hours. And yet here she was, anxiously watching the clock, feeling her compensation atrophy, amortizing away into nothing as the hours slipped past.

There was, perhaps, no winning.

*   *   *

The man who answered at the fifth house Desiree tried did not open the door all the way.

He peered at her suspiciously through the crack. He was seventy-five, perhaps, with gray hair under a golf cap. Somewhere inside, a TV was playing; Desiree heard gunfire and someone screaming.

"Yes?" the man said sharply.

He was not to be charmed, this one. She did not try to charm him.

"Good evening," said Desiree. "I'm looking for a friend of mine. She's having a bit of a mental-health crisis, and I'm trying to track her down."

"Ah," said the man. "Sure." He opened the door the rest of the way. "I know just who you're talking about."

FRIDAY

14.

Mom? Hey. *Mom.* Did you already check your e-mail?"

Grace woke up grudgingly, blinking and looking around. "What?"

"Do not check your e-mail, please."

"River. Come on. What time is it?"

It was still totally black outside, no sliver of light peeking around the shades; Grace fumbled for her phone and groaned. Six thirty in the morning, the darkness still refusing to acknowledge the existence of daylight. November in Maryland.

River stood in the open doorway of Grace's bedroom, framed by the pale light of the hall, hands on their hips. Grace groaned again. What was even happening?

"Mom," River said loudly, as if dropping the word from a great height. "I'm serious. Do not open your e-mail."

"Jesus, Riv. I just woke up. I didn't even wake up yet."

"Good. I really need to talk to you before you read this." They were holding their phone in its ridiculous Minecraft case, holding it straight out in front of them, brandishing it like a weapon.

"Can you hold on, please? Can I have one second?"

Grace struggled into a more or less sitting position. She felt everything: the soreness in her butt from all the driving; the lingering pain in her spine; the bone-weariness of having stayed up too late, slept too little. An incipient urgency for coffee called out from deep in her veins.

"Jerry is totally lying about this whole thing," River announced.

"What thing? Who is Jerry?"

"Can I turn on the light?"

River didn't wait for an answer. They stomped over to the wall switch, and the bedroom filled with light from the big overheads. Grace threw her arm over her eyes like a vampire. The light felt like heat. She was trying to place what she was feeling, the dull body-wide ache and disorientation, the sense of not quite being able to piece together what she had been up to yesterday: the surreal deep dive into C. P. Stargell's "Incarnating the Arrow" and then the long drive to the Hanover Regional Medical Center and the useless interview with Dr. Steve.

The whole thing came to her in flashes, with tinges of embarrassment and regret but also a sort of underlying excitement like a layer of light shining and shivering beneath her skin.

The feeling was like being hungover, Grace thought, blinking in the harsh bedroom light. It was like waking up after a night of partying. In truth, however, Grace had never really done much partying in her undergraduate days and none at all in law school. It was like she was recalling a memory she had never actually had.

She'd gotten home in the middle of the night and lain awake for an hour or more, vibrating, staring at the ceiling, listening to the silent sounds of the sleeping world. She told herself that she could *feel* it, what

Dr. Stargell described in that article: *time*. Not time the abstraction that measured the days, but time the *physical thing,* time that was part of her body. Lying sleepless, she became aware of it in her system, fizzing inside her like champagne bubbles: the individual moments of her existence, flickering microscopic particles, electric and alive.

And Grace's restless mind imagined what it would mean, to have *more*. More hours at the exhausting end of a day or in its hectic middle, hours that would be hers to do with as she wished, to use as a refuge or as a chance to, for once, catch up.

Or *years*. Extra years added to life's end or extending its middle, telescoping life open, making it last.

Eventually, finally, Grace had slept — and now, in the harsh light of morning, the whole thing felt ridiculous. A mad scientist's hypothesis, untested and untestable, buried in some obscure academic journal.

Except, of course, there was the woman in the Hanover hospital bed with the Goldenstar port, scared and helpless, certain that someone was after her. Yes, Stargell's theories were untestable, but *something* had happened to that poor woman. Something was *still* happening to her.

River plonked down on the bed beside Grace, tossing their phone onto the night table. River was fully dressed, in baggy jeans and a flannel button-down, glaring at Grace through their nonprescription lenses. Grace yawned and sat all the way up. She was in her oversize No Doubt T-shirt and underpants, the sheets sprawled around her.

"Okay, look," River said. "Here's the whole deal. And you promised you wouldn't freak out."

"What? No, I didn't."

"Basically, Jerry is being lame."

"Who is Jerry?"

"Jerry Falmouth?"

"The vice principal? *Dr.* Falmouth?"

River nodded, and Grace said, "You can't call the vice principal Jerry."

"Fine. Dr. Falmouth. Happy? Dr. Falmouth says I'm suspended."

"River! What?"

"It's just a half-day suspension."

"*Just* a half-day suspension? Are you kidding me?"

"I didn't *do* anything." Suddenly River sounded like the little kid they once were; their eyes were wide with outrage and filled with trembling tears. As was so often the case, River's outsize confidence revealed itself in moments of stress to be shot through with anxiety.

"Jerry—sorry, Dr. Falmouth, okay?—sent this whole long e-mail, but I really want us to talk about it before you start reading it. Because there are totally two sides to this story."

Grace reached for the night table and felt for her own phone, but River yanked it away and tossed it to the other side of the bed, into the sea of rumpled sheets.

"River!"

"No, let me just tell you. Let me explain. Okay? Before you start getting ready for work, because when you're getting ready, you don't listen."

Oh my God, thought Grace. *Work.* She couldn't believe she had to go to work. The idea of her job, her office, the third floor of the FDA building in Silver Spring, seemed like it belonged to some ancient prehistory of her life. Her job now was finding that young woman from the hospital; her job was making sure she was okay—figuring out exactly what had happened to her and protecting her from future harm.

The last thing she wanted to do was return to her wobbly office chair at the CDRH, go back to the world of the 510(k) applications and Kendall's black cherry yogurts labeled with passive-aggressive notes on Post-its in the break-room fridge.

River had launched into an elaborate recitation of their version of events. There was a graphic novel in the school library about systemic racism, and someone named Ms. Watkins had moved it to the "request only" section after a parent had complained about its depictions of violence. But then a freshman named Derek Mooney had demanded the book be moved back out to the main section. Derek was Black, and he argued that the book was being banned, which was not okay, and so River and some other students had come to stand in solidarity with Derek and formed a human chain around the library.

"Hang on." Grace was having trouble focusing on the story. She got out of bed. "Wait. I really have to pee."

The story had some obvious holes in it. For one thing, she had never heard of Ms. Watkins. The school librarian was a man. He was tall with no wedding ring and looked like he worked out. Grace remembered him.

"Mom? Are we talking about this or not?"

"What's the title of the book?" she asked.

"I don't know," replied River huffily. "Does it matter?"

"Are you serious?"

"Yes. What?"

"You got suspended for protesting injustice and you're not sure what book it is?"

"Just a half a day! I told you. What was I supposed to do?"

"*Nothing!*" said Grace. "You were supposed to do nothing."

River harrumphed, and Grace caught a glimpse of herself in the mirror before she sat down to pee. That didn't sound great, did it? *Nothing?* They were supposed to do nothing?

"Wait. I didn't mean . . . River, can you just give me one second?" she said.

Grace struggled with this particular aspect of a parent's job: how much to encourage her child's questioning and boundary pushing, how to know when they were just being a troublemaker for the sake of being a troublemaker. River had always been a brash, elbow-throwing kind of kid, averse to all forms of authority, which Grace found admirable but which also scared the shit out of her. The world was just such a complicated place and there were all kinds of rules and rule-makers out there. All kinds of potentially dangerous outcomes that River, in their youth and idealism, couldn't see or didn't want to see. So, yes, Grace was annoyed that River had gotten themselves suspended, but beneath Grace's annoyance, as always, there was worry, and not just worry but fear.

"It's just that there are times when you have to—" she started, then turned on the water to wash her hands. "Wait—hang on."

But River didn't hang on. They opened the door and stood staring at Grace. "Times I have to do *what?*"

"Times you can't do exactly what you feel like."

Grace came out of the bathroom, and River shadowed her to the closet.

"Oh, okay. And what are those times?"

"River."

"Wait, lemme get a pen. I wanna get 'em all down."

"River!"

River stomped away, leaving indentations in the shape of their Doc Martens in the carpet. While Grace was trying to pick out a dress, River was replaced by Kathy, who stood in the doorway—well, more like *leaned* on it, holding herself up awkwardly by the doorjamb—wrapped in her ancient flannel bathrobe.

"Mom?" said Grace. "Are you okay?"

"I'm fine."

"Where's your cane?"

"I'm *fine*. What is going on?"

"I'm staying home today," River declared angrily, ducking under Nana's arm and flopping down on Grace's bed. They had gotten their Nintendo Switch and started playing, defiantly staring at the small screen.

"Oh, yeah?" said Kathy. "Is it some kind of Native American Person Day?"

River rolled their eyes, and Grace said, "Mom, come on."

Kathy grinned innocently, adjusting her grip on the doorframe. Maryland was not among the states that had replaced Columbus Day with Indigenous Peoples' Day, but the idea had lodged in Kathy's mind as an egregious example of liberalism gone wild.

"Actually," River said smugly, eyes locked on the Switch, "I stood up for something that mattered to me, and I am being punished for it. I got a half day of suspension."

"No," Grace corrected. "You got yourself involved in something that was none of your business—"

"Of course it's my business. Jesus, Mom, would you—"

"And now there are consequences."

Grace pointed a finger at River, and River pointed a finger back at her. "Seriously, Mom? If you can't see the problem, maybe you're part of the problem. Have you ever heard that expression?"

"Don't be sanctimonious."

"Don't hide your head in the sand."

"Wait a second," said Grace, shifting her attention from the ethics of the situation to its practicalities. "What does a half-day suspension mean? Do I need to come home from work to take you to school at some point?"

"I'll take them," said Kathy immediately. "No sweat."

"It's not a big deal," River was saying. "None of this is a big deal. If they don't want me at their stupid school, then I don't want to be there."

"Mom, you can't drive," Grace reminded Kathy, although her immediate thought had been *Yes, great, fine.* But the doctor had told them it wasn't safe, and if Kathy drove River to school, she would undoubtedly go straight to Costco afterward.

"Of course I can," said Kathy.

"Great. Done," River said. "I'll stay home this morning with Nana and then she'll drive me."

"Wait. Stop." Grace could feel the two of them ganging up on her. "The point is, you're in trouble—"

"For no reason."

"Don't talk over me, and you *are* in trouble, which means you don't get to sit on your butt all day watching soap operas with Nana."

"Game shows," said Kathy sourly while River tossed up their arms in outrage. "I watch *game shows.*"

"Whatever, Mom." Grace glared at her mother. "They're being punished."

Grace continued looking for an outfit that wouldn't make her feel like a dowdy middle-aged person. It was useless. She stood before three extremely boring work dresses in three shades of tan, all of which she felt like she'd already worn this week. How could this be? When, exactly, had she become this person, a timid woman in a dull tan dress sourly telling her kid not to rock the boat?

"Here's the plan," she said suddenly, grabbing one of the dresses. "River, you're going to come with me to my office."

"What?" said River. "No! I am *not* coming to work with you."

"You are. You absolutely are."

"River can stay home," Kathy put in. "We will be fine."

"No."

Grace shook her head decisively, much more decisively than she felt. She was already feeling miserable about returning to her desk and to the

Sleeper's Friend application. The last thing she needed was her snarky, gender-nonconforming teenager whining at her side and stealing Kendall's yogurt from the communal fridge.

"Mom, no," River huffed. "Seriously. I can't go to your office. Your office is the most boring place in the world."

"Well, how do you think I feel?" said Grace. "I have to go there every day."

She stormed toward the shower, ending the conversation before she could reconsider. "You're coming to my work. And you can't make trouble. I'm right in the middle of a big project."

15.

River seethed in the shotgun seat for the entire twenty-minute drive to the FDA satellite office, arms crossed tightly across their chest, face pressed against the window, their body as far from their mother's as humanly possible. Normally they would be absorbed in their phone, but Grace had taken it away and put it in her bag, which only added to River's sense of mortification and outrage.

As for Grace, usually after she yelled at River and put her foot down about some issue, she became desperate for her child to say something that let her know it was okay, that indicated that even if they were mad, they were not *really* mad, that they would forgive her, that this core enduring relationship of Grace's life had not been permanently riven. But today Grace's thoughts were elsewhere. Today she let the hot emotions of their argument fade into the background and just drove, staring absently out the windshield, watching the shopping centers and town-home complexes go past like individual filmstrip frames.

"Hey, can I ask you something?" she said.

"What?" said River icily.

"Have you done any cosmology yet?"

"Do you mean cosmetology?" River's contemptuous tone was softened by confusion. "Like, skin care?"

"No. Cosmology. Like — the origins of the universe."

"No, Mom. I have not done any *cosmology*. I'm in high school."

"Yeah, no, I know," said Grace absently. "Right."

She turned off Rockville Pike onto the service road that led into work. The security guard sat in a small kiosk while the gate arm rose to let in cars and lowered again.

Grace rolled down her window, held her security card up to the little black box, and called, "Good morning, Marco," as the gate arm slowly chugged up.

"Morning, Ms. Grace," called Marco in return, and she drove through. River snorted, and Grace looked over.

"What was *that*?"

"Nothing."

Grace scanned the rows for an empty space, sighing. Irritated, she repeated herself: "River. What?"

"That guy hates you. You know that, right?"

"Who? Marco?"

"The guy at the gate."

"Yeah. Marco. River, what are you *talking* about?"

"I'm talking about how that guy has to pretend that the two of you are friends of some kind."

"He's not pretending. He likes me."

"No, he doesn't."

Grace was not enjoying this conversation. She was also not enjoying the fact that there weren't any available parking spaces. After working here for fourteen years, Grace might have thought herself entitled to her own assigned space or at least access to some sort of special section of the lot, but that wasn't how it worked. As she rolled slowly past another chock-full row, Randy the new guy was climbing out of his silver Tesla; he waved at her with early-bird exuberance. She smiled.

"Okay, fine, River. Why do you think Marco doesn't really like me?"

"Because acting like he likes you is part of his job. Which is super-dehumanizing, when you think about it for a second. Not only does capitalism force people from marginalized communities into menial jobs, it basically requires them to be pleasant and polite and act all deferential to people like you. Like they're trained seals."

"Marco's not a trained seal."

"I didn't say he was."

"I get Marco a Christmas card every year. With a Starbucks gift card."

"Oh my God, Mom."

Grace started to turn into an empty space, but no—there was a motorcycle in it. She stopped to back out. "Jesus Christ," she muttered as a green Jeep Cherokee whipped past her, probably to get to the only remaining space before she did.

"Mom, the first step in changing an unfair system is admitting that you are one of its beneficiaries. It's bad enough the guy has to sit in a little box all day."

"I'm not a beneficiary."

"Mom."

"*I* sit in a little box all day."

The green Jeep pulled into a space just in front of her, exactly as she had predicted, and Grace cursed. It was 8:57. If she didn't find something soon, she'd be late.

"River, is this how you're going to be all day?"

"It is," said River, and Grace glanced at them and saw that River was smiling, just a little bit, and Grace stuck her tongue out at them—and then, as if the minor melting of the ice between mother and child had sent a signal to the universe, a parking space materialized, a capacious and unreserved spot close to the forecourt and the main doors.

"Amazing," said Grace as she pulled in. "Oh. Wait. River, hold on. Wait here."

"What?"

Just as she'd turned off her engine, Grace had spotted Lou Fleming parking his own car, an enormous Ford Explorer with a rack on the top and ski-resort bumper stickers. Lou, of course, *did* get his own space, steps from the entrance.

"That's my boss. I have to talk to him real quick," said Grace, unbuckling her seat belt.

"Why?"

"I want to catch him before we go inside. Wait here."

"*That's* your boss?"

Grace threw open her door and, stumbling a little, slung her bag over her shoulder. This was perfect. She hadn't exactly formulated the intention to talk to Lou until she saw him, but now she thought, *This is perfect.* She could grab him right here, catch him off guard, get what she needed before the day even started. Perfect.

"God. That guy's mustache is *ridiculous.*"

"Okay, see, this is why I want you to wait here. One minute, okay?"

"It seriously looks fake. That's a *real* mustache?"

Grace closed the door on River and hustled to the forecourt, where a line of flagpoles stood sentry outside the building's entrance, their three flags fluttering limply — the United States, the State of Maryland, and the Food and Drug Administration. She gave Lou a tentative one-handed wave as he came toward her, juggling his work bag and travel mug.

"Grace," said Lou, checking his watch as he approached, still fumbling with the strap of his satchel. "Fancy meeting you here."

"Ha-ha. I know." And she sort of lurched in front of him, putting her-self awkwardly in his way. "Hey, before you head in, can I just really quickly run something past you?"

"Can't see why not."

Lou's glasses were fogging up with cold; he slipped them off, wiped them, and put them back on. He examined Grace in a way that made her wonder what she looked like.

"It's this thing from the other night," she began. She lowered her voice. "The business with the portacath."

"The what?" He blinked.

"The pictures they sent? From that hospital near Baltimore?"

"What?" Lou peered absently at Grace through his glasses, which were already re-fogging. "Oh, that whole thing." He nodded, remembering. "I think I mentioned that got canceled. Did I not tell you?"

"You did. Yes."

"Okay, then." Lou reached out awkwardly, his arm unnaturally thick inside his heavy coat, and patted her on the shoulder. "So I'll see you upstairs?"

He waited for her to step out of the way, let him go inside and start his workday. But Grace found that she couldn't do it. She felt a prickle of sensation along the lines of her body, a blurry heat filling her head. A sharp breeze fluttered the flags above them.

"No," she said, too quickly, and then stopped and smiled. "It's just that, uh—I just can't get the darn thing out of my craw."

"I'm sorry to hear that." Lou looked past her, toward the building and the safe haven of his office. Clearly he was thinking of his comfortable chair, of the dull but satisfying business of scrolling through his e-mail while sipping his coffee. He was a man of regular patterns. "But what, exactly, is caught in your craw?"

"The young woman, Lou. I think she's in trouble." Grace stopped, then corrected herself: "She *is* in trouble."

Lou's eyes went wide behind the glasses. "What are you talking about?"

"So, look. I went up there last night, Lou."

"You went where?"

"The hospital. In Hanover? That we got the request from?"

"Wait — you *went* there?"

Lou's confusion deepened into bafflement. It was one thing to get a work question stuck in one's craw; it was quite another to take a long drive to a random hospital in search of the answer to a question that had been withdrawn. Clearly, to a man like Lou Fleming, the idea of putting in that kind of time and energy on something — on *anything* — was bizarre to the point of being unnerving. "But — but why?"

Grace flicked that question away, jumped to the next one. "She ran off, Lou. That's why they rescinded the info request. Because she disappeared. She thinks someone is chasing her."

"Chasing?" Lou rubbed his fingers across his brow, really digging them in, like he was trying to pull his skin off his face. When he stopped, he gazed past her again, up at their third-floor offices and the nice, normal, boring day he was looking forward to. "Who would be chasing her?"

"That's what we have to figure out."

He opened his mouth to respond to her, then said, "Oh. Hello."

Grace swiveled. "River. I asked you to wait in the car."

"It's okay," they said. River was wearing Pokémon mittens, part of some complicated ironic adolescent-nostalgia fashion statement beyond Grace's comprehension. "Mr. Fleming, right? *Such* a pleasure to meet you."

"*River,*" Grace said warningly.

"What? My name is River," they said, segueing into their chirpy intro speech. "I'm nonbinary, and I use they/them pronouns."

"Aha," said Lou. "Well, that's fun."

"It is!" River chirped. "It is fun."

River thrust out their hand and Lou shook it, smiling uneasily. If he'd been flummoxed by Grace's unaccustomed forthrightness, her confusing appeal for help with the young woman in Hanover, he was utterly perplexed by this odd small person in silly mittens pumping his hand like a car salesman.

"River is unwelcome at school this morning, so they're going to hang out with us. Right, honey?"

"You betcha," River agreed with a hearty thumbs-up. "It's terrific. If you don't mind my saying, I am obsessed with your mustache."

"Uh — thanks?"

Lou gingerly extracted his hand from River's; Grace at this point thought he might just sprint away. She had to grab hold of the conversation, steer it into place.

"So, Lou," said Grace. "What do you think?"

"What do I think about what?"

"About looking into the identity of this woman. Tracking her down."

"What woman?" asked River, swiveling their head back and forth between Grace and Lou. Grace said, "Don't worry about it," and River said, "Wait — what woman? Is someone hurt?"

Grace sighed. "River, please." This was why she had wanted the kid to wait in the damn car. "It's not a big deal."

"It sounds like it is."

Grace kept her attention on Lou. "Seriously, Lou, I think we have a responsibility here."

Lou exhaled, shook his head tightly. "Do we?" The look on his face was one Grace remembered seeing on her husband's face during the years of their marriage: The cornered, wheels-spinning expression of a man of whom some response was required that he would not or could not provide. "I don't think it *is* our responsibility. This thing just landed on my desk, you know. It wasn't our thing."

"What *thing?*" said River. "Is this about that weird shit in your notebook?"

Grace ignored them, kept her focus on Lou. "Yeah, no, I know, it just landed on your desk, but it did land there, and I think we have a — an *ethical* and a *moral* obligation, and maybe even a *legal* one, to help this person."

"Legal?" he said. "Whoa."

"Can't we reach out to the seventh floor?"

"The OCI? No." Lou shook his head firmly. His eyes bulged with alarm. "Our department generally does not deal with investigations."

"Not generally, but maybe in this case we do."

Lou kept shaking his head, adamantly uninterested in any interaction with the FDA's Office of Criminal Investigations. Grace had never dealt with them either, but she knew they had a whole staff of special agents charged with looking into the illegal use of FDA-regulated products and turning offenders over to the DOJ.

"This just isn't our business," Lou said, and Grace said, raising her voice, "It *is* our business. It is literally our business! We do medical devices! This woman has got a medical device in her chest. I mean, Lou! Come on!"

"Mom?" said River, and Grace said, *"What?"* and realized she was talking very loudly. Standing here in the forecourt beneath the flags and basically screaming at her boss. Lou had retreated a little, hands raised, eyes darting, as if he and Grace were veering toward some form of actual physical altercation.

Restored to herself, Grace felt the sharp sting of embarrassment at

Lou's discomfort and River's confusion. Her child was looking at her strangely, like Grace was possessed or something, operating outside the defined parameters of her own personality.

"Lou," she said softly. "I'm so sorry."

"Hey, you know. No, uh——" He cleared his throat. His cheeks were flushed. "No biggie."

"No, really. So sorry."

"You're passionate. We love passion around here."

But he was done. She had given him a chance to leave and he took it, lifting his bag back over his shoulder and adjusting his hat, turning away from her toward the door. "Tell you what. Write up a request. I'll take a look at it."

"That would be great."

"Meanwhile, let's stick with the bread and butter, huh? How's that cert application cooking? On the sleep-apnea thing?"

Grace nodded, looking down at the pavement. "Cooking pretty good," she muttered.

"Okay, super," said Lou, and Grace kept her focus on the ground, conscious of River's eyes on the side of her face. "See you upstairs."

16.

"This is untenable." Allie stared at herself in Missy's bathroom mirror with tears in her eyes, her hands clutching the sides of the sink. "It's un-fucking-tenable."

And even that, even saying those words made no sense, because that wasn't how Allie talked; to slip in *fucking* as an intensifier between two syllables, *un-fucking-tenable,* that was pure Ana, Ana who barely knew the word *untenable*, some kinda fucking SAT-word bullshit, but who loved to say *fucking*, loved to see how it made the adults around her squirm. *Un-fucking-tenable* was Ana all day long.

Ana was in here with her. Inside her mind, Ana and Allie sharing space, in conflict, in chaos, grinding together nerve on nerve.

"You okay in there, hon?" called Missy through the door.

"Uh. Yeah," Allie called back. She was not, of course. Far the fuck from it.

Missy was working on something at the kitchen table. She had been up before Allie, her laptop open, drinking coffee. She had tried to show something to her, but Allie couldn't focus on Missy. She couldn't think straight.

Because she and Missy had sat talking for another hour last night, and the longer they talked the more Allie became aware of Ana stirring inside her mind, Ana's consciousness taking shape in and around the preexisting shape of Allie's. Each new memory catalyzing a dozen more, Ana's past leaping to life in small sections — math class in fifth grade, her mom's elaborate wedding in colors of cream and gold, making noisy punk music with Missy in her basement, her mom's long sickness, the angry form of sadness that had made Ana so desperate and wild. All of these things Ana now remembered inside the crowded space of Allie's mind, and meanwhile whole sections of Allie's past disappeared from view, falling into the depths like broken bridges, sinking into the water.

Now, this morning, she was Allie and also she was Ana, and the grinding inside her chest was constant, one thing crushing against another, and it *hurt*. Allie stared at Ana in the mirror and moaned because it was un-fucking-tenable.

She stood in her bra, looking at her body; she inspected the tattoo on her left arm and shoulder. She loved it. She touched it with her fingers. She and her husband had gotten them together, on their honeymoon —

No.

What?

Honeymoon?

Husband?

Allie's head fuzzed out and then came back. She felt with her fingertips the hard flat patch of skin on her chest. It was rough, like a callus, marking the location of the portacath like the disturbed earth atop a grave.

"Son of a bitch," she heard Missy say through the door. "What the hell?"

She ignored her friend's voice. She wasn't ready to engage again. Every time she talked to Missy, it intensified the perplexing and painful process happening inside her head.

She was Allie and someone was trying to put Ana into her, or she was Ana and someone had jammed Allie inside, and something had to give. It had to stop. The memory that had come to her of that long-ago night in some hospital had grown clearer, but not clear enough. She could almost see it; she could hear it and smell it and feel the chaos of the night. The bustling and the beeping of the machines and the floor-cleaner stink of the hospital hallway.

And someone beside her bed telling her to relax, telling her she didn't need to worry. *Don't worry, honey. You're in good hands. This is Dr. Stargell.*

"Hey," called Missy. She was outside the bathroom door, knocking hard. *"Hey."*

"Gimme a sec," Allie called, heaving breaths. She pulled on her shirt, her mind racing with an adolescent kind of shame, while Missy banged on the door again.

"I got it."

"You got what?"

Allie held herself steady on the rim of the sink with one hand, reached out with the other to unlock the bathroom door.

"Allie?"

Missy cracked open the door and poked her head in.

"I gotta show you this. I think it's—I don't know what it is. But it's definitely something."

Missy's thick hair was wrangled into a low ponytail, which was how she had to wear it to work; she was a server at some terrible family restaurant on Baltimore Avenue. She was holding her laptop, balancing it awkwardly on her forearm like a waitress delivering a pizza.

She trailed her friend into the living room, looking over Missy's shoulder. She was Allie. She was Ana. On the screen there was a PDF of some newspaper or magazine article, dense with text.

"I did a little Googling. Tried a couple different spellings."

"Of what?" said Allie.

"The name you said," said Missy.

Missy tilted the screen toward her, but she was already reading it. She was Ana. She was Allie. She stared at the article, at the title on the masthead.

What the hell was the *Journal of Applied Metaphysics*?

17.

So, wait. Are you going to tell me?"

"Tell you what?"

"Come on, Mom."

They were on the elevator, and River, who had sat in sullen silence the whole way to work, now would not shut up. "Tell me what the deal is with this missing girl."

"It doesn't matter because there is nothing we can do."

"Yeah, but you have to tell me."

"Nope. I don't."

But she knew the kid would never quit. Would never give up. So instead of marching directly across the open-plan office to her desk, Grace stopped River by the elevator bank and said, very quickly, "Look. There is this girl—not a girl, a young woman—who came to our office's attention, okay? She had a port placed in her chest."

"A port?"

"A portacath. It's a surgically implanted medical device that facilitates giving and taking fluids from a patient."

"Very sci-fi."

"Not really." Grace shrugged. "It's a common medical device. Cancer patients, for example, are often ported so they don't have to keep getting lines put in. But, um——" Grace stopped. She lowered her voice and said, "But, see, this one, this port, in this woman . . . oh, hey, Randy. How are you?"

The new guy strolled past the elevators in a sharply tailored dove-gray suit, grinning ear to ear and smelling faintly of soap. "Cannot complain," he said. "Absolutely cannot complain."

"Is that guy serious?" River said, too loud, and Grace scowled at them.

"Come on, Riv. This is my work."

"So what were you saying? About the port?"

Grace opened her mouth to answer and then realized that she was about to say something out loud for the first time. River waited. Grace glanced at the elevator doors to make sure they weren't opening, then back at River.

"Mom? What?"

"It seems like maybe this particular port was inserted as part of—— part of a *procedure*."

"Procedure?"

"Yeah."

What a sinister word that was, Grace thought, *procedure*. It whispered of sterile rooms, of scalpels gleaming under cruel light.

River was waiting, looking at her bug-eyed. "What kind of procedure?"

"Basically, I found this article about a . . ." She didn't want to say *procedure* again. "A novel form of medical intervention. And the author of the article, he worked at a facility that was using a very unusual model of a port. And now this woman turns up in a hospital with that exact kind of port. And she's baffled and disoriented and fearful. What I assume is—"

"They did this procedure on her."

Grace nodded, and River asked the obvious question.

"What kind of procedure is it?"

Grace took a deep breath and then just said it: "A procedure to extract something they call the durational element. Which is basically . . ." She stopped. She looked at River, who was waiting. "Time. A procedure to extract time."

"Time?" River started to laugh but then looked at Grace and stopped. "Mom." They grabbed Grace's arm. "Are you fucking with me?"

"I am not. These people think that time is, like, a thing. Like part of our physical structure somehow, and it can be extracted."

"Whoa," said River, and Grace nodded.

"Yeah. Whoa."

And she was smiling, just a little bit, because it had been hard to say that, but River had made her put it out there, and Grace was grateful.

River wrinkled their brow thoughtfully. "What would that even mean? To take time from someone? So they, like, just exist for less time? Does that mean that you could also, like, *give* time to someone? So that they would have a longer life? Or, like, more time on a test or something?"

"These are good questions," said Grace. They were, in fact, exactly the questions she'd been asking herself, though she didn't say so.

"Jesus," said River with a gasping sort of laugh. "This is actually *extremely* sci-fi."

"Yeah," said Grace. "I guess so."

River grinned and Grace shrugged. It was such a relief to have let this whole bizarre thing out of her head and even more of a relief that River had reacted not with disbelief but with intense and fervent curiosity. It always made Grace happy to see it was still there, under the veneer of prickly adolescent cynicism: that bedrock characteristic of River's, where everything was exciting and everything could be true.

"And it comes out through this port thingy?" River asked. "Is it, like, a molecule? Or a—wait, an atom? How does it *work?*"

"It doesn't."

"What?"

"No, I just mean that it's not real. I mean, the port is real, the woman who got ported is real. But I don't think the durational-element stuff—time as a physical thing—is real. Someone out there might believe it, but people believe a lot of crazy stuff. As we know."

"Okay," said River softly.

"So that's the story," said Grace. She had put her bag down, and now she picked it up again and started to cross the open-plan floor to her office. But when she realized that she was walking alone, she turned back to River.

"But, I mean," River said, "are you *sure* it's not real?"

"Come on, kiddo," Grace said. "I have to get to work."

As they entered Grace's tiny office, she felt the familiar sinking feeling of being there. The potted plants. The smeared window with the vertical blinds. Kendall Johns at his desk, listening to his tinny classical music, typing with almost uncanny focus, eyes glued to the screen.

"Good morning, Grace," he said. "Would you like me to turn my music down?"

"No, that's okay. Kendall, this is River, my child. River, I'd like you to meet my officemate, Mr. Johns."

"Kendall is fine," Kendall said tentatively as if not entirely sure his Christian name was something he was comfortable providing to an adolescent. River grinned their great big new-people grin and stuck out a hand.

"Hi," they announced. "Great to meetcha."

Kendall smiled tightly and nodded. He displayed none of Lou's confusion or unease with River, just the same distant formality he showed everybody.

"And are you with us today for some sort of school project?"

"Nope," said River. "I got suspended. I'm being punished for exercising my right to free speech. Actually, Kendall, you might find this interesting—"

"Okay, honey," said Grace warningly. "Let's let Mr. Johns do his work."

She laid a silencing hand on River's shoulder. She wasn't sure she needed the child expounding on their antiracist crusade over the graphic novel to her African American officemate, of whose politics Grace was entirely ignorant.

"You know what?" said Kendall, looking out into the main part of the office. Jan Ko was flittering about, casting glances in, curious about River and interested as always in Kendall. "Maybe I'll go ahead and set up in Jan's office for the time being. I can access my computer via remote desktop."

"Oh, Kendall," said Grace. "Are you sure?"

Kendall nodded rapidly: never so sure of anything in his life. As Kendall collected his things, Jan watched through the glass, eyes keen with excitement.

After Kendall had slipped wordlessly out of the office, River slung their backpack beside Grace's desk and plopped down cross-legged on the carpeted floor. "So," they said. "What are we going to do about the woman?"

"What?"

"The woman in the hospital room who they drilled a hole into?"

"They didn't drill a—it's called a portacath, honey, I told you."

River waved away the correction. "Fine. But how are we helping?"

"We're not."

Grace settled into her chair and it gave way with its light pneumatic hiss, sinking down a half an inch as she rolled into place behind her desk.

"Oh," said River. "Well, then, I guess I misunderstood. Because I thought you just told me that this chick was running around somewhere with a bunch of time zapped out of her head, and I suppose I thought some people might find that, like, *concerning?*"

"River, come on."

"What?"

"I told you, no one took time out of anyone. It's not possible."

"But you did say that she was a victim. And she was scared, and alone."

Grace looked away from River. She turned on her computer and kept her eyes on the screen as it went from dead black to gray-green.

"And," said River, well into it now, righteous and relentless, "when we were outside and you were trying to get Mr. Mustache to help, it sounded like you gave a shit about it."

"If you heard what I said, then you also heard what Lou said, which is that there's nothing we can do. So I'm going to do my work, and you're going to sit and do homework. What homework did you bring?"

"I have to read *The Great Gatsby.* Which is a nightmare."

"Why? Because it extols the virtues of capitalism or something?"

"No, because it's fucking boring."

"Would you watch your mouth, please?"

River was digging around in their backpack, talking over one shoulder. "I just don't understand why you're going to give up on helping that woman. Because you're too scared to help?"

"River," said Grace, sharp and tight, but then she didn't know what to say next. Her cheeks burned as if River had slapped her. The stupid computer was waiting for her to enter the password, and she found she couldn't do it. She brought her fingers to the keyboard but didn't type. Somehow, starting her workday felt like surrender.

She swiveled 180 degrees and stared at River. "Look," she said. "There are aspects of this you don't understand."

"Okay." River had found *The Great Gatsby* in their backpack and tossed it on the ground beside them. "You always say I'm so smart. Explain it to me."

"A person can't always do everything they might want to do, sweetheart, and that's just the way life works." As she said it, Grace knew she sounded like someone. Who did she sound like? She sounded like her mother. "I have responsibilities. I have a job."

"Granted. But, first of all, you hate your job."

Grace glared at them. "I do not hate my job."

"Of course you do, and please don't patronize me. You do! I can see it in your eyes every day. I can literally see it in the curvature of your spine."

Grace winced and sat up straight, pulled back her shoulders, and balanced her head carefully on her neck. Then she sighed and said softly, "River, I hear you. I do. But I'm just not sure what else I can do on this. I drove to the hospital and talked to the doctors, but the woman had already left. I don't have some kind of private investigative service. How would I even find this person?"

"Well, I mean, have you tried . . ." River cocked their head, pausing for comedic effect. *"Trying?"*

Grace sighed. "What is that supposed to mean?"

"It means sometimes you have to stick your neck out on shit."

"Easy for you to say!"

"Yeah. I guess so. Maybe." River shrugged. "I'm just a kid, right? But maybe people trying hard and not worrying so much about the consequences is how things actually change. And, conversely, maybe everybody just doing what they're supposed to do is how the rich stay rich and the poor stay poor and nothing changes."

Grace smiled, despite herself. God love this kid. God love them. "And how exactly did this turn into a lecture on oppressive structures?"

"That's how structures work, Mom. Everything is part of the structure. So? Come on. What have you got? Are there any clues?"

"No." Grace sighed. "Not really."

"Where's this hospital she was at?"

"Hanover," said Grace. "Near BWI, kind of."

"Okay." River spread their hands apart, gave Grace a pitying look. "So that's a *clue*. Right? If the person appeared out of nowhere at a hospital near Baltimore, most likely she's from somewhere around here—not, like, Wyoming. And wherever she got to, she's probably still somewhere in the area. Don't you think?"

"Oh my God," said Grace, "I hate you," but she said it to sound like *I love you*. Because River was right and they knew they were right, and Grace wanted this—she wanted herself to be wrong and River to be right, and who better to push and prod at her, who better to *force* her to do the righteous but reckless thing, than her own right and reckless child?

"Okay," said River firmly. "And do you have any kind of physical description?"

Grace nodded. "A picture, actually. Although—"

"God! Mom!" River jumped to their feet. "You have a freakin' *picture?*"

People outside of the office glanced over at the sudden noise, and Grace smiled uneasily, gave the room an *Everything's cool* wave. Maybe they would think it was Bring Your Child to Work Day, for some reason. Not for everyone. Just for Grace.

"A couple pictures. But they're not that helpful. You'll see what I mean."

Grace, giving up on work for now, took out her phone and scrolled until she found the pictures she'd taken of the photos on Lou's desk. She pulled up the one that was a close-up of a woman's torso, from just above the breasts to the bottom of the neck, a very skinny woman, wiry at the neck, pale unblemished skin dotted with small freckles. A tattoo high on her left arm, going over her shoulder.

"That's her."

As River looked at the strange picture, at the naked torso of a woman washed out by the hospital lights, their cocksure expression faltered. They looked chilled. "Jesus," they whispered.

Grace laid a reassuring hand on River's arm. "It's okay, sweetie. Maybe we should forget it? For the moment."

"No," said River. "Can you send it to me?"

"What?"

"I can find her. *Send me the picture.*"

Grace looked at River, and River looked back, their face set and determined, and Grace saw herself in the face of her child, a mirror of her own confusion and fear and determination, and she felt the hard clutch of love in her chest.

"Okay," she said.

River nodded sharply and stuck their hand out, palm up, fingers slightly curled. "I need my phone."

And they did. River found her, and it didn't even take very long.

While Grace got to work, at last, on the Sleeper's Friend application, settling in to compare its innovation claims with the specs of existing sleep-apnea products, River sat back down, their back against the wall in their intent cross-legged pose, bent forward, thumbs accelerating into a familiar blur.

Every so often, Grace heard a curious grunt or a small bright *bing* from River's corner of her office, but eventually she decided that River had suckered her or forgotten about it and was over there playing Word-Whizzle or hate-scrolling on Instagram, silently engaging in arguments with former friends or minor celebrities. Grace just sighed and kept working—she could not fight that battle right now. The kid wasn't at school, but neither were they at home watching *The Price Is Right* with their grandmother. That would have to be sufficient punishment for the time being.

At exactly ten o'clock, Grace watched through the smudged window as Kendall Johns rose from the seat he'd taken at Jan's desk to go and refill his coffee in the break room. She knew it was exactly ten o'clock because that was the time Kendall refilled his coffee every single morning. Five minutes later, right on schedule, Kendall drifted back to Jan's desk, holding a freshened cup of coffee in his STAR TREK: VOYAGER mug.

And then, five minutes after that, River said, "Mom?"

Grace looked up as River slid their butt onto one corner of her desk and slapped the phone down, face up, beside her.

"Yes?"

"I've got it."

"You've got what?"

"The girl. The woman."

Grace's mouth dropped open. "Slow down. Wait. What do you mean, you've got it?"

"I mean I've got her name, her birth date, her place of birth, and the town where she grew up." River waggled their eyebrows over the top of their glasses. "Is that not the sort of thing you were looking for? Mom! Hey!"

Because Grace had popped up from her chair and was hugging River as tight as she had hugged them in a long time, and River sat there stoically, suffering themselves to be hugged.

The sleuthing was not all that complicated, River kept saying as they walked Grace through it, but Grace knew damn well she couldn't have done it in a thousand years; she wasn't a digital native, as River was, and neither did she have her child's nuanced and sensitive perception of the world. Never, for example, would she have homed in on the most distinctive piece of the picture — River had taken the image of the woman's torso and isolated and enlarged the tattoo on her left arm and shoulder.

What had looked to Grace like a pair of indistinct triangles were in fact ears.

"Ears?" said Grace.

"Yup," said River. "Bunny ears." Still sitting on Grace's desk, River raised two fingers and separated them into a V. "But here's what's cool. I did a Google Images search of the tattoo because it looked like commercial art. It's a logo."

"A logo?"

"Yup. For a band."

River had created a searchable version of the image — not the woman's entire shoulder, just the tattoo itself — and copied it into an app called Freehand where they could trace it and clean it up. With that step done, the series of circles and triangles was more clearly a repeating chain of *V*s and *R*s, the logo, as River now triumphantly proclaimed, of an extremely short-lived mid-2000s punk band called — "Wait for it," River said with a goony smile — "Vulvateen Rabbit."

Grace blushed, and River laughed out loud. "I know. Brilliant, right?"

This strikingly named band with the distinctive logo had, sadly, left no recordings, or at least none that had survived on Spotify or Bandcamp.

The record of its existence seemed confined entirely to a handful of mentions in local news outlets, such as the *Washington City Paper*, and a couple of zines with limited press runs, one of which River had found through a deep dive on the website of something called the DC Punk Collections at the University of Maryland.

Grace listened to River recount all this, marveling at the resourcefulness of her child, astonished that someone so enterprising and clever could still perform so unevenly at actual school. The nice thing was that River's earlier sullenness and irritation had melted away entirely in the excitement of the project. It was sort of a miracle and more or less the best-case scenario of dragging the kid to work with her, but Grace was hardly going to remind River of how pissed they'd been.

"But wait," Grace said when River had wrapped up their reporting. "So she was a fan of this particular band. How does this help us?"

"Oh, I'm glad you asked," said River with fresh excitement in their voice. They leaned over Grace's shoulder, seized control of the mouse, and navigated swiftly to the profile of Vulvateen Rabbit that had appeared in the *City Paper* from 2012, previewing a show at a place called Club Soda. "She wasn't a *fan* of the band. She was the bass player."

River leaned in, and Grace leaned beside them. The photo caption listed the names of the band's members. River zoomed in once again until the screen was largely taken up by the pixelated picture of a face.

"You found her," whispered Grace, and River dropped all the silly comic salesmanship from their voice and said simply, "Yeah. I found her."

They scrolled down to the caption and pointed to it. "Ana." Grace read the rest of it. "Ana Jessica Court." She frowned.

"Mom? You okay?"

"Yeah," she said, "of course," but she was not. Dr. Steve had said the patient gave her name as Allie.

But it was her—there was no question. The certainty of it took Grace's breath away. She looked back and forth from the picture on the screen to the one she had on her phone, the picture of the photo from Lou's desk. In the hospital photos, she was ten years older than she was here. But it was her.

There you are, she thought. *Oh, honey, there you are.*

She bent further forward, holding on to the edge of her desk, staring into the eyes of Ana Jessica Court. The girl in the picture, wearing a black jumpsuit and a defiant smirk, tilting the neck of her electric bass toward the photographer, was flanked by two other teenage girls making rock-and-roll poses. Full of potential.

Poor thing. Grace looked into Ana's eyes, fierce and determined. *What did they do to you?*

"Mom?" said River again, and looked worriedly at Grace. "Mom?"

"I'm okay, baby," said Grace. "Seriously. This is amazing. Thank you."

"But wait," said River, pivoting back to their cheesy-pitchman voice. "There's more."

The next article they pulled up was from the *Washington Post* Style section a dozen years earlier: June 12, 2000.

And there she was again, Ana Jessica Court, transformed by the unwinding of years into a little girl, now in a fancy pink dress, at the end of a long line of women and girls extending out from a radiant bride. In the picture, Ana was only three or four years old, but you could see it in her stance; you could see it on her face—it was the same girl who a decade later would be the bass player in Vulvateen Rabbit. Looking sternly into the camera, pretty and thin and defiant and with the faintest trace of a smile turning up the edges of her mouth, clutching the handle of a wicker flower basket like she would one day hold the neck of her guitar.

At the center of the picture, of course, was the bride, beaming in a heavily brocaded cream-colored wedding gown that flowed around her like a waterfall. Beside her and entirely overshadowed was the short and bushy-haired bridegroom, a plump and earnest fellow smiling broadly at the implausibility of having secured himself such a lovely woman. River rattled off some specs about the happy couple — it was the second marriage for Rachel Court and the first for Martin Ajax, who was some kind of asset manager in the District — but Grace was hardly listening. She was captivated by the little girl with the blond ringlets and the itchy-looking dress in the outer orbit of the wedding picture. Staring right at the camera on Mom's big day.

No idea of what was coming.

"Okay, this is good," said Grace. "Can I go talk to them? Are they in the area?"

"Well, you definitely can't talk to the mom," said River. "Rachel Court-Ajax died. She was diagnosed with a rare blood cancer in — let's see. In 2011. She died in the summer of 2014."

"Cancer," Grace echoed, looking again at the bride in the picture, her shoulders back and her hair just so, flushed with joy. "How do you know?"

River typed some more and then leaned back so Grace could see. Another *Washington Post* article, this one from the autumn of 2014, accompanied by a large picture of Martin Ajax — still plump and earnest but the thick black hair streaked with gray, the big wedding-day grin softened by grief. The article was about Rachel's Place, some kind of all-purpose community center and free clinic that Mr. Ajax had opened and dedicated to the memory of his late wife.

"Okay," said Grace softly, and stood up. "Okay."

Her heart had not stopped hammering; her body had not stopped moving. She buttoned her coat and tugged her hat on. It was like a target was flashing before her—now there was somewhere to *go*.

"Hey," said River. "Wait. Where are you going?"

She stopped. It seemed so obvious.

"I'm going to talk to Ana's stepfather," said Grace. "I'm going to go talk to him right now."

18.

This is just bizarre," muttered Allie, who was Ana. "I mean, it is so bizarre."

"Yup. Hard agree. The absolute weirdest," Missy called back from the small bedroom area of her studio, cordoned off by a flimsy decorative screen. She was rummaging in her underwear drawer, where she kept her emergency supplies: her passport and a small stack of twenties and the little Smith & Wesson .38 she'd gotten on the advice of a friend after things got very dark with Tony and he kept threatening to come back in the night. She also had an old burner phone, though. She kept saying she knew it was here somewhere. Her plan was to find the phone and charge it up enough to give to Allie before she left for the restaurant. Missy had to be at work in an hour, and she wanted a way to keep in touch with her very odd houseguest.

Allie was sticking around for now. (Ana. Ana was sticking around.) Until they figured out her deal, she was staying.

"Aha," said Missy. "Found it." She came into the kitchen with the black

clamshell phone, dropped it on the table, then rushed back to finish getting ready for work.

As Missy kept bustling around her in the small apartment, Allie sat at
the kitchen table with her hands pressed flat on the sides of her head,
staring at the screen of Missy's laptop. She was still puzzling through the
dense columns of text that made up "Incarnating the Arrow: Toward a
Substantive Vision of Time," by Dr. C. P. Stargell. It was slow fucking
going for Allie and for Ana, the two minds circling and overlapping
inside the single mind, memories arriving and disappearing in a rum-
bling chaos. At some point Allie had given up figuring out how to get
back home, stopped trying to remember where home was. When she did
try, when she strained to picture her bed or her work, whatever her work
was, or her husband, if there was a husband, new memories of Ana's
would arrive instead, aligning and affixing themselves in her mind:
childhood memories of spinning in circles with her mom on her wedding
day, teenage memories of her and Missy shoplifting beers from the Safe-
way in Gaithersburg. Her fingers, she found, had begun to walk in the
air, making the shapes of bass lines.

Meanwhile, she struggled through the opening sections of the Stargell
article, which had to do with the Big Bang, the nature of matter, and the
slow expansion of the universe. Occasionally she copied some text out of
the article and pasted it into a search engine in another tab, trying to figure out what the hell was meant by "the dance of quarks" or "isolated
baryonic matter," wondering what any of this had to do with the fact that
she — that Ana — had apparently died in a car accident ten years ago and
had now returned with her identity in some kind of psychic free fall.

No, Allie protested, *that's not right,* because from her perspective it was
she who had been interloped upon; it was her identity that had gotten
broken and scrambled — although increasingly she did not know what
her perspective was, increasingly her sense of Allie-ness was dissolving

into a wider sea of Ana, and it hurt—it fucking *hurt*—and she kept reading, puzzling through these dense paragraphs about the nature of time before getting into this whole long section about mankind's misapprehension of the relationship between perception and time, and it was all a lot to take. Understatement of the fucking year.

Meanwhile Missy was muttering, "Fuck, fuck, fuck," from where she stood at the kitchen sink, slopping dirty water over the sides. She was supposed to wear a blue polo shirt with the restaurant logo on the pocket, but the polo was still dirty from her last shift, so she was giving it a quick hand-wash.

"I'm really sorry, dude," she said. "But I can't lose my job. Are you going to be okay here?"

"Yeah."

Missy wrung out the shirt haphazardly, sending droplets across the kitchen floor. "Ah, shit," she said, and Allie glanced over and Ana smiled because Missy hadn't changed.

"I absolutely can't get fired. My dad keeps saying I can come and live at home, but that is like—no. No, thank you. All sorts of strings attached on that one." She stopped at the table to read briefly over Ana's shoulder and shook her head. "So weird. But seriously, stay as long as you want. Eat what you want. There's not much. You're gonna be okay."

Allie felt that this was wrong. Ana felt very much like she was not going to be okay.

The dark rippling pain was still spasming across her chest, and her mind was a twisting mess, and she had hoped and expected that this article would give her some answers, but it hadn't. It didn't. All this complicated science about the birth and growth of the universe, all these metaphors for how we perceive time—was it a river? Was it sand in an hourglass?—it was all just making Ana's head hurt even worse.

Allie. My name is Allie. God damn it.

But then Allie — Ana — Allie — then she got to the end of the article, and a light went on. Something clicked.

"Oh God," said Ana. "Oh my fucking God."

"What?" called Missy.

She had turned on the water to get in the shower, but now she came back out, clutching a towel to her chest and casting a quick nervous glance at the clock above the kitchen sink. She looked over Allie's shoulder at the paragraph she was pointing to — the same one that had stopped Grace in her tracks yesterday morning, sending shivers down her spine like a slow cold rain.

The next phase of this project, Stargell wrote, *must be directed toward confirming that the durational element can be identified, isolated, and manipulated.*

"You see it?" Ana said to Missy. Missy nodded, but Ana pointed to the word and read it aloud. " 'Manipulated.' "

"I mean — shit. So you think . . ."

Ana didn't respond right away. It was clear. Nothing was clear. But it was clear.

"I don't know what I think. I got hit by a car, you said," said Ana. "I mean, Ana did," said Allie, and Missy nodded.

"Hit-and-run."

Ana had no memory of a car accident, exactly. No memory of impact or pain. Just the hospital, just the reassuring touch, just *You're in good hands. This is Dr. Stargell.*

"So what if this Stargell guy, you know — got hold of her body. Somehow."

"Jesus," whispered Missy.

But that was what had happened. Ana was suddenly sure of it, and it felt good to be sure of something. She got up from the chair, paced back and forth. "I got hurt, and this dude, instead of healing me, does some kind of mad-scientist bullshit to my body."

Missy was staring at her. Allie was saying *me*. Healing *me*. *My* body.

Missy had more or less made up her mind, no matter what her *heart* was telling her, that this unusual houseguest was just a confused girl who bore an uncanny physical resemblance to her old friend Ana. But she was becoming less and less sure of that, and it made her heart twist and tumble in her chest.

On the other side of the apartment, the water was still running, steam coming out from under the bathroom door.

"This doctor," Ana was saying, "he puts this port in me to — to — I don't even know what the word is. *Take. Remove.*"

"*Extract,*" offered Missy softly.

"Yeah." Ana stopped pacing, whipped her head toward Missy. "*Extract.* Jesus. I mean — it's fucked up, but what if I was in a coma or something? What if I was in a vegetative state? And the doctor took out my remaining time to, like — give it to someone else. Like a — like a donor. A time donor. Is that insane?"

"I mean —" Missy smiled cautiously. "Yeah. Kind of."

The pain rose and tightened in Ana's chest; she gritted her teeth, and meanwhile, Allie — who was inside the cage of Ana just as Ana was inside the cage of Allie — Allie moaned and bridled and wondered if that meant she was the recipient.

It was the only thing that made sense, but none of it made sense. Nothing did.

Ana moaned. Allie couldn't bear it. Ana was in maximum distress. Whoever she was, she was horrified and scared. She pushed shut the laptop and slapped her hands down on the table. Missy watched, her hands at her mouth.

166

"This is fucked," the stranger announced. "My mind is fucked. My body is fucked. I'm *fucked*."

"It's okay," said Missy. "Seriously. We're gonna figure this out."

Meanwhile another new memory returned with the force of a slamming door, a pure, clean Ana memory as vivid as electric light. Something her stepdad used to tell her when she was maybe nine years old. He was such a classic *dad* back then, all corny and confident and silly, white sleeves rolled up over tan forearms. Before Mom got sick and he was consumed by hospitals, by grim determination, by grief. *Baby, the answers are always out there* was what she remembered him saying. *You gotta know where to find 'em.*

That was it. That was right. She had to find the answers, and she did know where to find them.

"This Stargell character," said Ana. "I'm gonna track him down. You think I can track him down?"

"Honestly?" said Missy with a grin. "How many C. P. Stargells can there be?"

19.

I feel like a horse's ass," said Martin Ajax with an apologetic chuckle. "I swear this is not normally how I dress to meet with government regulators."

"Please don't feel bad," said Grace. "I didn't call or anything."

"Well, sure, I know," he said, smiling over his shoulder as she trailed him down the hall. "But come on. Let's have some professionalism, people, right?"

He laughed again, shaking his head with good-natured self-deprecation. Over Grace's objections, Ajax's assistant had pulled the founder and executive director of Rachel's Place out of a pickup basketball game in the community center's big gymnasium. Now Grace was trotting behind him, heading from the gym to the admin offices in the building's other wing. Ajax wore baggy basketball shorts and a bright green Rachel's Place T-shirt, vividly sweaty at the armpits, with a hand towel slung around his neck.

The community center was airy and expansive, with long skylights lining the ceiling. Bright wintry light followed Ajax and Grace down the hallways, past bulletin boards and kids' artwork and doors that opened onto meeting rooms, classrooms, a room filled with small painted chairs and child-size musical instruments.

"Oh, whoops," said Ajax after marching them confidently down one hall only to double back and try another. "You would think after all these years I'd have mastered the maze in here. I wish I had time to give you the whole tour."

"Oh God, no, that's not necessary, Mr. Ajax," said Grace.

"Don't misunderstand," said Ajax, "I love giving the tour." He glanced over his shoulder, beaming proudly. "And, please — it's Marty."

It had been a little over ten years since the *Post* ran the article about the tragic beginnings of Rachel's Place — how super-wealthy asset manager Martin Ajax had turned his grief over his wife's death into a mission to help one community in Northeast. But Ajax was the same slightly chubby, bushy-haired man from the photo that had accompanied the article; the hair was white, but he had the same small mouth and big, sweet eyes. The impression of youthful vigor was underscored by the cheerful puppy-dog energy with which he made his way down the halls, bobbing on his heels and poking his head into rooms to say hello to staff members.

"So you're here from the FDA, Barb said? Are you just wanting to look at the paperwork or do a site visit at the clinic?"

"Uh, neither, Mr. Ajax," said Grace. "Actually."

"It's Marty. I mean it. What does that mean, *neither?*"

A curious note had slipped into Ajax's throaty voice, but he was immediately distracted when they rounded a corner and he stopped to high-five a commandingly tall white man with a buzz cut and neck tattoos.

"There he is!" the man called appreciatively, throwing up his arms in happy surprise. "Marty, my man. How's it hanging?"

"Easy, Kev. Mixed company." He turned back to Grace, pointed at the giant. "Ms. Berney, this pipsqueak is Kevin Helms, who runs some of

169

our after-school programming. I don't know if you've ever seen a saint in the flesh before, but here's your chance."

"Shut the eff up, old man," said Helms, squeezing Ajax in a crushing bear hug. "You're the damn saint."

Ajax laughed as the two of them peeled off from Helms and kept walking, Ajax now digging an ID badge from his shorts to beep into the administrative suite. "That man came in these doors three years ago after a dozen on the street. Criminal record down to here, total junkie. I know we're not supposed to call them junkies, but boy, oh, boy. Okay. Here. Sit."

"Thank you."

Grace perched on a folding chair in Ajax's small office while Ajax mopped his forehead and tossed the towel into a bin. Then he bent down to a minifridge, one of a very few items of furniture in the spare office, and came out with two waters. He tossed one of the waters to Grace, who caught it awkwardly out of the air.

"Whoa! Nice snag! Gimme one sec here, would you?"

"Of course."

Ajax bent forward at his desk, his lips moving silently as he read something off the screen. Then, satisfied, he screwed the top off his water bottle and set it down on his desk with a light crinkle of cheap plastic. Grace took a polite sip of her own water, realized her nervousness was making her very thirsty indeed, and gulped the rest. Ajax's office was covered with small bits of art and personal items; a cartoon calendar was tacked up, open to November, showing a turkey in a football helmet.

"So," she said.

"So," he said. "Right. FDA." He popped back up and scratched the back of his head as he examined his wall of filing cabinets. "I'm guessing you're here about our opiate-replacement program, yeah?" He leaned out of the room. "Hey, Barb?"

"Wait," said Grace. "No."

He swung back into the room. "You're not?"

"I don't do drug regulation. I'm with CDRH."

"Oh. Okay." Marty came away from the file cabinets, his brow slightly furrowed, and plopped back down in his chair. "CDRH."

"You've heard of it?" Grace said hopefully, and Ajax gave her a naughty schoolboy's smile, caught in a lie.

"No, I have not."

Grace smiled and found that she was blushing. Ajax's voice was pleasant and honeyed, but with the throaty underlay of a man who had smoked for years and maybe still snuck one every once in a while. There was an offhand charm about Ajax, with his basketball shorts and his little charitable empire. Grace knew she should just blurt out the business she was here on, but she found herself tongue-tied and uncertain.

"So. CDRH?" Ajax prompted, his grin broadening. "Or do you want me to guess?"

"No. God. Sorry, Mr. Ajax."

"*Marty.* Seriously."

"Marty." Grace blushed more. She fussed at the collar of her shirt. "CDRH is the Center for Devices and Radiological Health. We regulate medical devices." Grace was thinking of Dr. Steve, of all the other times she had had to explain her obscure home agency.

But Ajax was nodding with interest that was either sincere or expertly feigned.

"Sure, sure," he said. "Devices. I thought you were . . . never mind. It's just, sometimes we get FDA folks who work with the DEA folks. The controlled-substance teams."

"That's not me. I'm different. I'm—"

"Yup. CDRH. Got it. Sorry for the miscue." He snapped and then wagged a finger at her like he was catching on to a trick. "So this is about the Exeter patch, then?" He frowned. "Usually our guy on the regulation side is Barry Perez. Do you work with Barry?"

"Uh, no. No, I don't."

The name had a vaguely familiar ring, but Grace couldn't be sure. The total staff of the FDA was larger than the population of 35 percent of American counties. That was a fun fact someone had told her once.

"Well, I'm sorry you came out here," said Ajax. She could see that he was distracted by his computer screen, whatever new e-mails had started to filter in. "But, really, anything about opiate-replacement issues, I can give you the guy's name from the DEA. If it's the Exeter or one of the other delivery products, you should check with Barry. He's kind of our man on the inside in terms of that stuff."

"Let me start over," Grace said.

"Unless—I mean, if you just want to review our paperwork on the Exeter real quick, it's not a problem. I don't know why I'm being weird about it." Ajax didn't wait for a yes or no. He popped up again, went back to the file cabinets. "I can dig 'em out."

Grace didn't know what the Exeter was, and it didn't matter, but Ajax was frowning, prospecting with his fingertips along a row of filing-cabinet handles, deciding which drawer to pull out. He struck Grace as one of those people who never stop moving—pacing from room to room, leaping in and out of chairs, walking briskly with knees up through parking garages and restaurants.

"Oh, where is the damn thing," Ajax muttered, yanking open one drawer as he slammed closed another.

"Mr. Ajax, I'm so sorry," said Grace, "but I'm not here about your medical-device regulation."

He kicked closed a drawer and glanced at her, perplexed. "You're not?"

"No. I'm here about your stepdaughter."

Ajax had been crouching to pull open yet another filing-cabinet drawer, and now his entire body stopped. He just *froze*. It was like he was a hummingbird hovering through the world at his heightened metabolic rate, and then he suddenly became a *picture* of a hummingbird, caught mid-motion, frozen in the sky.

"My *stepdaughter?*" Ajax repeated, rising slowly. His voice rich with disbelief. "Hold on a minute. What *is* this? Who are you? You're *not* from the FDA?"

"No, I am. I am from the FDA. But this is about your stepdaughter."

"About — Carolee?"

"Who?"

"My *stepdaughter*." He gaped at her, confused, like he was doing the "Who's on First?" routine.

"Oh. No. I'm so sorry." Grace's mind raced to catch up. "Carolee is your daughter — your stepdaughter — from — from a current marriage?"

"From a current marriage?" he echoed, incredulous at what Grace instantly recognized as her bizarre choice of words. "Yes. My stepdaughter's name is Carolee Harmon and she lives in Rochester, New York. She's got no business with the FDA. She's got no connection to my work at all. Now, I'd really love it if you would tell me what this is all about."

Grace's mouth opened and closed like a fish's as she alit upon the mortifying possibility that she had screwed this whole thing up, and this man Ajax had no connection at all to the missing woman from the hospital photos. What was she relying on, really? What had brought her here other than some bread-crumb clues collected by her sixteen-year-old child?

And what was she even investigating? What the hell *for*?

Grace felt a pang of keen longing for the uncomplicated comfort of reviewing 510(k) applications, for her chair and her office and the dull unthreatening ever-presence of Kendall Johns.

But it was too late now. Martin Ajax stood directly in front of her, his hands planted on his hips. "What *is* this? Who are you?"

"Hang on, Mr. Ajax. Wait."

This time he did not tell her to call him Marty. Grace tugged out her laminated ID badge and held it aloft, like a cross wielded to ward off a vampire. Ajax took it in his fingers and glared at it.

"Okay. So—" Ajax paused. He let the badge drop and breathed deeply, looked at her carefully. "Starting over. You're from the FDA, and you're here about Carolee?"

"No, Mr. Ajax," said Grace. "And I'm sorry. I do apologize, because I should have been more forthright from the outset."

"Yeah, I guess so."

"But I'm actually here regarding Ana?"

"*Ana?*"

For the second time in two minutes, Ajax stared at her in startled silence, caught by new information, trapped in a hollow mouth of time. After a long moment, he exhaled once, a stunned half-sigh, and said, "My God, *Ana.*"

"So she is your—I'm right? She's your stepdaughter?"

"She was. Ana was the daughter of my first wife, Rachel. But she's dead. She passed away."

"I understand that," said Grace. "Rachel was—it sounds like she was an extraordinary woman."

Ajax put a hand over his chest. "They're both dead," he said. "Ana is dead also, and God rest her soul."

"I'm sorry?" Grace's heart stopped beating, started again. The room around her, and Ajax's flushed, perplexed face, faded in and out of view. "What do you mean?"

"What do I *mean*?" For one second, it appeared that Martin Ajax was about to cry. His chin quavered, but he mastered himself with visible effort, nostrils flaring, and continued, his voice lowered and carefully controlled: "Ana was struck by a hit-and-run driver walking home from a music club in 2013. She died."

"No, she didn't," said Grace, the words tumbling out even as she understood how horrible they were, how insensitive and bizarre. She just heard herself saying, *No, she didn't,* like some kind of lunatic ghoul, and then Ajax said, "Get out."

Grace stumbled to her feet. Ajax pointed at the door of his office. "Get out of here right now."

Grace wanted to protest, to explain how and why she had tracked him down and what she needed. She wanted to explain about the odd assignment she'd been given, to find the manufacturer of a portacath, which turned out to be Goldenstar Therapeutic Technologies, how she had subsequently become concerned with the fate of the young woman in the photos, and how she had identified Ana Court as the person she was looking for. At the very least, she could show him the pictures on her phone of the scared-looking woman in a hospital bed in Hanover and ask if he thought that might be her.

But to do so, to do or say anything else, would be cruel. Nothing but terrible cruelty. And it didn't matter. Martin Ajax was through with her.

He said it again: "I want you out of here." There was no amiability left in his voice, no ambiguity in his command. "Go," he commanded, and Grace obeyed.

She found her own way out of the labyrinth of the community center, feeling flushed and foolish and defeated, with a warm sheen of anxious sweat at her armpits and waist.

She made a wrong turn somewhere near the central recreation area where she had first caught up with Martin Ajax, circled back, and nearly collided with a young couple pushing a stroller who had just come through a wide door. Both the man and the woman were very thin, with tired, worn faces; the woman's hair was pulled back in a scraggly ponytail.

"Excuse me," said Grace, and the woman muttered, "You're fine," while the man yawned and smiled tightly.

Grace lingered at the door from which the couple had emerged. It was marked INTAKE/RECOVERY, and Grace instantly understood that through this door must be the opiate-replacement clinic Ajax had assumed that Grace had come to inspect. She glanced over her shoulder at the disappearing couple. The woman was pushing the stroller slowly down the hall with one hand while with the other she fished around in her bag for something. Her husband or boyfriend had his hand gently on the small of her back. Were they drug addicts? Grace wondered. She resisted the urge to stare, thinking, as she always thought when in the presence of people who were so vividly down on their luck, how fortunate she was, for all her dissatisfaction and disillusionment, to have a job and a family. And a sturdy place to be in the world.

"Can I help you, miss?"

A sharp-eyed young woman in nurse's scrubs had appeared beside her, clutching a clipboard and scowling.

"No," mumbled Grace. "Sorry. So sorry."

She left, head down, and found her way to the exit. Grace thought admiringly of Marty Ajax, who had turned his tragedy into this brightly lit infrastructure of Good Samaritan–ship. She should do more — she should run after that young couple and their child, see what she could do to help them. Then she remembered these were the ones who *were* getting help. They were getting help right now.

20.

River, meanwhile, sat alone in Grace's office, gnawing on a thumbnail, reading *The Great Gatsby,* except not really reading it, not even really pretending to read it. Scanning two paragraphs, closing the book, checking their phone, picking up the book again. They sort of couldn't believe Mom had left them in this boring weird office and gone without them to seek out Ana Court's stepfather. It wasn't like River's investigative brilliance had revealed the dude's existence in the first place or anything.

Whatever.

River's other problem was that every time they glanced out the office's window, they risked making eye contact with that dude Kendall. Their mom's sad-sack officemate was still sitting in exile in the big main room, awkwardly jammed in at the edge of his coworker's desk, while River was in here kicking it alone, like a teenager in a Disney comedy who through some contrivance becomes the boss of a company.

So now River, already frustrated at being stranded with F. Scott Fitzgerald while Mom was off playing fucking Sherlock Holmes, was doubly agitated by their ongoing effort not to look out the little window and see baleful Kendall staring back at them; God forbid they had to go pee and actually walk past the guy.

River sighed heavily. They picked up the book and scanned another couple paragraphs: loveless marriages, hollow aspiration. Cocktails. *Got it, F. Scott.*

They slapped the book closed and pushed it away, wincing as the paperback slid like an air-hockey puck into the no-man's-land between Mom's and Kendall's desks. Grace had explained how protective he was of his side of the office, a small-mindedness symptomatic of the capitalist system's corrosive effect on the psyche.

River rolled their eyes, but not at Kendall. Who was River, after all, to be passing judgment on this man? Kendall had a whole life of which River knew nothing, and it wasn't fair for River to be writing him off as some corporate drone. Not to mention that River understood that their mom's work wasn't really corporate America, it was *government* America; it was the faceless bureaucracy of the regulatory state, not the faceless bureaucracy of the consumer machine—much less the faceless bureaucracy of Big Law, where River's father earned megabucks protecting the interests of death-dealing pharmaceutical companies.

There were differences among things. There was nuance in the world.

The truth that River knew deep down, and honestly not even that deep down, was that their mother was not some soulless shill. Grace had not sold out to the quote-unquote "man" or any dismal shit like that. If anything, it was River's dad, David, who was the soulless one; Grace at least had the decency to feel conflicted about the choices she had made, to long for something bigger and better, in ways that she probably thought she kept hidden from River.

Like many kids who judged their parents harshly, River nevertheless often approached decisions first by wondering what Grace would do.

River stood up, turned away from the window, and paced back and forth a couple of times. They actually had quite a bit more homework to do than they had let on — not just reading *Gatsby* but also three problem sets for chemistry and a math quiz to study for — but they felt absolutely incapable of focusing on any of it.

They sat down at Grace's computer and turned it on, which just meant they turned on the monitor — the computer itself had been left on when Grace abruptly left the office to go talk to Martin Ajax. The multiple Safari tabs were still up, and River, leaning forward on the desk, navigated back through the pages of history showing the hunt that had led them to Ana Jessica Court.

River lingered on the Style section picture of the wedding with the beaming bride in her brocade gown. Wedding photography reinscribed traditional gender norms in ways that were almost too over-the-top to be critical of. River returned to the *City Paper* article about the band. Vulvateen Rabbit. Hilarious. *A+, ladies.*

River had no mandate to continue pursuing this matter on their own, but they felt in their gut that they had to. As the minutes ticked by and they were trapped here behind the office glass like a fish in an aquarium, they felt like all the homework and all this other shit, *The Great Gatsby* and the problem sets and the math, even the theoretically entertaining things they might do instead — dicking around on the internet or weighing in on a group chat, all the small bits of business that made up life — all of it seemed suddenly essentially useless. A lot of life was just useless, wasn't it? Just various ways to get through the time.

When something mattered, it was like two wires touching. You could feel the spark of it. It lit shit up.

River zoomed in on the picture of the band and reread the caption. Ana Jessica Court was one of three names. Ana was the bass player, but there was a lead guitarist and a drummer too. The drummer was a girl with a nose ring and a GI Jane buzz cut with the incongruous name of Felicity St. Rouge. The guitar player, with thick black hair secured in a knot with a chopstick, was Missy McDermid.

River stared at the screen. They gnawed on their thumbnail some more, smiling just a tiny bit. Finding people was easy. It was quite possibly the easiest thing in the world.

They glanced through the glass again just as Kendall Johns happened to look up; he regarded River with cool civility for half a second and looked back down. River reached out and ran their fingers over the weathered cover of *The Great Gatsby*.

River gave the book the finger and dug into their pocket for their phone.

Missy answered on the first ring. Or first vibration, actually, because her phone was in her palm. "Thank fucking God," she said with a start and answered.

Normally Missy would never answer a call from some random number because it was always some bullshit, someone wanting her to donate to the Fraternal Order of Police or inquiring about refinancing a home she didn't own. Worst-case scenario, it would be Tony, her ex, calling from a strange number to catch her off guard. But as it happened, Missy was waiting for an Uber, and when the phone vibrated she assumed it was her driver. It was one of those times when the car that was supposedly on the way kept canceling, and then it would say, We are finding you a driver, and then after a new one was finally assigned it, too, would disappear.

So when the phone rang, Missy was already twenty minutes late to work and thrumming with nerves. The possibility of being late for work was not the only thing sending her anxiety level through the roof—there was also the question of why the hell had she given Ana her fucking van in the first place?

Missy had instantly regretted it. She handed Ana the keys and said, "Good luck," and then stood watching the old Ford panel van putter down the street and turn right onto Baltimore Avenue, and asked herself what the fuck she had been thinking.

Friends help friends. They loan each other cars. But was this woman really her friend? Though she looked like Ana and sounded increasingly like Ana, the stranger was still calling herself Allie half the time. The only thing Ana *did* seem sure of was that she had to track down this Dr. Stargell and demand to know what had been done to her.

And now that Ana had gone, Missy felt doubtful that it was her. She'd probably been right in the first place, and this was just some disturbed girl who looked like her old best friend—her *dead* best friend—and she didn't even really look *that* much like her. Or did she? Missy was having a hard time now sorting it all through. What she knew for sure was that she had handed Ana, or whoever the hell it was, an old burner phone and fifty dollars in cash and her only means of transport, and the girl had made vague promises to return it all as soon as she could. And the gun, Missy reminded herself sharply. She had also given Ana—Allie?—whoever she was—the Smith & Wesson that she kept in her underwear drawer for emergencies. Which this obviously was, it was obviously a desperate emergency, unless of course she had just armed some random nutcase and sent her off in her own van to murder a stranger.

"Great move," said Missy to herself. "Brilliantly done."

And now a series of Ubers were refusing to come to her marginal neighborhood, and Missy was going to get fired, leaving her carless and jobless all in the space of one glorious November day. It was this kind of impulse control and first-class decision-making that had gotten her where she was in the world, living alone in a shitty section of College Park, working as a server at a lunch-rush hamburger place, earning fifteen bucks an hour plus tips while fat businessmen stared at her boobs.

So when her phone rang, she'd answered right away. "Hello? Are you here?"

"What?"

"What?" The person on the line didn't sound like an Uber driver. It sounded like a teenager.

"Yeah, hey, is this Missy McDermid?"

"Yeah," said Missy. "Who is this?"

"Okay, so. Look." The stranger took a deep breath. "My name is River, and this is going to sound totally insane, but are you friends with someone named Ana Court?"

"Wait." Missy had been looking anxiously down at the street for a car, but now she stopped and leaned her head against the window, feeling the cold pane on her forehead.

All Missy's doubt fell away. It was her. She fucking *knew* it.

"I'm — sorry." There was a tremor in Missy's voice when she said, "Who did you say you were?"

The conversation was circular and comical. This person River said they were working with was a woman named Grace Berney who was some kind of federal agent, trying to track down Ana Court.

"We're worried about her," River said, and Missy could barely speak.

"Yeah," she whispered. "Yeah, me too."

"We have determined that she may be in some danger," River went on, and Missy got the distinct impression of a kid using that voice that kids used when they were trying to sound official. "And we are hoping you have some information that might point us in the right direction."

At this, Missy brightened. Yes, she had probably made a mistake by letting Ana go off alone in search of Stargell. But the idea that, according to this kid, there were other people looking, actual government people out there trying to solve this unsettling and scary problem, was a powerful relief.

"I do, actually," Missy said, clamping the phone between her cheek and shoulder as she walked over to the table where she'd written down the address. "I know exactly where she's going!"

Whoever Dr. C. P. Stargell was, he had made a handful of real estate transactions since 2014, in each case using a different LLC instead of his real name. In general, the guy seemed careful to leave very few traces online: no social media, no public posting, no pictures. But Missy and Ana had managed to dig up what appeared to be his current address, in an obscure town in the eastern part of Maryland, and now Missy gave the address to River, who eagerly wrote it down.

"Amazing," they said. "Thank you."

"Oh, wait," said Missy. "I've gotta go."

She hung up. Someone was knocking at the door.

It made no sense, of course, that the Uber driver would be knocking on her door—she'd never gotten a notification that a driver had been assigned, for one thing, and of course he or she would be waiting out in the car on the street, not knocking on the door of her second-floor apartment. But whether because she was still in the confused haze of the phone call about Ana or because of her now-palpable anxiety about not getting to work on time, Missy didn't even crack the door with the chain on it and check to see who it was.

She yanked the door open and said, "Thank God you're —" and then stopped, taken aback by the unusual appearance of the driver: a short woman in a white shirt and some kind of black pantsuit, dark-haired and beautiful except for the thick pad of gauze taped over one eye.

21.

"How are you, Ms. Grace?"

"How are *you*, Mr. Marco?"

"Can't complain, my dear. How was lunch?" As always, Marco was hanging his whole upper body out the window of his little kiosk, waving cheerfully. Inside the gatehouse, he had the *Washington Post* open to the sports page. "Bring me a cookie?"

"Aw, shoot," Grace said with automatic cheerfulness. "Plumb forgot!" She smiled apologetically, even though this was just another of Mr. Marco's fun routines and even though she hadn't actually been to lunch.

He wagged a teasing finger and said, "Two cookies next time, okay?"

"You got it," Grace said, and leaned slightly out of the driver's seat, holding up the stippled plastic card to the black box on the metal post.

The light flashed red. Grace by habit had lifted her foot from the Altima's brake and started to roll forward. When the box didn't beep, she jammed her foot back down on the brake so she wouldn't crash into the gate arm.

"Doesn't wanna work, huh?" Marco said cheerfully, standing up after having just settled back into his chair. "Try her again."

Grace stuck out the card again, reaching back at an odd angle from where the car had inched up. She held it to the black box, and again nothing happened. It blinked red. She adjusted the card and tried a third time, feeling a squirm of panic.

"It usually works," she said, looking up helplessly at Marco, who was frowning. "I mean — yeah. It usually works."

Marco shrugged, leaned out of the kiosk again, and gestured for her to try once more. She did, pressing the plastic slab right up to the box with which it had successfully communicated every weekday for a million years.

Nothing happened. Grace was literally sweating; she swiped her winter hat off her head and stuffed it into her coat pocket while Marco came out of his little box muttering to himself, "Okay. This is officially weird."

Marco was surprisingly short and big around, with a rolling waddle; he wore some kind of supportive brace on his left leg, which Grace had never noticed before — she realized, actually, that she had never seen him outside his little kiosk before and felt embarrassed at having insisted to River, just that morning, that she and Marco were somehow good friends.

Now Marco leaned toward the box with a frown of concentration and poked at a couple of the buttons on its rear side, although it did not look to Grace like he was doing so in any particular order. Then he straightened up, shaking his head, and held his hand out to her.

"May I?"

Grace handed him the card through the window. In her rearview, two or three cars were waiting to enter the lot. Rhoda, an older woman she sort of knew from the fifth floor, was leaning out of her window, squinting through her glasses, trying to get a look at what was happening.

"I'm really sorry about this," Grace said as Marco held the card up to the box. Grace wasn't sure what she was apologizing for, but it somehow felt like she had made a mistake. Maybe she had demagnetized the card by putting it through the washing machine, something she'd once heard could happen to credit cards and hotel key cards.

Marco blew on the card. He wiped it on his sleeve. He waved apologetically to the cars that were stacking up behind Grace. Then he gave her a quick nervous *Here we go* smile and tried the card. Nothing.

Grace drummed her fingertips on the steering wheel. What the hell? She had to get back to her desk. And River was up there waiting for her to return. Suddenly, she felt like a prisoner trapped below the surface of the Earth while life above continued without her.

"Listen," she said, "maybe you could just—"

"Yes," said Marco. "You bet. I'm not supposed to, but I guess we better do that. We'll hook you up with a new card tomorrow, Ms. Grace."

Something in the way he said it sent up a little flare of shame inside Grace's heart. She felt it burn red onto her cheeks. *Marco's just trying to eat his lunch. He's trying to sit in there and sip his large Sprite from Shake Shack and read his sports page in peace, and here comes this lady with some bullshit for him to deal with. Some friend.*

Marco dug into the front pocket of his work shirt and came out with a different card, the same thick plastic as hers only cream-colored instead of tan and without the smiling photo of Grace on it. Marco held the card up to the communicator box, and the gate arm obligingly began to rattle up.

"Open sesame," he said and Grace exhaled, and she was so relieved to escape from the situation that she lurched forward again and nearly smacked into the arm before it was elevated enough for her Altima to get under it. By some miracle, the parking spot she'd vacated was still open, and Grace reclaimed it.

A flare of pain shot up from her lower back just as she unbuckled, and she had to sit for a second, breathing through her front teeth.

Out of her car at last and walking toward the garage stairs, Grace found herself thinking about Martin Ajax. Huffing with exertion from his basketball game, sweetly attentive to every aspect of his little non-profit fiefdom. Bustling around his office, popping up and sitting down again, tapping his fingers on his cluttered desk, chugging water from a bottle out of the minifridge. Freezing in place only at the mention of his lost stepdaughter; slowing to a stop only at the mention of his dead beloved family.

No one will be sad like that when I go, thought Grace suddenly, sadly, and then chastised herself for such self-pity. *Of course they will.* Pushing open the door to the stairwell, Grace glanced back at the gatehouse, where Marco had settled back down with his sports page. One by one, the other cars glided through with no problem, the gate arm smoothly sliding up and down like a conductor's baton.

Oh, she thought, and then, *Oh no,* although she wasn't sure why.

It was only when Grace got to the third floor, only when she stepped out from the elevator lobby and into the open-plan office, that things began to fall into place.

People were gathered in small groups, hovering at desks or whispering in clumps by the copier closet, by the restrooms. They were staring at something happening on the far side of the big room, and as soon as Grace got close, she could see that what they were looking at was her own small office, which was crowded with people.

River was pacing back and forth outside the office door, one hand pushed up into their spiky hair, the other hand holding the stem of their glasses, their eyes squinched up nervously, their cheeks flushed. Grace walked faster, her heart leaping from her chest toward her loving, nervy child.

"Honey?" called Grace, and everybody stared at her. Grace didn't care. "River, honey, what's going on?"

"Oh God, good. You're back. Okay." River gestured anxiously at her, wheeling their hand in the air: *Come on, come on, hurry up.* "I told them to stop. I tried to stop them."

Grace joined River at her office door and took their hand and squeezed it as she peered inside.

"Excuse me?" she said. "Hi. Can I help you?" A pair of large men in coveralls and heavy boots were in the middle of packing up her office; they looked like they'd been at it for a while. Her filing cabinet was on its side like a felled tree, her computer monitor was facedown on the desk, and they were in the process of strapping the computer tower onto a standing dolly like it was Hannibal Lecter. The two men looked up at Grace as she entered but didn't answer her or stop working.

"I told these guys they can't do this," River said. "And that they had to wait for you to get back. It's not okay to come into someone's office and mess with their stuff while they're not here." River cupped their hands around their mouth to make a megaphone and said it louder so the men could hear. *"It's not okay."* But then River's tone shifted, and they rubbed at their forehead with their fingers. "I'm sorry, Mom. Mom, I don't know. It might be my fault."

"What might?"

"I don't know. I made a phone call."

"What?"

Whatever was happening, it had flipped River into some kind of low-grade panic attack; they were pacing back and forth in a tight, agitated circle, chewing on their nails, staring with frantic hatred at the two men in coveralls. "I used your name."

"What?"

"I made a call. I was just trying to help. I don't know what happened."

"It's okay." Grace put her hands on River's shoulders and looked them in the eyes, something she used to do all the time when River was little and spinning out of control after getting a bad grade or losing their retainer on the bus. "It's going to be okay."

River nodded. Breathed deeply, in and out.

The workmen, meanwhile, were aggressively ignoring not only River but Grace herself, going about the business of dismantling her office of fourteen years like it was no big deal.

"Grace. Hello." Kendall Johns was standing protectively at his own desk, watching the proceedings with a pinched, displeased look. "Do we have any idea what's going on here?"

"I sure don't," she said, and then tried again with the workmen. "Excuse me, hi? Can you — sorry, can you stop that? Can you put that down? That's mine."

They were putting her framed pictures into a banker's box. While she watched, one of the men turned her coffee mug full of writing implements upside down over the box, and the pencils and pens tumbled into it. It felt like an anxiety dream, like she was in some sort of soundproof bubble, staring helplessly as her world came apart before her eyes.

Kendall looked on with one hand up to his face, clutching his chin, his lips screwed to one side.

Grace stepped closer to the workmen and said, "Pardon me," as loud as she could. "Could someone *please* tell me what's happening here?"

"Yeah," said the smaller of the two men, glancing at her sideways, hissing at the interruption. "Sure." He had a thicket of curly dark hair, and a breast-pocket patch identified him as Sanderson. "We got a work order says to clear this office out. We're supposed to move the contents to short-term storage down in the basement."

"Storage? But——"

"And is it just *her* side of the office, or . . ."

Kendall trailed off when Grace looked at him, then cleared his throat. "Just trying to clarify the situation."

"This is my office," said Grace. "I work here. Is it possible there's some mistake?"

There was no mistake. Grace knew this already; she knew it in the pit of her stomach and in the marrow of her bones. She had known it the instant her card hadn't worked on the gate box——something was happening. Something had happened. She shivered. Instinctively she reached out for River, who moved in beside her with fists clenched, her ferocious androgynous adolescent henchperson.

"I told you," they said. "This is BS. You can't just move my mom's shit around. My mom's worked here for a long time."

Sanderson gazed curiously at River for a moment; Grace could see him processing their size and aesthetic, and she prayed that he didn't decide to make a crack. This was the last thing the situation needed. The other man, whose breast pocket didn't even have a patch, had kept on working through this whole conversation, and now he was busily wrapping Grace's computer cord around and around the computer tower. "Listen, I don't know. They tell me where to go, I go. Can I get a little space here, please?"

"But who? Who told you?"

Sanderson sighed again, tugging a piece of yellow paper from the same breast pocket that identified him as Sanderson. He unfolded it and presented it with mock solemnity to Grace.

She just had time to see the words *work order* and today's date before he whisked it away again.

"Well, hang on," said Grace. "Can I actually look at it?"

"You gotta let her look at it," River echoed. Sanderson ignored them and glared at Grace. "Lady, come on. We've got a job to do."

"Yes," she said. "It's funny, because I also have a job to do, and I can't do it without my computer."

Sanderson shrugged. Grace felt herself becoming heated and tried not to.

From across the open-plan office she could see Lou Fleming making his way over, his usually placid face rigid and sheened with sweat. He gave her an awkward *Hang on* kind of wave, and Grace felt another bloom of fear in her stomach.

Just to Lou's left was another man, a man she sort of recognized, a short man with a thick comb-over and bushy eyebrows and a dark blue suit. They were walking together, except not exactly together because the shorter man was out ahead of Lou by maybe a foot or two, Lou trailing behind him, one hand jammed in his pocket and the other smoothing and resmoothing his mustache.

She knew that man. She had seen him before. Where had she seen him?

Kendall Johns looked pointedly at his watch, then up at the workmen. "Gentlemen, I don't mean to be rude," he began, and Grace for a moment thought he was going to stick up for her. "But I do wonder how long this office clearing will take?"

"Jesus, dude," said River, swiveling angrily toward Kendall, and Grace murmured, "It's okay, honey," although now she was focused on Lou and the other man, both of whom had come to a halt just outside the office door.

"Lou," said Grace. "What's going on?"

He held up both hands, wincing apologetically behind his mustache. Lou Fleming was the most conflict-averse person Grace had ever known, and now he looked to be in deep pain. He looked like someone who had stubbed all his toes at once.

"I just got a call about this, Grace. I just did."

"About what? What is going on?"

"Well, it looks like someone put a flag on your file."

"What flag? What—"

"I guess someone raised a concern about that whole business with Greenberg."

Grace laughed and then immediately stopped laughing. "Wait. You're not serious. Are you serious?"

Lou looked serious. He looked downright solemn. "You do remember all that?" he said.

"Of course I remember. But that was—I mean, it was . . ."

She trailed off. She hardly knew what to say. The whole thing with Art Greenberg had been seven years ago, maybe eight by now. It had been her first regulatory review involving a new class of heart valve, and she had been paired with an older reviewer named Art Greenberg to mentor her on the ins and outs of that particular technology. But it turned out that Greenberg had taken some kind of small-potatoes kickback from the device's manufacturer, a company called Midwest Heartwise. When the bribe was discovered, Greenberg tried to blame everything on Grace in a desperate bid to save his own skin.

To prevent this kind of violation, there were all sorts of strict regulations, none of which Grace had ever even come close to breaking. In that case, her only mistake had been trusting the other reviewer, whom she hadn't even wanted to work with in the first place. The point was, the Greenberg business had been years ago, it had been exhaustively investigated, and Grace had been cleared of any wrongdoing.

"So, yeah, look, I'm not sure why this is all cropping up now," said

Lou, and shrugged helplessly. "But I got an e-mail about it just a few minutes ago."

"It was all dismissed," said Grace, hating the sound of her voice, the high pleading register. "Remember? It's not even supposed to be in my file. It was nothing, Lou, you know that."

"No, yeah, hey, *I* know that. Of course. This isn't coming from me. I guess there's some kind of shake-up going on upstairs, some kind of global review, and someone got something up their you-know-what on this Greenberg thing. This, uh..." He cleared his throat. "This old thing."

Grace reached out to River, who was standing beside her, quivering with alarm. She took her child's hand and squeezed it, wanting them to know this was okay but not really sure that it was.

"It's okay, honey," she said anyway. "I promise."

Lou nodded as if she had been talking to him. He flashed his pathetic watery grin at River too.

"Hiya," said Lou, then turned back to Grace. "Look. You're gonna be on ice for, I don't know—a week, maybe?"

"A week?" said Grace. She had never been suspended before. She had never had so much as a negative performance review.

Lou shrugged and looked to the other man, the guy with the combover, who had been standing close by with his head tilted down, his hands shoved in his pockets. He nodded noncommittally. "Maybe a little longer," he said. "You know how the wheels turn. A month, maybe?"

"A *month?*" said Grace. "Of suspension?"

"Suspended with pay," added Lou quickly. "Like a little vacation, really."

Grace didn't laugh. She squeezed River's hand harder, and River squeezed hers back, and the two of them stood in silent communion while Lou squirmed and the nervous little man with the combover just nodded up and down, solemnly ratifying everything Lou said.

194

His hairstyle was really asinine, the sort of preposterous gesture of vanity that makes women wonder if men are somehow unaware of what they look like. As she thought that about the stranger's hair, Grace remembered that she had had the exact same thought before about the same man, and then she knew who he was, and all the pieces slammed together.

"It's Barry, right?" said Grace abruptly, and the man stopped nodding.

"Yes, it is," he said. "Have we met?"

"Once," she said. "Very briefly. At the Christmas party."

"Oh, sure," he said with zero actual recognition in his eyes.

"Barry Perez," said Grace. "Isn't that right?"

"At your service," he said, and stuck out his hand, and Grace shook it. It was limp and moist. It was like his hand was a fish. Even as she was letting go of Barry Perez's weird hand, Grace tilted her head toward River, touched her forehead to River's, and said in a small and sharp voice, "We're gonna go."

River didn't even answer. They just nodded once and when Grace started walking, they started walking too, both of them departing abruptly from the conversation.

"Uh, Grace?" called Lou. Grace kept going. "Grace, we actually need you to hang out here for a moment." He was talking now to her back. "Grace. Hey. Grace?"

Grace didn't stop, and neither did River. In fact, at the same moment, they broke into a trot, speeding up in lockstep like a pair of wind-up toys. "Hey!" Lou cried. And so did Barry Perez — "Hey!" — and then Grace said, "Go, go, go!" and she and River started sprinting at the same instant.

She had met Barry Perez at the all-staff holiday party one of the years she had for some reason thought it would be fun or emotionally healthy to attend. Perez had been wearing plush reindeer horns and a piano-key tie, but it was definitely him; that hair was impossible to forget. She had a faint but indelible memory of him tilting his head forward slightly to peek down the front of her red crushed-velvet top.

He was one of the business liaisons. He was Martin Ajax's guy on the seventh floor.

Perez shouted, "What the hell?" as Grace and her child rapidly closed the gap between themselves and the exit. River was no speed demon in their chunky jeans and big black Doc Martens, and Grace hadn't been an athlete even in her long-ago youth, but the two of them were moving now, baby, zooming past the rows of desks and Grace's baffled and startled officemates. They rounded the corner of the last row of desks, burst out of the open-plan area and into the elevator hallway, and Grace slammed at speed into fresh-faced Randy in his dove-gray suit who had just come out of the copier closet, knocking the kid backward and sending his armful of documents up in a cyclone of regulatory paperwork.

"Whoa!" cried Randy as he landed on his ass, but Grace didn't miss a beat, reeling back and dancing around him, and River just hurdled over him at a thousand miles an hour while the papers drifted down toward the carpet.

The office was in an uproar. People were shouting and pointing, and Lou Fleming and Barry Perez had at last come unstuck and were rushing after them, running unevenly, ducking around desks and shouting, but it was too late, and they were too far behind. Grace used her elbow to bang the long flat bar that ran horizontally across the midsection of the big steel EXIT door, and it flew open. She let River rush through first and then spared one quick glance behind her and saw, from all the way across the chaos of the open-plan office, Kendall Johns in their shared office staring after them in open-mouthed astonishment.

Then the emergency-exit alarm clanged and she was flying down the stairs after River, who was actually leaping from landing to landing, whooping and kicking their legs. They were already two stories down the stairs when she heard the mighty slam of the door closing behind them like a gunshot, like a cannon, the echoing bang of everything changing forever.

22.

Missy stared, confused, at the beautiful stranger standing in her doorway.

"Oh. Are you — no. Are you my Uber?"

The woman didn't answer. She tilted her head slightly and slowly smiled. Her one good eye gazed carefully back at Missy, gold and green like a lizard's. Missy's insides shivered slightly. *Was* this an Uber driver? What was this?

"Can I help you with something?"

The woman still didn't speak, and Missy was getting a very bad feeling, but it was already too late.

"Is she here?" the woman asked in a voice as cool and hard as polished stone, and Missy started to swing the door closed but the woman kicked it back open and the cheap thin door smacked into the side of Missy's face, drawing blood.

She was saying, "Wait — wait —" but the stranger took her by the throat and walked her backward, kicking the door closed behind her.

Missy grabbed at the hand that was locked on her throat. She gurgled, trying to speak, but the woman was crushing her airway. Missy blinked rapidly, her eyes watering.

The woman banged Missy's head against the wall, and she saw bright flaring lines of red and white. She tugged crazily at the hand holding her throat, trying to pry it away, and the word *Please* bubbled up from her gut and tried to come out but couldn't.

Still holding her by the throat, the stranger smacked her with the other hand and then let go. Missy doubled over and spat up weakly, just a run of thin bile, and the woman brought her knee up into her face. Missy felt the sharp crack and blast of pain as her nose broke, and she fell to the floor and watched blood explode out and onto her carpet. She sobbed and screamed, lying on the ground.

"My goal here," said her assailant in the same cool dark voice, "is to get the information I need as efficiently as possible. Okay?"

"What?" Missy said thickly. She had the heel of her hand to her nose; blood cascaded down her wrist.

"I am past my deadline. It was important to establish that I can and will cause you pain in order to ensure that you answer my questions quickly."

Missy nodded. She whimpered. She was still clutching her face, warm rivulets of blood coating her forearm.

The woman lifted Missy and put her up against the wall with a knife to her throat. It was a short knife with a black handle and a thin silver blade. Missy felt the knife's edge pressing into the flesh of her neck; any harder and it would cut into her.

"Will you answer my questions quickly?" the woman said.

"Yes," Missy managed. She had never been so scared in her life. Not even close. She felt vomit in her stomach, churning, ready to come up. She turned her face to one side so she didn't have to look at the knife or at the lady's one green eye.

"Your friend came to visit you, right?"

Missy stared at the intruder. Every instinct in her body lit up: *Say no. Say no. Say no.*

"No," she said.

The woman angled the little knife so it dug in slightly, just enough to break the skin, and Missy whimpered. She squeezed her eyes shut tight but tears slipped out of them, trickled down her cheeks in hot bright lines.

"Your friend came to visit you, right?" she repeated, and Missy said "No" again, and the woman pulled the knife away from her throat, and Missy trembled and exhaled, and then the woman slashed her once across the face.

Missy shrieked and Desiree stepped back, satisfied. It had been a quick sharp slash from a spot beside the right eye, down the right cheek, and across the bridge of the nose. Missy kept screaming; the noise was loud and terrible. Desiree waited impatiently for the screaming to stop.

There were people in her line of work who enjoyed delivering pain. There were those, for example, who were working out old traumas, or who were just plain sociopaths.

Desiree counted herself in neither category. But there were situations where a quick jolt of terrible pain was the fastest route to getting what was required; this, she had judged based on past experience, was such a situation.

Her watch was at sixty-one hours and twenty-two minutes. But she had forced herself to stop running the numbers on this job. It had long since become a catastrophe, from a pure remuneration perspective.

But neither could she stop. The job had become something else entirely. Something new. "Okay, Missy," she said, and held up the knife. Missy jerked backward, her hands over her face. Her face was a mask of blood; her hands came away covered in it. Her blue work polo was sopping with blood.

She would talk now. Desiree knew it. Her refusing at first to talk had been an admirable resistance, a gut instinct not to turn over a friend. But weapons were simple machines. Simple machines saved time. "Your friend *did* come to visit you. Right?"

Missy was incapable of speech. She nodded.

"She was here?"

Missy nodded some more. Her eyes were stuck on the knife. Desiree put it down on the carpet. Missy brought up one arm and wiped some of the blood off her face with her forearm. She was crying heavily, her tears mixing into a mud of blood on her cheeks.

"Okay," said Desiree. "And where is she now?"

Missy didn't try to lie anymore. She had obeyed a trembling courageous impulse to protect her old friend, but she didn't even know if it *was* her old friend, and when the lady had cut her, it had hurt so much. Now she needed it to be over. She had exhausted all her reserves of courage and defiance and all she wanted was for this woman to leave without hurting her again.

So as the cold-eyed woman listened without reacting, crouched beside her on the carpet, Missy explained as much as she could. How this woman Allie had shown up at her house last night, how Allie had turned out somehow to be Ana also, and how she had helped Ana figure out that some sort of experiment had been done on her a long time ago, and her mind had been confused—*intermingled*—with someone else's mind.

The woman listened in total silence, although when Missy risked a glance at her, she saw that she was paying avid attention, some sort of deep curiosity flickering in her working eye.

Missy finished the story, ending it with a name and an address on Maryland's Eastern Shore.

Desiree didn't write it down. She didn't need to.

She did, though, ask a single question: "An experiment, you said. What kind of experiment?"

"I don't, I mean . . . honestly, I didn't really understand," Missy said, trembling. "Something to do with . . . with *time*."

"Time," said Desiree, and something turned over inside her. Something began to shift, dig its way up from her insides, like a tree birthing itself from cold soil.

"Please," Missy was saying as Desiree straightened up and picked the knife up off the carpet. "Please don't cut me anymore."

"I won't."

Missy needn't have worried. Desiree wasn't psychotic. She was a professional. She had the information she needed, and there was no purpose in causing further pain to Missy. But there was no version of leaving her here alive that did not risk slowing down Desiree's forward progress. Not now; not when she had an address in hand.

She tucked the knife away and with her other hand she drew the 9-millimeter from her purse. She shot poor Missy once, right through the heart.

23.

Put on your seat belt, River," said Grace as she clicked her own into place and jammed the starter button of the Altima.

"What is happening?" said River. "What is going on?"

"*Seat belt,*" Grace repeated, loud, and River clicked it as Grace threw the car in gear and backed out of the space.

The jig was nearly up right there in the FDA parking lot because her rear tires caught on a patch of ice and the back end of the Altima fishtailed and almost slammed into the Jeep parked in the next space over.

"*Whoa,*" shouted River, and Grace said, "It's fine, it's okay, we're okay," but it obviously was not okay. They were *fleeing* from her office. They were essentially *escaping*. River was breathing deeply in and out the way they had been advised to by a school therapist in fourth grade. Grace just focused on driving, clutching the steering wheel with both hands at ten and two and lurching to the exit lane; the gate arm swung open and Grace caught a glimpse of Marco staring and waving with confused friendliness as she zoomed past.

"See?" murmured Grace through her clenched teeth, punching the accelerator and turning on her blinker as she merged onto Rockville Pike. "He totally likes me."

Grace's hands were trembling slightly on the wheel, and she looked down and saw that it wasn't just her hands; her whole body was shivering. She gunned it to the limited extent that the Altima would allow itself to be gunned. Glass office towers and batches of identical townhomes raced by outside. She didn't really think that Lou Fleming or Barry Perez would, like, come after them, and she was fairly certain the FDA's Center for Devices and Radiological Health didn't have some kind of roving hit squad to handle escapees.

The idea that they were being followed was insane and impossible, but the whole thing was insane and impossible, so Grace drove quickly and carefully for fifteen miles, looking in the rearview mirror and switching lanes a lot like she had seen people do in movies, until she was satisfied that no one was on their tail.

"Are you all right, River?"

"I guess I am. Are *you* all right?"

"I guess. Yeah."

Grace winced as a constricting band of pain tightened around her lower back. She was really going to have to see a doctor when all of this was over. And then she almost laughed. When it was *over*? What did that mean, when it was *over*? She had just sprinted out of her office in the middle of the afternoon, had *literally* run away from her boss and some higher-level goon from the seventh floor. And before that she had watched them packing up her computer. What kind of *over* was she talking about? What health insurance would she have so she could go see an orthopedist? What would be left of Grace when she was done with the mystery of the girl with the portacath?

In forty-eight hours she had blown up her entire life — she just hoped it was worth it.

"You sure you're okay, honey?" she asked again.

"Yes."

River had removed their glasses and was cleaning them furiously on the hem of their shirt.

A tailgating pickup truck maneuvered around them and the Altima shuddered in its slipstream.

Grace glanced at River. "You have your seat belt on?"

"Mom, you can see that I do."

"Okay, good."

"Mom?"

"Yeah?"

Grace's mind was jittering and rushing. They were far enough away now. She didn't want to be driving anymore; she slowed and flicked on her turn signal.

"Mom? Are you going to tell me what's happening?"

"I am," said Grace. "Yes."

She took the next exit. She guided the Altima onto a quiet side street, put the car in park, and turned to River to tell them what she knew, or thought she knew.

"It's Ajax," Grace told her. "Ana's stepfather. He did it."

"He did — what?"

"He was the one who called the FDA and got me suspended. It was him."

"What? Why?"

Grace wasn't sure. She was still trying to figure that part out. "I went in there to ask him about Ana, but apparently Ana is dead. She died in a hit-and-run ten years ago."

"What?"

Grace held up one finger: *Wait.* "And then he—he pretended to be angry and upset that I was asking about his dead child."

River scrunched up their face. "How do you know he was pretending?"

"Because as soon as I left, he must have talked to Barry Perez. That guy who came in with my boss? Ajax called in some kind of favor to get me in trouble. To stop me from asking questions."

"Whoa," said River.

"I know," Grace said. "He's worried that I'm looking for her. He's worried that I know she's alive. Or, I guess..." Grace paused. She shuddered a little at the surreal magnitude of what she was saying. "Alive *again.*"

"Mom," said River softly, and again Grace said, "I know."

"Are you saying..."

Grace looked at River. "I don't know. I really don't."

Two hours ago, she had told River that it wasn't real. Yeah, sure, maybe someone believed that you could get time out of a person's body, and maybe someone had ported that girl to try to do it. But you couldn't *really* take time out of someone, she'd said. It wasn't *real.*

But now Grace wasn't so sure.

Across the street was an abandoned gas station, all of its pumps covered with OUT OF SERVICE yellow hoods.

Ana had died in 2013, except now she had returned to life. But how?

Time, of course, was the answer. Someone had given her time.

Or taken it.

Grace shut her eyes and shook her head. As soon as Martin Ajax realized Grace was asking about Ana, he had with one phone call shut down her amateur investigation and her whole professional life.

Grace felt seasick with the suddenness and strangeness of it all, but she did her best to explain it to River, and River was not fazed; River was right here with her, nodding fervently, their eyes alive with concern and fascination. That made it better. Not good, but better.

"So, wait," River said, collecting their thoughts, still nodding. "So, okay. You think he's the one who did the—what are we calling it? The experiment? The time procedure?"

"I don't know." Grace considered it. "No? Yes? Maybe I do think that. Definitely I think the original idea came from the doctor, this C. P. Stargell. But at the very least, Ajax knew about it. Maybe he was the one who arranged it. Either way, he's afraid that if someone finds out the truth, you know—"

"Then he's fucked." Grace didn't bother scolding River for language.

"Yeah. Exactly. Then he's fucked. God, I have to find her," Grace concluded. "I have to find her fast. He's looking for her too."

She was thinking of Dr. Steve describing the patient as confused but also scared, sure that someone was coming after her.

"Looking for her . . ."—River lowered their voice, though it was just the two of them in the car—"why?" Across the street, a battered Chevy pickup pulled into the station, slowed down at the defunct pumps, and pulled out again.

"God knows," said Grace. But a dozen possible answers swam darkly through her mind, none of them good. Grace's stomach hurt. She didn't know what to do. "River?"

"One sec." River was digging in their pocket, shifting around in their seat, and now they pulled out a piece of paper, like a magician producing a rabbit from a hat.

"River? What? Why are you smiling?"

"Because," they said, *"I know where she's going."*

"What?"

*   *   *

River had of course been bursting to tell Grace all about Missy McDermid from the second they'd hung up the phone. But then those assholes had come with their handcarts and started packing up the office, and then they'd had to bust out through the fire exit, and the whole thing had turned into the fucking *Great Escape.*

But now River walked their mom through all of it: How while Grace was at Rachel's Place, they'd gotten antsy and started making some phone calls, running their own little side-hustle mini-investigation to track down Ana. They'd ended up connecting with this chick Missy, one of Ana's old bandmates, and confirmed not only that Ana had been with her but that Ana had just headed off in search of the mysterious C. P. Stargell.

And, River concluded with a flourish, they even had the address. They dramatically unfolded the scrap of paper and handed it over to Grace.

"I'm sorry," River said. "With all the excitement and everything—"

"No," said Grace, looking at the address. "Do not apologize."

Grace, her hands very slightly shaking, put the address in her phone. C. P. Stargell lived in a very small town on Tilghman Island, which sounded vaguely familiar. It was somewhere on the Eastern Shore, the southern end of the peninsula, maybe. Deep in tidal Maryland.

"You're incredible," Grace said to River.

"Am I?" River smiled crookedly. "Yeah, no, I guess I am."

"You are." She seized her child and squeezed them closely. "I'm so glad you got suspended."

"Har-har," said River. "All right, let's go. Are we going?" River patted their knees excitedly.

"No," said Grace. "*We* aren't."

"What?"

Grace was shaking her head. She would not take River any further.

208

Whatever else was happening, the last two days had tipped Grace over into a part of her life she never knew was waiting for her, and there was real fear in it, and danger, and the whisper of death. She was not bringing River.

"Sorry, doll. It's not up for debate. But wait—hang on one sec."

Grace took her notepad from her purse and jotted some notes on the top page, printing as neatly as she could. Something else had occurred to her. It was a terrifying prospect, and she hoped she was wrong about it, but she needed to know. She needed to know as soon as possible.

Grace said, "There's something else."

"Something else?" said River petulantly.

Carefully Grace tore the paper free from her notepad and held it out to River. "There's something I need you to do—and it's important."

24.

Ana twisted a lock of hair with her right hand and kept her other hand on the wheel. Ana wanted to go fast, to get there now, and Allie struggled with the steering, keeping the giant Econoline van between the highway lines. It rattled and rattled the faster it went. Allie blew out a long steadying breath; Ana shook and muttered and tugged at her hair. Both alive in here, two minds chattering, everybody at home. Ana muttering, "Come on, come on, come the fuck on," Allie focusing on the road, steady as she goes.

The rattling old coffin of a panel van rumbled eastward toward the Bay. The burner phone Ana had borrowed from Missy was just some basic clamshell with a prepaid plan and no maps app to guide her from College Park to the address they'd found for C. P. Stargell. So Missy had done it old-school, printed out the directions to the desolate nowhere place south of Salisbury and off the southwestern tip of the Delmarva Peninsula.

Allie-Ana.

Ana-Allie.

Aliana, Anna Lee; anonymous; alien; alive.

The mind all full of chattering backtalk, a constant clatter, a battling landscape, a sky full of stars. She was a farmer's daughter from Ohio with three older brothers on an old tire swing wearing a thin dress with daisies on it, except Ana had no swing and no siblings; she'd had a cat and never had a cat; Allie had loved skating and Ana had tried it once and nearly broke her fucking leg; and Allie was in the basement of the campus library sweating out her senior thesis on effective mathematics instruction for preteens, and Ana was jamming it out with Missy onstage at some talent show in an American Legion hall in Silver Spring. All of Ana's fierce defiant Ana-ness clustering and clanging against all of Allie's confused, uncertain Allie-ness, hot angry spots of unreconcilable self-understanding, shifting and bursting like spots on the sun.

Rachel was real. Her child was waiting for her to find her way home. But among all of these memories was one that was pure and crystalline and strong as a signal on the FM band, and every once in a while it would bubble to the surface and Allie would lay hold of it and smile and murmur, "Rachel." A sense memory more than a visual; a feeling, the tiny weight of a wriggling body nestled in the crook of an arm.

But then Ana shouted, *"No,"* and *"Stop* it," because Rachel was not a baby at all, Rachel was her mother, who Missy had gravely informed her had died. The fucking cancer that had been sapping away at her for three years finally got what it wanted in the summer of 2014, a year after Ana herself had been struck by a car and killed.

"No," she said again, "fuck that," and then she screamed it, pulling the central *uh* sound in *fuck* into a long guttural groan. She *wasn't* dead. She was driving over the Chesapeake Bay Bridge and screaming, and people in cars in the other lane looked over uneasily. Allie clutched the steering wheel, working at staying steady, working so hard that her forearms trembled.

If what Missy had told Ana was true and she'd been hit by a car in 2013, then what the fuck was she doing here? What was the time between 2013 and today? *What was now?*

Ana couldn't scream anymore. It burned at her throat. Allie let go of the steering wheel and then banged it with the hard flat heel of her hand. *"Fuck."*

Tilghman Island was a fishing village trapped in time, Tidewater cottages and a boxy white church and a series of tiny marinas separated from the mainland of the Delmarva Peninsula by a two-lane bridge with high rusted fencing on either side.

Allie adjusted her speed as she navigated the narrow lanes and squinted into the darkness as she made the last set of turns, closing the distance to Stargell.

It was twilight now. The sun had faded as she drove, and the little town didn't seem to have a single streetlight to stand against the deep-red sky.

Ana passed a series of desolate, isolated landmarks: a roadside farmer's stand, a bait shop with a gas station, and finally a blink-and-you'll-miss-it right turn onto Hermit Crab Lane. The headlights of the van were weak and watery, catching patches of blue mailbox and scraggles of bare trees as she came around curves. After a couple windy miles, Hermit Crab Lane narrowed and then petered out into a gravel driveway. Whoever this C. P. Stargell was, he lived in near-total isolation. An old farmhouse set back from the road, backing right up onto the Bay.

Allie rumbled the van to a stop halfway up the gravel drive, and when she killed the engine, she could still feel it trembling in her chest. This was the address. She looked up at the house. A tin weather vane spun listlessly on the peaked roof, catching glints of the twilight.

She flicked open the glove box and got out Missy's Smith & Wesson. Missy had told her, half apologetically and half warningly, how small the gun was, but it felt big to Ana, heavy and dark in her hand. Allie turned it over once or twice. She had been hunting a few times when she was a girl — long, dull duck-hunting trips with her dad, shivering for hours in the uncomfortable boots. She remembered it vividly. Not Ana. Ana had never held a fucking gun in her life.

Someone rapped against the driver's-side window, and she jumped.

"Put it down," a voice said. It was a woman's voice, low and steady and in control, coming muffled through the glass of the window. "Put down the gun. Go on, now."

Ana looked at the woman addressing her. A Black woman, easily in her late sixties or early seventies, with reading glasses dangling from a thin gold chain. She had tapped at the window with the muzzle of a rifle. Now she tapped the window three more times.

"Down," she said again. "Down on the seat."

Very carefully, Allie lowered the Smith & Wesson to the shotgun seat and released it. She looked back at the woman, who was staring at her down the length of the rifle.

"Now . . . now . . ." The woman stopped. Her expression had changed. Confusion swam in her eyes.

But she managed to keep giving instructions. "Now, please — please step out of the van onto the lawn. Come on."

The woman moved back from the window and opened the van door, and Ana undid her seat belt and stepped out into the night. It was gloomy and dark, a tidal tang competing with the smell of swampland.

The woman stared at Ana, holding her rifle with two hands. She was in a thin housedress, pulled tightly closed against her body, but also heavy black boots. Allie was still in the worn-out Nikes she had stolen from some poor nurse in Hanover two days and a thousand years ago. The ground was icy, long Maryland grass coated in frost, and it bit into her ankles above the sneakers.

She could hear the distant slap of low-tide waves cracking against wooden pier legs. A dog barked once, and then again.

The woman, still holding her rifle, lifted her glasses and put them on. "My God," she whispered. "Ana?"

"Who are you?" Allie said.

The woman lowered the rifle entirely, brought a hand up to her chest as if in pain. "Is it really you?"

"Are you Stargell?" Ana said, but she knew that it was her. The eyes— the face. A doctor standing beside her, at her bedside, an unsmiling Black woman, while everybody told her to relax, it was going to be fine . . .

"Are you fucking C. P. Stargell?"

"You're alive," said Stargell, and sank down onto her knees, letting go of the rifle, which fell onto the muddy lawn. She was clutching her chest and staring up at Ana, like she didn't understand what she was seeing— and, Allie thought, like maybe there was some kind of grinding pain pushing through her chest.

Ana grabbed the rifle from where it had fallen in the long grass. The handle was wet with the moisture of the lawn but she held it steadily on the other woman, her mind leaping and crackling and her heart full of fury and fear.

And Ana who was Allie, and Allie who was Ana, felt the surging grind of pain in her own chest, the tearing sensation like her life was being wrung out of her, and she screamed.

"It's you?" she demanded, holding the rifle just inches from the other woman's face. "You're Stargell?"

"I am," said the woman. "God forgive me, I'm Clare Stargell. Oh, Ana—oh, honey—"

Ana roared. She stepped forward and jammed the muzzle of the gun into her forehead. "What did you do to me?" she said. "What the hell did you *do?*"

25.

Desiree drove eastward on State Highway 50 from College Park toward the Eastern Shore.

She had cleaned Missy McDermid's apartment of evidence and taken what few valuables the woman had to make it look like a burglary: a laptop and an iPad; a handful of cheap jewelry. One small person's store of prizes, and nothing that added up to anything.

Desiree drove toward the address that Missy had provided.

She did not listen to music or to the radio. She drove in silence, sitting upright, as she had when the target was in the back seat, sixty-three hours ago. The sunset was behind her, casting long shadows on the road as she drove.

When her phone rang, she answered it.

"Oh, good. Hi." Desiree put the client on speaker and put the phone on the seat beside her. His voice came out tinny and distant, as from the bottom of a great well. "I'm wondering if we've got any sort of update."

"I'm on the way to get her now," Desiree said. "She's in a small town on the Eastern Shore of Maryland called Tilghman Island."

"What?" The client sounded skeptical. "What the hell is she doing all the way out there?"

When Desiree said the name Stargell, the client groaned. "Oh, Lord. You're kidding me," he said, and then again, "You're *kidding* me. All the dead shall rise. All the dead shall rise again."

Desiree didn't know what this meant. She didn't much care.

"Okay, look," the client said then. "I'm gonna go out there with you. I want to be there."

She looked around the interior of the Buick. She didn't like company.

"Are you there? Hello? I need you to pick me up."

"The plan was for me to contact you when I had her in my possession to arrange for delivery."

"Yeah, well—I'm the boss, right?" Desiree frowned with irritation at the phone. She did not like the word *boss*. She was a freelance contractor. She set her own rates and made her own hours.

The client's voice rose and fell in volume as he bustled about whatever room he was in. "Yeah, no, this is good. I'll come with. I'd like to make sure this thing gets done. That no one makes a run for it, anything like that."

Desiree twitched at the implicit criticism. She did some rapid internal math. Right now she was approaching Bowie, Maryland, well on her way to her destination. Circling back to get the client in Northeast Washington in evening traffic would cost her at least two hours, round trip.

"I would require additional compensation," she said.

There was a brief, astonished pause before the client said, "What?"

"My job is to deliver you the woman. I am not a chauffeur."

The client let out an exasperated hiss but relented. "Fine," he said.

There was a brief pause and then he said, "Okay. Here. There's a Denny's off 450, just before you get to Annapolis. Pick me up there."

Desiree furrowed her brow. "Is this a joke?"

She was half an hour from Annapolis. The client was back the other way. How did he think he would get to this diner before she did?

"Really," said the client, with a note of amusement in his voice that Desiree did not like. "Just tell me what car I'm looking for."

When she had relayed the information, Desiree thumbed off the phone and continued to drive in silence. Was the client having her on? Jerking her around for his own amusement? She only hoped he wasn't wasting her time for some private joke of his own. She had long since begun resenting this fussy, wheedling client with his airy sense of entitlement. This was always a part of it, though. An occupational hazard. When you work for others, you are never fully free. You can call yourself a contractor or a freelancer, but the person writing the checks is the person with the power.

Desiree's life since she'd discarded her birth name and took the first of the many identities that preceded "Desiree" had been relatively uncomplicated.

This was how she preferred it. Given the things she had experienced in the years before becoming the person she was now, before she successfully sloughed off the scarred skin of her childhood, she had wanted a simple and regular life. A life measured in assignments completed, miles traveled, and checks cashed.

Her life was defined by the work, and the work was simple geometry. A job was a triangle: there was a client, there was a target, and there was the sharp point that was Desiree.

But now, as the Buick plowed eastward and burrowed through the countryside, her feelings were complicated. She was feeling again what she had felt in Missy McDermid's apartment just before she had concluded that encounter by killing the girl. There had been some sort of procedure conducted on the woman that she was seeking, and it had something to do with time. That's what Missy had explained, or tried to explain, and that information had lit some fuse in Desiree, some queer internal light, glowing blue. It was showing her something, but Desiree with her one working eye was having trouble seeing clearly.

It seemed somehow to be *offering* her something more than this client, or any client, could offer. What it was, she was not yet sure.

She pressed the accelerator. She pushed the Buick past 85 to 90, and then past 95 to 100.

Martin Ajax leaned all the way back in his office chair, covered his eyes with his hands, and groaned.

"You all right in there, Marty?"

That was Barb, who sat in the outer office of the admin suite, just beyond his open door. Such a sweetie. Little bit of a busybody. She oversaw everything at Rachel's Place having to do with community engagement, the after-school stuff, everything forward-facing. Everything in the sensor-locked east wing, everything on the opiate-replacement side, Marty had a whole different staff for. It was a whole different ball game.

"I'm fine, Barb," he called back. "All good."

He let the front legs of his chair down and took a breath. This was not the first time he'd wondered what the hell kind of person he'd hired to find Ana. He'd been warned by the friend of a sort of friend who had recommended her that she was the type of person who did not quit until the job was done, which at the time sounded like exactly what Marty needed.

But he'd been too hasty, that was the thing. He hadn't properly vetted this character. Bad staff work. The truth was that from the second the signaling device inside that Goldenstar port had come back to life, from the second he'd known poor Ana was walking around out there somewhere, he'd been rattled. He was thrown off his game. Now he really just wanted to get her back, put this thing to bed.

"Ah, fuck it," said Marty, and stood up.

"Fuck what, Marty?"

"Nothing, Barb."

He slung his gym bag over his shoulder, went out the rear door of his office, and navigated through the warren of back hallways that let him escape unseen into the employee parking lot.

He got to his car, a handsome Audi, and crouched behind it, whistling between his teeth. He was excited now. This would be somewhat wasteful, but Ajax loved using the product. He was still in that puppy-dog phase where he relished any chance to use the miracle he had made.

He unzipped his gym bag and pulled out a small frosted-plastic case that contained a row of nine hypodermic syringes, each of them loaded with a liquid. The liquid was clear except for the almost microscopic flecks that caused the fluid to glitter when held up to the light. Marty selected one of the syringes and, with the ease of long experience, pushed the needle at its tip into the base of his neck and depressed the plunger.

No one was watching. It was twilight on a cold night in a remote part of Northeast Washington, and Marty, hidden behind his car, was doubly hidden by the curve of the building.

But if somebody had been watching—if they'd had some vantage point from the street or from the inside of Rachel's Place—they would have been astonished to see the man rise from his crouch and get in his car before, a moment later, both man and car disappeared.

26.

Grace had never heard of Tilghman Island, but there were plenty of parts of Maryland she'd never heard of, miles and miles of hinterland far removed from the gleaming suburbs that were as much a part of Washington as the rest of the state. She drove steadily east on Route 50 as the boxy glass office buildings of the DC outskirts gave way to the rural red-barn counties. As Bowie flashed by, and then Annapolis, Grace cast occasional anxious glances at her phone, where her Google Maps display was splotched with the worrying red of traffic along the route line. The arrival time kept ticking upward, more and more minutes piling onto the total.

Grace shifted in her seat.

She just needed the pain in her lower back not to get any worse so she wouldn't have to get out and stretch, and she needed the gas gauge needle to stay where it was so she wouldn't have to get off the highway to fill the tank, and she needed the arrival time to stop getting later and later and later. She needed time to *stop* was what she needed, stop and hold steady so she could find Ana before Martin Ajax did. Find her and protect her. Find her and give her back what had been taken from her.

Grace laughed suddenly, sounding slightly crazy to herself in the confined space of the car.

Because hadn't she, just this morning, insisted to River that the whole thing was a bunch of nonsense? Time obviously wasn't really a thing that could be extracted from a person's body, nor put into someone else's, no matter the theories of Dr. C. P. Stargell.

She had said that, yes, and it had to be true, yes, *and also* Ana Jessica Court had died in 2013 and then turned up yesterday in a hospital outside Baltimore.

"Stop." Grace shook her head tightly, admonishing herself.

All she knew for certain was that someone was in danger. What mattered most right now was just finding the person who needed help, and helping them. Everything else could be for later.

Grace took her eyes from the road long enough to thumb to her missed calls, but there was nothing yet from River. She'd put the kid in an Uber, given them specific instructions, and River had gone off to pursue the other aspect of this mystery. Yes, Ajax had lied about what had happened to Ana. But lies did not travel alone.

That was one Kathy loved, one of her all-time favorites: *Lies come in batches, honey. They travel in packs.*

Grace's suspicion was that Ajax was lying about more than what had happened to his stepdaughter, and she thought she knew why. So she'd directed River to reach out to Kendall Johns, to try him at work and at home and to keep trying until he answered and if he didn't answer to show up at his house and wait for him in person. Eventually, hopefully, Kendall would look up what she needed him to look up in the CDRH database and report back. Grace couldn't do it herself without her work computer, which they'd taken away, and even if she could remotely access the database, her credentials had been suspended.

Kendall would be reluctant; River would be persistent. Grace felt sure about both of these things.

The end result, Grace hoped, would be an intervention from the FDA's Office of Criminal Investigations. A warrant served on Rachel's Place in Northeast DC and another on Martin Ajax's place of residence. She started to imagine what they would discover, the full scope of what he was up to.

"Stop," she told herself again. *"Stop."*

She didn't know if it was real. She couldn't know right now.

Just find her. Find that girl.

Grace shifted in her seat and gritted her teeth against the pain in her back. It was getting worse, tightening and shifting, creeping its way up the ladder of her spine.

She addressed her own body like it was a stranger's body conspiring to trouble her. "Come on," she said. "Can I just get there?"

As if to mock her, the map on her phone took that moment to readjust the arrival time from 8:45 to 8:49. Time stacking upon time, new minutes added to the day. As she approached the Chesapeake Bay Bridge, Grace saw cars beginning to slow, brake lights glowing. And then, halfway across the mighty suspension bridge, with night falling and the moon reflecting off the waters of the Chesapeake Bay, traffic came to a total standstill.

"Oh, *come on,*" said Grace.

Also, she had to pee. Just a little bit, but she knew by long experience it was going to get worse, and fast. She flicked on her wipers; a very light snow was starting to come down, and through it she could see the haze of brake lights all around her. "Shit, shit, shit."

There was construction going on or there had been some kind of accident and a lane was shut down or both.

She craned up in her seat, trying to see around the traffic, but the movement of her body caused her back to cry out in protest, so she settled back, sighing. Grace's phone rang, and she nearly jumped out of her skin.

"Do we need eggs?"

"What?"

The question was so mundane and her mother's voice so gruff and matter-of-fact, it was like the call was coming from another universe.

"Mom? What are you talking about?"

"I'm at the Costco. The eggs are pretty cheap, but not if you're not going to use 'em."

Grace took the phone away from her face and stared at it like it was an alien artifact. "Mom, what the hell are you talking about?"

"I told you, I'm at the Costco."

"Mom!"

"What?" Kathy's voice sparkled with mischievousness.

"Did you *drive* there? You're not supposed to be driving. We discussed this."

"*You* discussed it. Look, the eggs are two dozen for six bucks. What do you want me to do here?"

"Look, Mom, I can't think about this right now. Okay? I'm—I'm really in the middle of something. I'm driving out to the Eastern Shore. There's a young woman who might have been subjected to some sort of unlicensed medical procedure a decade ago, and the person who did it to her is trying to make sure no one finds out. I have to get to this woman before he does."

"Huh," Kathy grunted. Red brake lights blinked on and off in the gray. Grace's wipers scratched across the frosted windshield.

"So you want the eggs or not?"

By the time Grace got off the phone with Kathy, shaking her head at the durability of the universe's base elements, she was deeply snarled in traffic on the bridge, and the need to empty her bladder had become urgent. People honked incessantly, as they always did, but Grace didn't bother. *Honking does no good,* she reminded herself, *it only makes you feel better, and it doesn't even do that.* So she inched forward as close as she could get to the bumper of the hideous Range Rover that had been in front of her for the past ten miles.

At this point it felt like her entire life had been spent here, at the miserable choke point that was the only reliable way down into the Eastern Shore. She was conscious of time dripping past, every instant adding to her sense that it was too late, it was already too late, and here she was locked in a sea of cars slowly moving across the endless bridge, the water of the bay a heavy dark churn below.

At last the traffic eased and she was on the other side of the water, and naturally the WELCOME TO THE BAY rest area was closed for repairs, hung with an apologetic black-and-yellow State of Maryland DOT sign. Grace muttered a curse, shifting once again in her seat, and managed to make it to the next turnoff...where the Flying J truck stop had only one restroom, and it, too, was out of order.

Grace hustled back to her car and resigned herself to pushing through until she made it to her destination: 7421 Hermit Crab Lane. As she started the Altima again, her GPS told her that she'd be there within forty-five minutes—at which point, besides finding C. P. Stargell and recruiting her in her effort to save Ana's life, she would have the world's longest pee.

For God's sake, Grace thought. *Is this what it means to be a real action hero?* En route to save the day, torn between the call of duty and the call of nature. The bitter mirthless chuckle Grace allowed herself caused a tiny bit of pee to slip out, so she stopped.

The road narrowed and then narrowed more, and then, squinting into the darkness, Grace saw the sign for the bridge that crossed into the tiny fishing village on the other side.

27.

I'm sorry," said Dr. C. P. Stargell, who had turned out to be this woman, this elderly Black lady in a plain blue housedress with tiny gold earrings and reading glasses on a chain. She sat in a kitchen chair now, inside the house, looking at Ana with wonder and with fear. "I am so sorry, Ana."

"Stop saying that," Ana hissed. She snarled.

Ana. Allie.

They were in the kitchen now. Her hands were unsteady. She was still holding Stargell's rifle.

"I am so terribly sorry."

"I said, stop *saying* that. *Please.*"

Ana stepped sharply toward Dr. Stargell with the rifle raised and she felt her body move as if to hit her with the gun, and Dr. Stargell flinched and jerked backward on the flimsy kitchen chair. Ana slid into the chair next to her and lay down the rifle on the table so it pointed at Stargell.

"I don't want you to be sorry. I want you to tell me what you did."

Dr. Stargell nodded slowly. "Okay," she said.

"Okay?"

"I will try."

"And I want you to fucking *fix* it."

To this, Stargell didn't respond; she looked up at the exposed beams of the kitchen and blinked her old, sad eyes. Ana scowled.

She had marched Stargell back into her house and pushed her roughly into one of the four plain vinyl kitchen chairs arranged around her rickety kitchen table. She wanted to be furious. She needed a target commensurate with her anger, the chaos in her mind, and the clashing grinding pain in her chest. But C. P. Stargell was a poor fit for her fury. Her house was old and drafty. It smelled like kitchen spices and dryer sheets.

"May I please get you some water?" Stargell said softly, turning her eyes back to Ana. "Something cold to drink?"

"No." Ana licked her lips. She cleared her throat. "Okay. Yes. Water."

She tracked Stargell with her eyes while the old lady moved across the kitchen floor to the tap. She was still wearing the heavy black boots. She walked with a slight bend in her back. The kitchen counters were stained Formica; at the center of the chipped table there was a salt and pepper shaker, a cow and a bull. Allie had imagined C. P. Stargell as this diabolical scientist who had reached into her body and fucked with her insides; instead, she was a dignified old lady in a flowered dress and glasses on a thin chain. She looked like someone's grandma.

"Here you are," she said and set down the water. Ana drank some, keeping her other hand on the gun. Her head was raging, Allie jockeying with Ana and Ana with Allie.

(But Allie was already beginning to slip away, wasn't she? At the sight of Stargell on the lawn, at the click of recognition, the beginning of understanding, Allie's grip on the cliffside had begun to loosen, hadn't it? Ana blinking, mad-minded, taking fuller hold.)

"Now I will try to explain," said Stargell. "I will do my best. You may call me Clare if you like, Ana. My name is Clare."

"Fine," said Ana. "Clare." She was working hard to stay angry. She needed to be angry. She needed answers. "Talk."

"Can you just—I wonder if we can put the gun away. I promise I am not going to run. I am not going to try to hurt you."

"You hurt me enough, didn't you?"

Now her anger flared, and Ana picked up the rifle and pointed it directly at Stargell, who flinched and put her hands up over her face, and Ana thought, cruelly, *Good.*

Let her understand. She wasn't going anywhere until Stargell quieted the storm inside her head. She laid the gun back down on the table.

"So what happened? I died, and you brought me back? My parents brought me to a doctor, and—"

"No." Stargell held up her hand.

At the word *parents*, Dr. Stargell had begun to shake her head, and when Ana got to *doctor*, she interrupted.

"I am not a medical doctor. I'm a scientist." Then, with a wry lopsided smile, she corrected herself: "I *was* a scientist. Now I'm nothing. I live alone in this house, as far from the world as I can get. Not a scientist anymore."

She tilted her head and gestured with one hand, taking in the small house, the Formica countertops, the knife block. The cute salt and pepper shakers; the clock above the kitchen door.

"But I was a scientist with a very specific area of expertise. One idea, really, on which I had built my professional life." Stargell smiled, very slightly, a wistful ghost of a smile, and raised one finger. "One idea. But for most of my life, that's all that it was. An idea. Very complicated, but also very simple."

Ana—Allie—knew all about it. She had sat in Missy's apartment and fought her way through "Incarnating the Arrow." She hadn't under-stood all of it, but she had understood enough.

"Go on," she commanded.

Haltingly and slowly at first, then fluidly, not looking at Ana, not look-ing at the gun that lay on the table, aimed at her chest, Dr. Stargell told her story.

She had not entered a field of science but created one. She had been a student of metaphysics and a student of applied chemistry, and her idea—entirely hypothetical, as big and paradigm-shifting as it was untested—was to create a process that could isolate and eventually extract what she called the durational element. Time was not abstract. It lay inside us.

As she spoke about her ideas and her perseverance and her trust in herself, Stargell sounded less scared. She began to sound proud. She sat up straighter.

Despite having an exemplary academic record and multiple degrees, despite being a gifted lecturer, she'd never quite found her professional footing. She bounced from position to position, from assistant professor to adjunct lecturer; in part, she knew, because she was a woman, and in part because she was a woman of color, but primarily because her ideas inhabited a unique intellectual space, somewhere between philosophy and chemistry and physics, outside the mainstream of them all. Wher-ever she presented her ideas, Stargell met only gatekeepers, uninterested and full of scorn.

But Clare Stargell was passionate; she was obsessive; she was right and she knew that one day she would be proven right. So she had pressed on, refining her notions, corresponding with interested parties, publishing in fringe journals, cadging whatever lab hours and resources she could from sympathetic or curious partners.

Ana listened, twitching, agitated. When she finished her water she stood and began to pace in a tiger's tight circles around the tiny kitchen.

"For the most part, of course, I was entirely dismissed. I was a crackpot. I was in over my head." Stargell's nostrils flared slightly at the memory of dismissal and disdain. "But this is a familiar story. Ideas beyond imagining that eventually are proved to be not only imaginable but incontrovertible. This is the story of science. This is the story of truth."

"So — what?" Ana demanded. "No one wanted to work with you, everybody thought you were crazy, so you go looking for a fucking guinea pig? Some poor person who wouldn't know what you were up to? And you found me?"

"Oh, no," said Stargell, snapping out of her reverie and staring directly at Ana. "No, no. You were *brought* to me."

"By—" Ana stopped pacing. She was directly behind Stargell, close enough to smell the scent of whatever the woman put in her hair, something sweet and floral. Ana knew. On some level, maybe, she had always known. But still she asked: "By who?"

"Oh, Ana," said Stargell. She looked at her with a tender smile. "Oh my goodness."

Don't worry, honey. A voice in a hospital room. A man's voice, familiar and calming. *You're in good hands. This is Dr. Stargell.*

"Marty."

Stargell nodded. "Martin Ajax. Yes."

Ana sat down roughly, pushed one hand into her hair. She put her other hand back on the butt of the rifle.

Marty wasn't her father, but he was. He was the father that she had known, and not a distant, uninterested father either, but one who was fun and funny and stern — a reader of bedtime stories, a fixer of snacks.

Until her mom got sick, and he changed.

Ana had watched him change, had felt it. His eyes had hollowed out, and his voice had become ragged. Like he was sick, too, worry and grief like a creepy infection.

Ana remembered what he was like then. He would have done anything to save his beloved wife. He would have tried anything.

(Allie was going quickly now. It had started in the mud of the lawn and accelerated as this conversation continued. As Dr. Stargell brought her story together with Ana's story, as the truth slipped into the room, bubbles of Allie were popping. Bits of Allie were sloughing away. Every time Ana blinked, a slice of Allie went dark.)

"No one would engage with my ideas," said Stargell. "They literally laughed at me. But not Martin Ajax." Even now, even in this context, Stargell could not keep the pleasure from her voice, pleasure at the memory of the day. The moment when everything changed. "He believed in my work. He saw the potential. And he had the resources to make it real."

Ana listened to this next part with a seasickness in her stomach, thinking about her childhood. About Marty.

"His wife—your mother—" Stargell looked quickly at Ana, then away. "Your mother was terminally ill. Martin, desperately seeking some answer, had read my work and wondered if it was possible to extend the time that she had left. And the answer was yes. It was *theoretically* possible. Once I told him that, he made it clear he would expend whatever resources were necessary to make that happen. We could do it. We could make it real."

Ana glared at Stargell. She gripped the rifle. Was this supposed to make her feel better, the fact that it was all done for her mom? Was this supposed to make her feel *good*?

"So you experimented on me. On a child."

"Not right away," said Stargell. "Not immediately."

She was shaking her head, defensive, holding up one finger: *Wait*. "I wanted it to be *me*. It had always been my intention to be the first donor myself. And Martin wanted to do it himself. He was spending all of this money, procuring material, the right kind of ports, the various apparatus I required. Marty at first insisted that *he* be the donor."

"So?"

"So it had to be blood," said Stargell. She looked directly at Ana, her eyes brimming with apology. "That was part of what I discovered as we got close. To isolate and extract the durational element was one thing, but a successful transfer required that the donor and recipient be blood relatives."

"And I was her only one."

Stargell nodded.

Ana had always been proud of this fact. Rachel's parents were gone. Ana had no siblings.

Little Ana, squeezing her mom's hand at the grocery store. *Just you and me, kid. Just you and me.* Her mom reassuring her after her and Marty's weekend-long honeymoon: *No matter what, it's still you and me at the center of it all.*

It was silent now in Clare Stargell's kitchen. The murmuring silence of nighttime; the distant nocturnal sounds of animals. Bullfrogs and night birds. Water rushing against the pylons of nearby docks.

"I was sixteen," murmured Ana, who, after all, was still only sixteen. Was and wasn't. "Just a kid."

"Yes, b-but, see —" Stargell stammered. She stared at the table. She was arguing even though she knew there was no argument. Arguing even from the depths of her repentance. "We were going to take a very small amount. To start with. There was no risk. There was really very little risk."

"Well, obviously there was!" Ana exploded in bitter laughter. She stared incredulously at Stargell. "Obviously there was!"

"You have to understand — you have to understand that it was worth it. I felt certain that it was worth it. From a scientific perspective. If this — if this had been successful —"

"Do you still believe that?"

"What?"

Ana jumped up. The chair clattered out from under her as she seized the rifle with two hands and jammed its muzzle against Stargell's forehead. Stargell let out a soft, terrified moan.

"Do you still believe that it was *worth* it?"

"No," Stargell managed.

She shook her head. Tears stood in her eyes. Whatever she believed or didn't believe, now she had the gun to her head, so she murmured, "No," and Ana pulled the rifle away but didn't put it back down. She pressed the fingers of her other hand into her forehead until she left divots in the flesh.

She looked out the front window of the house, out at the moonlit street, and thought about her stepfather. She had loved him a lot. They had been so lucky, she and her mom.

"What the hell, Marty," she muttered. "What the hell?"

They had drugged her. It was as simple and as sordid as that. A needle to the back of the neck, using a very safe dose of a common sedative that rendered her unconscious. And then they had taken her, not to a hospital, but to Dr. Stargell's private clinic, the many-million-dollar laboratory she had built with Martin Ajax's many millions. And Stargell had performed on Ana, for the first and last time, the procedure to extract the durational element from a living subject.

The idea — supported by decades of research but not, before Ana, any testing on any actual human—was that a single year could be safely extracted from a human donor and transferred neatly into another person. The year would come off the *end* of the donor's life but be inserted, or grafted, into the immediate future of the recipient. Another year for Rachel. Another year to live.

"So what actually happened?" demanded Ana. "You put the port in, and you hooked me up to a fucking—what? A machine? Yes?"

"Yes."

"Then?"

Dr. Stargell didn't answer. Ana stared at her. *"Then?"*

Dr. Stargell started to cry. She tilted her head down and tears fell freely, pooled, and slid across the table.

"It's hard—I must say, it's hard to explain."

"Try."

Dr. Stargell pushed tears from her eyes and spoke quickly. "You were there and then you were not there. Your body was on the table and then you were . . . you were gone."

"Gone? What does that mean, gone? I just *disappeared?*"

"You ceased to have duration, which is not precisely the same thing. It was not that you were gone, it was that the idea of 'you' no longer pertained. Your time line became inoperative."

"Jesus," muttered Ana. "Jesus fucking Christ."

But Stargell, even through her tears, had begun to speak excitedly. Despite the horror of the outcome, she was astonished by the miraculous complexity of the science. Her eyes flashed with fascination.

"Obviously, there was an error. Obviously we took far too much durational element from your body. And what I hypothesize is that, at that moment, an alternate reality came into being. Because we snipped your time line at that moment, because there was no longer an 'Ana' but there *had* been an 'Ana,' the universe had to—had to—" Stargell faltered, bit her lip for a concentrated moment, and then continued. "Had to construct an explanation."

"So the—the accident," Ana began.

"Yes! The accident." Stargell was positively excited now, like they were colleagues, brainstorming. "People don't just *disappear*. People don't just *stop being*. So I, along with everyone else, came to believe that you had died in a car accident. Not just to think so, but to *know* so. My mind stopped remembering that Martin Ajax and I had conducted that experiment on you. Only when you appeared tonight on my lawn did I recall it. Until tonight, in my memory, we never went through with the procedure. I decided it was too risky, Ajax and I argued, and I left his employ and retired. You *died,* Ana. You were struck by a car and you died. For all intents and purposes that is what happened because the universe needed an explanation for your absence."

Ana was listening, trying to understand.

"I still half-believe this is what happened," Stargell said. "Even as I'm looking at you now, and you're here in my house, alive. The two realities are existing together. It—" She pressed her hand to her chest. "I can feel it. It hurts. It's quite—really, it's quite fascinating."

Ana knew what she meant. But Ana did not find it fascinating.

(As for Allie—the flickering form of her that remained—Allie, too, had understood. With horror and with sadness, she understood now what she was—what she had never been.)

"I wonder," Stargell continued. "I wonder if a related phenomenon would occur on the other end, so to speak, when a person drops back *into* a time line, when their existence is renewed."

Stargell had given herself over entirely now to her curiosity. She rose from the table, one hand clutching her chin, to examine Ana carefully.

"I wonder, Ana, if the universe, in the same way it wove together a story of your leaving, would have woven a story of your return. Would have, in other words, created some sort of consciousness for you to inhabit, or believe that you were inhabiting. That would have felt to you like a fully lived existence, a *reality* that would survive until it made contact with *actual* reality."

Ana shook her head. She didn't like this. It was confusing. "Can you just talk in English, lady? Can you tell me what the fuck you're talking about?"

"When you returned to being, were you yourself? Or was there some other person that you believed yourself to be?"

Ana paused. Ana blinked. "I . . ."

(She trailed off, and in the ensuing silence, the last of Allie fell away and disappeared for good and forever — and the last fading flicker of her existence was a glimmer of love for a baby girl whose name she couldn't remember, who was just a light, a feeling, the smell of soap on a scalp and the push of little feet against the too-tight heels of a pale blue onesie. A name, some pretty name.)

"I don't think so," said Ana. "No."

The front door creaked open. Neither Ana, when she'd marched Stargell inside, nor Stargell, being marched, had bothered to lock it or even close it all the way.

"Hello?" said a chummy voice, a sweet voice, the happy-living-room voice of Ana's early childhood. "Anybody home?"

Ana swiveled toward the door, holding up the rifle, and before her mind remembered what she had just learned about Marty, her heart was glad at the sight of him. Just fucking *Marty*, her fond and funny stepdad, his hair as thick as ever, only mostly white now, his eyes dancing happily at the sight of her.

"Holy moly," Marty said. "It's true. You're alive. You're *back*."

Before Ana could answer, the woman standing directly behind Marty said, "Put the rifle down." It was the woman who had kidnapped her, small and striking and dark-haired. She had a thick pad of gauze taped over one eye. Ana flared with hatred at the sight of her. But she, too, was holding a gun, a small pistol pointed directly at Ana's face.

"Now, please," she said.

"Why don't you go fuck yourself?" spat Ana. Her hands, holding the rifle, trembled.

The dark-haired woman's expression did not change, but she stepped closer. Her hands did not tremble.

"Okay, calm down. Let's all calm down," Marty said. "Ana, honey, drop the rifle, okay? She's, uh . . ." He tilted his head at the dark-haired woman. "She's kind of a tough cookie, this one."

Ana glared at the kidnapper but dropped the rifle on the scuffed kitchen floor. Dr. Stargell was at the table, her eyes darting around the room.

"How could you do this?" Ana asked her stepfather, her voice choked with anger but also with grief, because she was an angry woman and she was a sad kid, she was both things and she was all of them. She was lost in time. "How could you do this to me?"

"Oh, Ana," Marty said softly, and then he turned to the one-eyed woman. "Shoot them," he said. "Shoot them both, please."

Desiree nodded once and opened fire.

28.

Grace's body was stiff and aching, and her bladder was crying for release, but at last she had landed at 7421 Hermit Crab Lane.

It was an old farmhouse, silhouetted against the moon, with lights on in the first-floor windows. Grace pulled into the narrow driveway and saw that someone had gotten here before her; a big SUV was parked a little farther up. The large vehicle's slick silver modernness had an air of menace, looming in front of this rural home like a landed spaceship.

Grace peered through her windshield. As she sat asking herself whose car that could be, fear and self-doubt seeped up into her from some black well at the very base of her being.

It's too late, she thought. *They're here. Martin Ajax caught up to her first, and what am I supposed to do about it? Who am I?*

She sat in the car, unsure what to do next. Her back hurt horribly. She had to pee like hell.

But she got out of her car and stepped into the cold night. Her cheap work shoes rustled on the gravel, and the sound startled her. Ahead of the SUV, an old white van was parked haphazardly, half on and half off the driveway.

That was Ana's car, then. That was Ana. Grace didn't know how she knew, but she knew that it was her. She looked toward the house. There were people inside, moving behind the windows. She couldn't tell how many.

Grace walked past the SUV and toward the van. She could feel her heart beating in her chest. The moon slipped behind a bank of clouds, and there was no streetlight; no light at all.

The driver's-side door of the van was open.

"Hello?" Grace whispered. No answer. A dull glow came from the small yellow globe of the cabin light.

Grace crept closer. A gun lay on the shotgun seat. A little black hand-gun, like you'd see in the movies. The glove compartment hung open like a mouth.

Grace pulled the van's door the rest of the way open and reached for the gun, thinking, *Ana, oh, Ana*, and then, just as her fingers touched the metal, she pulled back. Grace hated guns. She had always hated guns. David, her ex-husband, had dragged her to a shooting range once, insisting it was a basic skill that everyone should have. Grace had gotten as far as signing the waiver before changing her mind. No. No, thank you.

Now Grace stared at the small black gun, and a shiver chased itself up her spine.

Then her phone rang, and she screamed and immediately clapped her hand over her mouth to stop the scream.

"Mom?" It was River. The line had a slight crackle on it. "Are you all right?"

"Yeah. I'm — yes. Are you?"

"Yeah."

Grace could feel the miles between herself and River. She hated it. She hated being so far from them. She turned away from the van and the gun and looked toward the house and said in a low whisper, hoping River could hear her over the static, "Honey, were you able to —"

"Yes. I got him. Listen."

"Kendall? You —"

"Mom. You were *right*."

The louder River talked, the more the line crackled and hissed. Grace pushed a hand to her other ear, tilted her head to try to hear clearly. "You were totally right," River said.

"You talked to Kendall?" Grace's voice echoed back in a wash of chittering static. She flinched. "River? Are you there?"

"Mom? Are you there?"

"River?"

"Kendall called me back. He said to tell you it checks out."

"What?"

"He's going to file paperwork for an OTC investigation."

"OCI?"

"Right — yes —" River's voice was lost then in pops and hisses. But Grace heard enough to understand that her hypothesis had been correct.

She had hoped she was being overly suspicious about Martin Ajax. Dreaming up nightmare scenarios when the reality was bad enough. But no. Sometimes your darkest suspicions are correct. Sometimes the world is just as wicked as we fear it to be. Kendall had followed it up, and Kendall for all his faults was as careful and cautious as they come. It was as Grace had predicted. All of it was real.

"Oh, Riv," she said when River finished talking. "Are you okay? Where are you? Are you home?"

"Not yet. But I'm okay — are *you* okay?"

"Tell Kendall he can't go through Lou Fleming. He's got to —"

"He knows. I told him, but he said he knows. He's sending you an e-mail—to your personal account—with everything he found. He's going to call you later, when he's home. He—"

Abrupt silence, and then the line exploded in static. If River was still talking, Grace couldn't catch a word of it; it was all electronic clusters and robot noises.

"River," she said, "I don't know if you can hear me, but I want you to call me when you get home. And make sure Grandma got back from Costco."

There was a sudden clarity in the line, and River's voice burst through: "Grandma went to fucking *Costco?*"

Grace was about to say *Language, honey,* or maybe *Thank you, River,* or maybe even *I fucking love you,* but whatever it was, it was stopped by the sound of a gunshot from inside the house, and then a second gunshot, and then Grace's bladder released and she peed all down her leg.

29.

Ana wasn't dead. She knew she wasn't dead because her heart was beating, so hard and fast that it was like a frightened animal trapped in the narrow space of her rib cage. She wasn't dead even though the bitch with the one eye had fired directly at her and then fired once more directly at Stargell, but neither of them was dead. Ana wasn't even hurt, as far as she could tell. The sound of the gunshots echoed in the tiny kitchen. There was the hot burning smell of gunfire.

Ana turned to the kitchen table and looked at Dr. Stargell, who looked back at her. Nobody was dead.

Marty was not surprised.

"Hey, hey," he said casually. "What d'ya know?"

The shooter, too, was startled. She looked at Marty, questioning, and he winked at her — Ana saw him wink. The woman didn't like it. She scowled. Her gun hand twitched. She wanted to shoot more, but Marty waved her off.

He walked toward Ana, grinning warmly, and she jerked back. A few feet away from her, he stopped walking. He raised his fist and slowly opened it, one finger at a time.

In his hand were two bullets, nestled in his palm like baby animals.

"Ta-da," he said softly.

"What—" said Ana, and then the woman with the gun interrupted. "What just happened?"

"Exactly what it looks like," said Marty, still grinning. He was wearing an old T-shirt, baggy and grubby at the neck, and a hooded zip-up sweatshirt. "Desiree here shot both of you, but you're still alive because I caught the bullets out of the air."

He dropped them on the kitchen table, one bullet and then the other, a pair of soft metallic clicks. They rolled lightly, back and forth. Stargell looked at them and then back up at Ajax, but Ajax's eyes were on Ana, only Ana, and his smile was sly and self-impressed, awaiting acknowledgment, like she was still a little kid and he had pulled a quarter from behind her ear.

"That was scary, right? Sorry to scare you." He looked at Stargell. "You too. Hi, Clare."

Dr. Stargell looked at him in astonishment. "Martin," she began, but he kept his attention on Ana.

"I had to show you what we're talking about here, honey. I really wanted you to see what this is all about."

Ana couldn't get a handle on how she was feeling. She wanted to break Marty's fucking neck; she wanted to grab that rifle back up off the ground where Desiree had forced her to put it and shoot him in his smirking face . . . but also it was her stepdad, and her heart could not help responding with old fondness for the man who had read her books and taught her to ride a bike and tended to her dying mother with a crazy, obsessive kind of love. It was fucking *Marty*. Ana was riven, as she had been since he'd walked in the door, between her old strong love for the man who had raised her and the anger of understanding what he had done to her.

What was nice, though, was that underneath all of those contradictory feelings she had the pure pleasure of being alone in her own head. She could not remember exactly what the noise had been, but the noise was gone, and her psychic landscape was at peace. It was all just regular confusion now.

"This is what I wanted you to see," Marty said, "before we get into any of the rest of it." He pointed at the bullets on the table. "This thing that we've created. It *works*. We made it, and it *works*."

He grinned as he pulled out one of the other kitchen chairs and sat down across from Dr. Stargell. So he and she were at the little kitchen table now, and Ana was by the refrigerator, the rifle at her feet, and the cruel woman with the dark hair was by the door. Like it was a party, and the older people were seated.

"We thought we were going to be able to add time to people's lives, right, Dr. S.? That was the idea. That was the big dream, and that would have been amazing. But . . ." He gazed at the bullets he had snatched out of the air, now lying on the table. "What we can *actually* do? In a way? It's even *better*." He shook his head happily. "Honestly, Clare, you're not gonna believe it."

"What?" Stargell spoke softly, like she was barely breathing. "What does it do?" Again she was speaking from her pure scientist's curiosity, aside from and outside all of the dangerous circumstances, the bullets and the guns and the desperation. She wanted to know. She had to.

But Ajax was elusive. "I will say, Clare — you shoulda stuck around."

"Can we get to it, Marty?"

Ajax turned his head to Ana. "Get to what, sweetheart?"

"You're going to kill me. Yeah?" Ana screwed up her face. She spit out her words like nails. "You fucked with my body without permission, and now I'm back, and you're worried I'll tell the world what you did. Which I absolutely *will*."

Ajax was smiling, fondly smiling, listening to her with a parent's tolerant affection, and this only made Ana more furious. "You sent this lady to kill me, so let's go." She puffed up her chest and raised her chin. "Do it."

And Desiree looked to Ajax: Well?

But Ajax said, "No." He touched his heart, affronted, and pointed at the bullets on the table. "If I'd wanted to kill you, it would be done already. Obviously, right?"

"Okay? So?" Ana hissed. "So what, then?"

"Let's all sit down, huh?" said Marty. "Let's talk it through. Did Dr. S. here already walk you through the weird-science aspect? What happened to you, I mean? More or less?"

Ana didn't answer, so he looked at Dr. Stargell, who nodded. "I did. I told her."

Ajax gazed fondly at Ana. "God, sweetie, I thought you were dead. I—ah. Jesus." Marty winced and clutched his chest, breathed slowly through some kind of pain. "God. Sorry." He looked at her, puzzled, exhaling. "I don't know *what* I thought. I thought—"

He stopped. He laughed mordantly. Ana knew what was happening inside his head; it was what Stargell had explained, what Stargell herself had experienced: The universe had built an explanation for Ana's being gone, and now she was back and that explanation was grinding itself away. Marty stood there breathing, blinking, and Ana could practically see it happening: the hit-and-run accident began to pass out of his memory; it was already passing; it had passed.

"But, see," he said, "each GTT port has an embedded device that alerts us if it goes offline and lets us know when it's back. Three days ago . . ." He grinned, astonished. "Yours was back."

"But—wait, now," said Stargell sharply. "Are you saying that you kept working on this project, Martin?" She was startled. "Are you saying you *kept going?*"

"Oh, sure," he said, glancing over at her before snapping his attention back to his stepdaughter. "Of course I did."

Desiree, meanwhile, was listening. Ignored in her corner, forgotten about after the moment of violence in which she had participated. Neglected until more violence might be called for or until she was paid and dismissed.

But she was listening.

She was listening very closely.

"It started simple," Ajax explained to Ana. "I wanted to give your mother more time. That's it. I think Clare probably told you that. Yeah? Clare here's the scientist. I was just a man in love. I loved her, I was lucky enough to marry her, and I wasn't ready to face life without her. And I was rich enough and stupid enough to think, *Well, gee, maybe I don't have to.* Right? Maybe I can tack on some years. Maybe enough to find time for a cure. Ana? Honey. Come. Sit down."

Ana sat down across the table from Ajax as he kept talking.

"So I did some research, and my research brought me to Dr. Stargell here, and I dropped some money on her. Asset manager is not the most exciting job in the world, but if you're good at it, you might just find yourself with a lot of spare cash tucked away somewhere. So I invested in Dr. Stargell, and we built something."

"*I* did," Stargell said—quietly but forcefully. Meaning to be heard. "*I* built something."

Ajax shrugged amiably. "Well, that's a philosophical conversation, I guess, who built what, right?" He turned back to Ana. "No question, though, that after it went a little funky—after you, uh, you left us . . ."

Ana shuddered, and Ajax smiled in awkward acknowledgment of the term's insufficiency. "Yeah. I know. But listen—listen. I did, as Clare suggests . . . I kept going. I had to see what else was there. I had to see what it could do."

"You had to do no such thing," said Stargell, her eyes burning a hole in the side of his face. "Not after what happened."

"To the contrary," Ajax said, "I've never been one to stop at the water's edge, Doctor. And I am sorry you got cold feet. I would think that you, of all people, would've rallied to the idea that when it comes to the sciences, one must try, try again. We tried to help my wife, and we failed, and she died." Ajax stopped for a moment and gritted his teeth at the loss; he closed his eyes and opened them again and pressed on. "So then the question became, what are we going to do, having come this far? There was obviously enormous potential here. There was a fortune to be made. Investments had been made. *Sacrifices* had been made." He reached for Ana, placed a hand over her hand, and she pulled it away. He shrugged again: *Fair enough.*

Dr. Stargell was staring at him, aghast. "How did you—who on earth were you working with?"

"Come on, Clare. You're vain, but you're not that vain. I found other scientists capable of comprehending your work and moving the ball down the field."

"I don't mean what scientists," she said. Ajax looked at her blankly. "I mean what subjects. What *population?*"

"Oh," he said, and waved away the question with one hand. "We worked that out."

Ana listened to all of this, deeply uncertain. So much new information coming in so quickly. Her anger now tinged on all sides by confusion and sadness, and all of it made her feel alone.

God, she missed her mother.

"I'll tell you what, though, Clare, you really had a lot of stuff wrong," said Ajax. "Doesn't have to be a blood relative, for one thing." He wagged a finger at her as if chastising a mistaken child. "So that expands the donor pool *considerably*."

Desiree, still, was listening, and her one working eye roamed across their faces from where she stood watching in the darkness.

She was not only listening but reacting, growing new shapes inside the space of her mind. A new sense of the world was rising deep within her, one dangerous inch at a time.

"So, no," said Ajax. "The durational element cannot simply add years to someone's life. It cannot inch us toward immortality, as we'd once hoped."

As Ajax meandered toward his punch line, he tilted back in his chair, letting its two front legs lift slightly off the floor. Entirely calm, entirely comfortable. A man used to being in control.

"What the durational element *can* do is add time *into* time, so to speak. *Fold* time into time. Extra seconds within the space of a minute, extra minutes in an hour. A person on DE can move exponentially faster than those around him — or her. Sorry, ladies." He paused, winked, and went on. "Run faster, think faster. Do more. The possibilities — and I do apologize for being corny — but the possibilities are endless. They are endless, because the value of time is endless."

"My God," said Clare Stargell, and Ajax smiled at her. "You see?" he said. "See what I mean? You should have stuck around. We really were just getting started." Then he swiveled abruptly and took Ana's hands in his. This time she let him take them.

"Ana, are you understanding all of this? What we're talking about here? Because I know what I did was wrong. I know that I hurt you."

"Hurt me?" Ana said wonderingly. "*Hurt* me?"

It was such a brutal understatement. *Hurt* could not be the word, and Ana could not even conjure up what the word should be. "You — you — you fucking —" She seethed. She waited for words to come. "You stole my life, Marty."

He nodded, conceding, but *stole* didn't do it either. *Harvested. Seized.* The word *raped* was in the back of her throat, caught on her tongue like a burr.

Marty just waited patiently for these feelings to wash over Ana, and he nodded and nodded, his face dead serious, gravely acknowledging his misdeeds even as he tried to usher the conversation forward.

"Yes, see, I know what I did. But what I'm saying is, I want to make it up to you." He looked at her earnestly. "And you know what? I *can*."

He pulled something out of the zippered pocket of his hoodie. It was a small plastic case, like the kind they sell nails in at the hardware store. He set the case down on the table and clicked it open. Inside was a line of plastic vials, and in each vial was a clear liquid, glimmering with what looked like flecks of gold.

"This is a fortune, Ana," he said. "This right here. And we can share it. It's the future." He laughed self-consciously. "It's the actual future."

"What —" Ana began, and then there was a bang from the front of the house, and Ana turned to see a middle-aged woman in a puffy coat and a winter hat with a pom-pom at the top standing in the doorway. She was holding the small gun that Missy had lent her. "Everybody stay still," said the newcomer. "Stay — ow — damn it."

The woman had kicked the door open, but it banged against the opposite wall and swung back closed in her face. She opened it again, still holding the gun.

"Stay still, please."

30.

It was a shock of joy for Grace to see Ana in the flesh after all this searching.

Ana Court, her hair a mad unruly tangle and her eyes confused, sitting at a small kitchen table beside the familiar settled figure of Marty Ajax.

Grace almost cried out. It was like she had been looking for Ana her whole life. It was like coming home.

"Oh, Ana," she said. "You're alive. You're okay."

And Ana said, "Who the fuck are you?"

Grace let out a happy, surprised laugh. "My name is Grace Berney," she said. "I'm from an agency called CDRH," and then before she could explain what the letters stood for, someone appeared from the shadows behind the door and punched her in the stomach. Grace doubled over, coughing, and fell to her knees.

"Whoa, whoa," said Ajax, jumping up from the table. "Not necessary."

Grace clutched her stomach, bent forward, heaving breaths.

"Ms. Berney?" said Ajax. "You okay?"

Grace couldn't talk yet. Once, when she was ten, she had gone bike riding with the twins who lived at the end of the block, despite her mother's frequently expressed distaste for the "low-class" family. There had been a broken branch in the road, and it caught in her spokes and sent her hurtling over the handlebars and onto the ground. Grace was filled again with the startling, gasping pain of that accident and of Kathy shaking her head with grim satisfaction when Grace limped back home. Prophecy fulfilled.

Now Grace looked up, and the small pretty woman who had punched her was staring steadily down. She wore dark pants and a crisp white shirt and had a thick wad of gauze taped over her eye. She had a gun pointed at Grace. The little gun that Grace had taken from the van, meanwhile, had slipped from her fingers and lay like a dead fish on the floor.

"Desiree," Ajax said sternly. "Stand down. This nice lady means us no harm. Isn't that right, Ms. Berney?"

Grace managed to nod. Her breath was coming back to her. The woman with one eye—the one that Ajax had called Desiree—took a step back, and Grace rose slowly to her feet. This woman looked like she actually knew how to use a weapon. Grace glanced down at the tiny gun she'd come bursting in with, the one she had found in the van outside, and wondered if there were even bullets in it. She didn't know. She hadn't thought of it, and even if she had, she wouldn't have known how to check. Good God. What the *hell* was she doing?

It was too late now to retreat. That much was for sure. She looked again at Ana and then at Ajax. When she spoke, she tried to put as much steel in her voice as she could.

"You can't hurt her now," she said to Ajax. "Because I know where she is. And not just me," she added hastily. "I've—we've—I've alerted the authorities."

"The authorities," Marty echoed with mild amusement. "Meaning . . . the Food and Drug Administration?"

"Yes," said Grace. She looked at Ana with what she hoped was a reassuring smile. "It's okay," she said. "You're safe."

"Okay," said Ana. "But who are you?"

"Oh, honey," said Grace, and took a step into the room. Desiree moved to intercept her, and Grace stopped.

"Ms. Berney," said Ajax. "You're really very persistent, aren't you."

Grace noticed that there was someone else here, an older Black woman at the far end of the small table in a plain housedress and old-fashioned glasses. She sat half hidden in shadow, her eyes moving carefully from person to person. Grace almost gasped when she realized who she must be. How had it never occurred to Grace, who considered herself a dedicated feminist and who had learned to be attentive to personal pronouns, that Dr. C. P. Stargell might be a woman?

Ajax had walked halfway around the table and now stood protectively behind Ana. He placed a hand on her shoulder and she did not move to take it off.

"My daughter is in no danger." He smiled pleasantly. "I promise." He gazed down at Ana and said it again, to her this time. "I *promise*. I understand, Ms. Berney, that you in your admirable persistence figured out what happened to Ana, or some piece of it, and you found it alarming, which — hey — is totally understandable. You're just doing your job. Or somebody's job; I'm not sure it's yours. Anyway, you think I intend to harm Ana so the world won't discover what I've done to her." He looked archly to the other end of the table, where Dr. Stargell sat quietly. "What *we* have done to her." He looked back at Grace. "Right? Yeah? Something like that?"

Grace flushed, but nodded. The kitchen clock over the sink had a cat's tail that swung back and forth as the seconds ticked past. Grace wished

253

for just one moment of silence, so she could get her bearings. She wished she could talk to Ana alone. But Marty rolled smoothly on, golden-tongued and grinning.

"The thing is, though, Ana knows all this already. She knows now. I told her. I just told her! Right, honey?"

Ana didn't look at Ajax, but she nodded. Her face twitched.

"Yeah. She understands. She gets it. There was an attempt to save my wife's life, an experimental procedure, and—well, you know what they say." He gave his voice a light ironic spin: "Mistakes were made."

At that, Ana exhaled roughly, and Ajax hurried on. "But that's all ancient history. It's water under the bridge. And actually, the thing is, just before your dramatic arrival, we were discussing how Ana here might participate in my continued work. In its profits, that is. Turn this all into a win-win. Maybe even for Dr. Stargell here, if she'd like to participate."

"No," Dr. Stargell said immediately. Her voice was low and unfalter-ing. "I'm not interested."

Marty shrugged. He looked directly at Grace, raised his eyebrows slightly. "Maybe for you too, Ms. Berney."

Grace blinked. The implication was clear. No one had ever offered her a bribe before. Her brush with Art Greenberg's perfidy had been the closest she'd come. She'd never done anything unethical, and she wasn't about to start now.

"No," she said. "No, thank you." And then, rushing on, she said, "I'm here to take Ana away."

"No," said Martin Ajax. "No, you're not."

They both turned to look at Ana, whose hands were trembling on the table. Her eyes flashed with uncertainty. She had been through so much, Grace knew. She had gone away and come back. Grace could not imagine what it was like inside her head.

"Hey," said Grace softly. She took a careful step toward the table and held out her hand. "It's okay, honey. Let's go."

Again, Ajax said, "No." His face twisted to one side, and he tightened the grip of his hand on Ana's shoulder. "That's not an option that's on the table. We are going to work together. She is going to join me in my continued work. Right, Ana?" She looked at him, and then back at Grace. "As I said, I hurt her, and I've apologized, and it's all in the past."

"I'm not concerned with what you did in the *past*," Grace said. She flicked a nervous glance behind her at the small mean woman with the gun, then forced herself to continue, forced the courage to stay in her voice. "I'm talking about what you've done *since*. I'm talking about what's happening *now*."

Ajax stopped smiling. His face turned hard and sour; he looked like a child who had suddenly grown sick of the game that was being played. Ana looked closely at his profile; so, too, from her end of the table, did Stargell.

"What does that mean?" said Stargell. "What's happening now?"

Ajax frowned, his brow furrowing. "Whatever you think you have discovered, Ms. Berney, I am sure it's not quite so sinister as you imagine."

"Wait—what?" said Ana. She slid to one side in her chair, shaking Marty's hand off her shoulder. "What's she talking about?"

"Nothing," said Ajax.

"It's a patch," said Grace. "He's made it into a patch."

"Oh my God," Stargell murmured, shocked. "Oh my *God*."

"What?" demanded Ana again.

Grace explained what she had learned from River, who had learned it from Kendall, who had done exactly what Grace had asked of him— burrowed into the CDRH archives to pull the applications for the Exeter patch. That was the product Ajax had mentioned when Grace came into his office. When he thought she was merely a regulator, before he understood she'd come to see him about Ana.

The Exeter patch was a combination product, both a drug and a device, and the clinicians at Rachel's Place were administering opiate-replacement therapies through the patch, applying it to the arms of the dozens or hundreds of people who came through every day. Transdermal patches were often used in opiate-replacement therapy to deliver less dangerous, less addictive opiates, such as buprenorphine, into the blood-stream. The innovation of the Exeter patch—which was actually regulated not by the CDRH but by an affiliated agency, the Office of Combination Products—was that it created microscopic punctures in the skin that allowed it to simultaneously deliver medication and draw blood for testing.

Quite a clever product, in Kendall Johns's estimation.

It was, Grace understood, essentially a tiny, temporary port.

"My God," said Stargell, her voice low and shaky.

"What?" said Ana for the third time, and she slapped an open hand down on the table. *"What?"*

"He's taking durational element from the patients in the clinic," said Grace. "Right, Marty?"

Ajax didn't answer. He didn't have to. Ana, for the first time since Grace had come into the room, looked directly at her. Grace looked back at her steadily.

"Oh, well, look," said Ajax. "Sure. Yes. I have been extracting durational element from some individuals. My team and I identified an appropriate patient population, and we moved to take advantage of it. It's smart science, Clare."

"Martin," said Stargell. "It's unconscionable."

"Well, that's—I mean—" Ajax sighed. "*Unconscionable* is sort of a relative term, I think."

"Do they know?" Ana whispered.

"What?"

She repeated it loudly. Very loudly. "Do they know? Do the people in the clinic *know?*"

He shook his head and cast a quick look at Desiree as if reassuring himself that she was still there, her and her gun and her bullets.

"No. They don't know. Because, let's be honest — right? You ask people for permission, and people are gonna say no. Even the act of asking requires all kinds of approvals and regulations and — I mean, just ask Ms. Berney here how fucking slowly, pardon my French, but how fucking *slowly* those bureaucratic wheels turn. And meanwhile word gets out and suddenly you've got seven competitors doing the same thing you are." He shook his head, waved a hand in the air. "So, no. We've been playing it all a little under the table, a little off the radar. And by the way — it doesn't matter. The extracted amounts we're talking about are basically infinitesimal. And actually, Ana, honey, this is among the innovations I am excited to share with you. We don't have to take years from a donor. We don't even have to take *a* year. We've got it to a point where we are dealing with minutes. Moments. And you take thousands of these very small amounts from a large number of individuals, and you *combine* them, see?" He tapped on the plastic case full of vials that still sat on the table. "It is not a one-to-one situation, donor X gives to recipient Y. The product is manufactured from the durational element extracted from *many* donors."

"For God's sake, Marty," Stargell said, and he wheeled around on her, scowling.

"Oh, come on, Clare. Come on!" His voice had changed. And he was not smiling. "It is one thing to live in a world of theories. Huh? That must be a nice world in which to live. That must be very nice. And by the way—"

Ajax turned back to Ana, knelt before her, hands out.

"Just by the way, *eventually*, in the fullness of time, this product is going to give people control over their bodies in an absolutely unprecedented way."

Ana tilted her head, confused.

"There is this whole untapped source of value inside of people," said Ajax. "And what we are going to do—not yet, but ultimately—eventually—and we will do it—what we are going to do is provide a way for people—*regular* people, every person off the street, I mean—for regular people to *unlock* that trapped value. What we're talking about here is the emergence of a new asset class. A new form of value. And we don't have to mine it, we don't have to cut down forests for it, we don't have to pump it out of the ground. We're born with it. All of us! Everyone! Born with this *asset*, this thing, our *time*, and what we are doing—what *I* am going to do—is to make it possible for *individuals* to control their own store. Keep it, spend it, gift it. Whatever. It's yours. You should be able to use it how you want."

When he stopped, he was practically panting with excitement. He waited to hear what Ana would say. Waited for her, for everyone, to recognize the genius of what he had created.

Ana reached for the plastic box on the table. She tapped on it slowly with the tip of one finger. "But *this* time, Marty, this time here?"

"Yes?"

"This time was stolen?"

"I mean—Ana. Sure. If you want to put it that way, sure."

Still, Desiree was listening.

Her name was not Desiree. There was a different person inside her, layers down. Catching sensation, deep in darkness, still real.

And as she stood listening, it was finding its way to the surface of her. It was close. Getting closer.

Ana lifted her hand from atop the plastic case full of durational element.

Marty waited, watching her.

Desiree watched them both.

At last, Ana stood up.

"All right, Ms. Berney," she said. "That's your name, right?"

"Grace," said Grace. "You can call me Grace."

"Let's get the fuck out of here, Grace."

"No." Ajax rose unsteadily, shaking his head. "I'm sorry, but as I said . . ." He ran his hands through his hair. "We're not leaving. We're not done talking about this. This is a project that is really only just in its beginning phases," he said. "This is not a project I can allow to be jeopardized."

"Shut the fuck up, Marty." Ana spat the words out, a ferocious rush of words, and Ajax stepped back, startled. He pushed his hands into his thick white hair and tugged on it a little, as if there were something inside his head and he needed to pull it out. "Ana. Honey. I'm not sure you understand."

"I do," said Ana.

And she did understand. Her head was clear and open and quiet, and she understood completely. For the first time since she had swum to the surface of her own life, standing in Missy's apartment, her mind was absolutely calm and absolutely still. This was what she was.

"I want nothing to do with it," she told her stepfather.

Marty reached for her and said, "Listen — sweetheart —" and she spat in his face.

Ajax, at long last, stopped talking. The last bits of jocularity dropped out of him, all of the dad-joke sweetness. He looked at Ana for a long time. "I wish you hadn't done that."

He took the front of his T-shirt, tugged it upward, and wiped the spit off his face.

Then he turned away from her and nodded solemnly to Desiree. "Do it," he said. No superhero trickery implied this time, no fun with the catching of bullets. Pure intention. "Kill them all."

31.

Desiree, by that moment, was ready.

She did not have all the details figured out. All of that would come. She would make her move and decide the next and then the next one after that.

The first move was simple.

She raised her 9-millimeter pistol and shot Martin Ajax in the spine and he let out one startled yelp and pitched forward onto the linoleum, mouth open.

He did not catch the bullet, or dodge it. Whatever extraordinary capabilities were granted by the consumption of durational element, they were unavailing if the subject was looking the wrong way.

Ajax twitched and went still.

While the women watched, startled, Desiree swept the hard plastic case full of durational element off the table.

She held it aloft, and the fluid inside the vials sparkled gaily under Clare Stargell's kitchen lights.

"Okay," she said to Dr. Stargell. "On your feet."

Grace watched in horror. She was having trouble breathing. *No. No, no, no.* Her eyes searched the floor for the gun she'd been holding when she came in here. The little black handgun she'd taken from Ana's van.

"You are the creator of this technology?" the one-eyed woman asked Stargell. It was a statement that just barely curved up into a question as it reached its end. But Clare Stargell just gaped at her, confused.

The woman held her gun steadily on Stargell. "Yes or no?"

Dr. Stargell nodded rapidly, eyes wide, clutching the Formica countertop. Grace didn't know what the one-eyed woman was going to do. Desiree grabbed Dr. Stargell tightly by the throat, lifted her from her chair, and walked her toward the door.

"Take me," spat Ana.

"What?" said Desiree.

"I said take me, you fucking coward."

"Take you?" Desiree looked at her curiously, as if the words made no sense to her in the current context. "No." She tilted her head toward Stargell, whom she was still holding by the neck. "She will show me how to make more of this substance. I don't need *you*."

Grace understood what that meant: Desiree did not need Ana, and even less so did Desiree need Grace. *She's going to kill us,* Grace thought simply, even as Desiree aimed at Ana. *She's going to kill us both.*

And then Grace lurched into motion, throwing her body at Desiree and screaming as she did, screaming from adrenaline and nervousness and pure holy fear.

It was crazy. There should not have been enough time. Not even close. Desiree was a trained killer and she was six feet away. Desiree should have been able to shoot Grace easily as Grace charged screaming toward her.

But it was as if Grace had taken the durational element, as if the universe had folded more time into her own, and the moment stretched out. It yawned open, time within time, and she collided with Desiree and knocked her off balance the instant before she pulled the trigger and so her bullet went wild, even as Grace pushed Stargell down and covered the old woman's body with her own and Ana grabbed Stargell's rifle from the kitchen floor in time — *just* in time — to return fire.

Desiree felt the bullet enter her stomach. The impact drove her backward and her head smacked against the wall. As she sank down, she felt blood gushing from the wound, and she clutched her hands across her stomach, the fingers of her right hand interlacing with the fingers of her left, forming a poor barrier against the gout of blood from the hole torn in her center.

She felt herself draining from herself. It might take as much as forty-five minutes for her to die, she knew, but given the severity of the injury and the speed with which blood and thus oxygen were flowing away from her brain, she was likely to lose consciousness in under a minute.

No escape, thought Desiree finally. *There is no escape.*

Grace lay on the ground not far from her, shaking with pain. It felt like she'd been shot but she had not been shot. She'd just done something very bad to her back when she'd lunged for Desiree. She lay supine, staring up at the ceiling.

It was excruciating, the pain twisting like a hot cable down the length of her body.

Dr. Stargell was panting beside her. Grace couldn't turn her head to see if Ana was okay. She hoped that she was. Poor thing had gone through a lot already.

"Dr. Stargell, can you call the police?" Grace managed. "Can you do that?"

"Yes," said Stargell. "Yes."

Grace could see the clock with the cat's tail out of the corner of her eye, and she tried to focus on it. Each swish of the tail was a second passing. She felt the hard floor underneath her head. She let the moment surround her. She let time pass.

EPILOGUE:
SIX MONTHS IN THE FUTURE

Nana, come on. Don't be a jerk. Turn the sound back on."

"Ech," said Kathy. "What the hell are we even watching this for?"

"Are you kidding?"

"If we switch over, we can watch *Judge Judy* instead."

"You're such a jerk."

Kathy shrugged. They were going to sit here and watch goddamn C-SPAN, of all things? She stared with annoyance at the still shot of a congressional hearing room. Bunch of old farts wandering around in suits, yapping about this or that bull crap. Pretending to be important.

"Mom is testifying before Congress," said River. "You don't think we might want to check that out?"

Kathy rolled her eyes. "We already know what she's going to say."

River rolled their eyes back at her, but it was true. Grace had rehearsed her testimony a hundred times, standing in here in this stale small room where Kathy was laid up like a lump of ham, reading from her cue cards while River cheered her on or made nitpicky suggestions.

River snatched the remote and unmuted the TV, and Kathy harrumphed and resettled herself on her pillows.

It was bad enough she was stuck here in this hospital in the stink of other people's piss, pestered all day long by these daffy nurses who could barely speak the language.

It was the damnedest thing. She'd been changing lanes on Wootton Parkway, driving back from the CVS where she'd gone to do one quick errand, to pick up some Epsom salts for her bath. Grace was supposedly going to get the salts on her way home from work, but she didn't want to wait until seven or eight or God knows when to take a bath, and why the hell should she when she had a car and she was perfectly capable of driving the damn thing? Well, of course some redneck bozo in a pickup truck cut right in front of her, and she'd lost track of her hands on the wheel and spun off the road and woken up here.

And somehow or other, everybody had decided it was her fault, especially her daughter, who kept saying she was just glad Kathy was okay and that they had health insurance and all the other shit she was supposed to say, even though Kathy could just see the words *I told you so* dying to pop out.

"I was going to go to the store" was what Grace kept saying. "I was going to get you the salts."

No matter that the accident really and truly had *not* been her fault. That redneck SOB had flustered her, honking and shouting and trying to get around, and her damn car was all poky and unresponsive because Grace never let her drive it!

None of it mattered, of course. She knew damn well what it meant. Even as she lay here in this bed, enduring another week of tests and scans, watching the blotchy bruises on her body go from black to purple, she knew that she would never drive again. Her identity had changed forever. For almost sixty years, she had been a person who drove a car, who even was good at it and loved it, and now she would never be that person again. She had slipped from the shore of *that* identity into the open sea of this new one: old lady in a hospital bed waiting to be driven home, driven to the store, driven everywhere.

And it wasn't like you went *back*. You move from one of life's countries to another one, and you never go back.

"There she is! Holy shit," said River. And then Kathy saw her daughter on TV, and Kathy began to cry.

Grace Berney, moving carefully, plainly nervous, was being led to a seat at a long table behind a little placard with her name on it while one of the younger of the old farts spouted off pompously. Ana Court was seated beside her, thin and nervous and apparently chewing gum.

"It's especially distressing when you consider that the regulatory bodies that should have been providing oversight were nowhere to be *seen*," the man said. "In all of government, there seems to have been exactly one person who was curious about this."

Suddenly Kathy's daughter's face filled up the television screen, smiling uncertainly. Kathy blew her nose and said, "Ugh." Grace was wearing too much makeup. She looked like a clown. Who told her to dress that way to be on television?

Behind Kathy, River cheered.

"Go, Mom!"

"Hush," said Kathy. "I'm *watching*."

"Oh, *now* you're watching."

"I said quiet, child." Kathy belched softly, then watched in silence as her daughter was formally invited to make her introductory remarks to the Senate committee.

"My name is Grace Berney, and I work at CDRH, the Center for

269

Devices and Radiological Health, part of the Food and Drug Administration. The woman beside me is Ana Jessica Court, and I believe you will hear from her a little bit later on."

Grace was reading a prepared statement, and Kathy winced to see Grace's hands shaking slightly as she held her papers. A few beads of sweat appeared just below her hairline.

"There you go, honey," whispered Kathy. "You're all right. You're doing great."

"Nana? You say something?"

"Hush."

"Are you crying?"

"No, River. *Hush.*"

"It was through my work at CDRH that I first became aware of the existence of what is now being referred to as DE, or the durational element. The, uh — the — "

She paused, flushed, and looked down at her notes, seemingly confused.

"Come on, kid," growled Kathy. "Come on."

On the TV, Grace cleared her throat. She steadied her hands. It was like she could hear her mom.

She flipped to the other side of her paper and kept reading, peering at it closely to avoid looking up, and eventually she found a kind of rhythm, flipping forward page by page as she told her story. Sometimes the idiots on the committee interrupted to ask questions or make short dumb speeches in the guise of questions, but for the most part they just listened.

"I wish she would talk more slowly," said Kathy at one point, and River said, "Nah. She's doing great."

Kathy harrumphed, allowing it. She couldn't say anything else for the moment; she was overfilled. Tears ran down her old cheeks in hot narrow lanes, and her breast was choked with a happiness that was a kind of pain. Her own child was appearing as a hero, and she had lived long enough to see this, and she would not live forever, which was unbearable, but okay too.

"Nana?" said River, crouching next to her. "You all right?"

"She oughta try and sit up straight. She's on television, for Chrissake."

As the hearing wore on, Kathy became tired and began to drift in and out of sleep. At some point, Grace concluded her testimony, and other people were invited up, one by one. First Ana Court, then a series of experts, various kinds of scientists. A man from the FDA named Barry Perez stammered out a series of incoherent answers in response to pressing questions about the relationship between his office and "this man, Ajax, who we have heard so much about."

A tweedy and professorial gentleman with the unlikely name of Jeffrey Wingo, from the National Institutes of Health, accompanied his testimony with a tripartite chart showing illustrations of deep space, diagrams of the human genome, and a blur of mathematical equations.

And though Kathy MacAlister had taken enormous pride in Grace's testimony, and though she could have fooled herself into confusing that pride with hope, she was no dummy.

She saw where it all was, and she understood where it was going.

The senators in their mortuary suits, with their thundering glowers, were going to rant and rave, they were going to demand accountability from the FDA and punishment for those involved in letting this illegal, exploitative, and potentially catastrophic experimentation occur out of the public eye and for private profit. And Grace Berney would be lauded until the cows came home for her resourcefulness and courage in revealing this illicit scientific activity.

But now it was public. Kathy let her eyes drift closed. She couldn't watch anymore. She couldn't bear it.

Now all had been revealed. The world knew about it, and everybody would gnash their teeth and tear at their hair, but one thing Kathy knew was that there was no driving the horse back into the barn.

The science of it was above her pay grade, but Kathy understood a few things about the world. She had known a lot of people. Bosses and workers, owners and renters, liars and thieves. She knew what happened next. Time had become a thing to which value could be assigned, and anything with value would be bought and sold, it would be stolen and hoarded, it would be leveraged and bundled and amortized.

The ending had been built into the beginning. The worst outcome had become a possibility, and all possibilities become real if you wait long enough.

Kathy mumbled, and River said, "Nana, are you okay?" and she couldn't answer. Her husband had died in an accident in a coal mine. Her parents hadn't had the money for her to finish college. Five years from now, poor people would be selling the hours of their lives to buy insulin or asthma medication or gas for their cars.

Ten years from now, it would be worse than that.

Kathy drifted off to sleep until the congressman leading the hearing banged the gavel for quiet, and the chamber was filled with the low hum of a motor. The hum came from an electric wheelchair that was maneuvering slowly into the room.

The man in the chair had thick white hair and a plump, cheerful face. He drove slowly up to the witness table, stopped, and adjusted the stack of papers on the table before him. He conferred with a small cluster of sharply dressed lawyers assembled around him. Ahead of his pending criminal trial, he'd posted an enormous sum in bail and had been released on his own recognizance. Meanwhile the grand jury's investigation into his role in the development of the durational-element technology was running in parallel with this congressional investigation, so it was understood that there were certain questions that Mr. Ajax would not be at liberty to answer.

But to look at him, adjusting the chair into position behind the table, grinning, with his sleeves rolled up, Martin Ajax hardly seemed reluctant to testify.

"Mr. Chairman," he said. "Good morning. If I may begin?"

"Turn it off," said Kathy to River. "Turn the damn thing off."

River raised the remote to do so as Ajax looked directly into the camera and the future he'd made.

ACKNOWLEDGMENTS

Thanks first and foremost and always to Diana, Rosalie, Orchid, and Milly. I don't know what I would do without you.

Thanks to Joelle Delbourgo and Joel Begleiter, agents and friends.

I read a lot of delightfully strange stuff while I was writing this one. I am particularly indebted to James Gleick's *Time Travel*, Richard Muller's *Now: The Physics of Time*, and the fantastic anthology *The Time Traveler's Almanac*. If I work backwards, the first kernel of *Big Time* was in the *Twilight Zone* episode "A Most Unusual Camera." Highly recommended.

Thanks to James McKinney at the FDA for the walkthrough on medical-device regulation. Thanks to old friends Ray Scholl and Sarah Leshner Carvalho, both of whom provided fascinating insight on areas of expertise that didn't end up in the novel. (In a parallel universe, Ray, there's still a small aircraft crash landing in here somewhere.)

This book is dedicated to my editor, Josh Kendall, who seems always to know where I'm trying to get before I do. He and his colleagues at Mulholland make it a joy.

Onwards!

—Ben Winters, Los Angeles 2023

Ben H. Winters is the *New York Times* bestselling author of *Underground Airlines, Golden State,* and the Last Policeman trilogy, among other works. His books have won the Edgar Award, the Philip K. Dick Award, the Sidewise Award, and France's Grand Prix de l'Imaginaire. Ben also writes for television and lives in Los Angeles with his family.